ENGAGING
THE BILLIONAIRE

The Winters Saga
Book Eight

IVY LAYNE

GINGER QUILL PRESS, LLC

Contents

THE BILLIONAIRE CLUB

PROLOGUE
ANNALISE

He lay in the hospital bed, eyes closed, his chest rising and falling with every breath. He was alive. That was something.

Life had taught me to expect the worst. When I'd been summoned to the emergency room, my head had been filled with disaster. Death. My stomach already twisting, my heart sick with grief. But Riley wasn't dead.

He was unconscious, and his arm was broken, but that was it. The nurse told me he'd woken once, to ask for me, and was simply sleeping. I was having a hard time believing her. I'd been sitting by Riley's hospital bed for hours, holding his hand. Waiting.

If this were normal sleep, he would have woken. Wouldn't he?

The white bandage wrapped around his head was a jarring contrast to his tanned skin and dark hair. Riley couldn't be hurt. Riley was strong and smart. Riley was everything. Since the day we'd met, he'd taken over my life. It seemed impossible that anything, even a pickup truck and a drunk driver, could slow him down.

The nurse came back in, narrowing her eyes at the sight of Riley, still asleep.

"Shouldn't he be awake by now?" I asked.

She spared me a sidelong glance as she checked his vitals and made notes on the chart. "Not necessarily. The doctor can tell you more when he does rounds, but your boyfriend has a concussion and a broken arm. So far, that's it. No internal bleeding and his brain isn't swelling. I would have expected him to be up by now, but I don't think there's cause to worry."

She patted my shoulder as she left. I didn't think you were supposed to go to sleep when you had a concussion, but it seemed ridiculous to question the nurse. I knew nothing about head injuries, and she was a medical professional. If she wasn't worried, I shouldn't be either. I knew that. It didn't seem to make a difference. I wanted Riley to open his eyes.

His dark lashes fanned against his cheeks, hiding the green-flecked hazel of his eyes. I loved Riley's eyes. They were the first thing about him to capture my attention.

I'd been watching him for two months before we officially met. He sat three rows ahead of me in Intro to Psychology. Three rows up and just enough to my right that I could stare at his profile when I was supposed to be paying attention in class.

One day, as he stood to grab his backpack, he'd looked up, and his eyes met mine. Warm, light hazel framed by the kind of long lashes men never appreciated, and women envied. A strong blade of a nose, dark hair a little too long, and the hint of a tattoo peeking up from the collar of his gray T-shirt.

He was prime eye candy for a girl like me. He wasn't too pretty. None of that highly polished, pampered look I'd been over by the time I hit my teens. I'd grown up around rich boys with their expensive haircuts and overpriced watches. Designer clothes didn't do it for me. The way that gray T-shirt stretched over his arms definitely did.

He slung his backpack over his shoulder, locked those hazel eyes onto mine, and winked. My heart stopped in my chest. By the time I'd recovered, he was gone. I'd never looked forward to a class as much as I did the next session of Intro to Psych. He was there, in the same seat he always took—three rows up and four to my right.

The class went by in a blur. I took notes, but later I realized none of them made sense. I spent most of my time studying the curve of his ear, the way his hair was a little too long in the back, curling up over the collar of his T-shirt, this time a faded navy blue with the logo of a classic rock band on the front.

His jaw, the side of it I could see, was clean-shaven and strong. His shoulders were broad, and his left arm was just muscled enough to be sexy. I could tell you I didn't sketch the edges of his tattoo, visible below the T-shirt sleeve, but I'd be lying.

That time, when he winked at me, I had just enough composure to smile back. I leaned down to grab my own backpack, and when I looked up, he was gone. Again.

We played that game for another week, and suddenly it seemed like I saw him everywhere. Checking his mail at the student union, waiting in line in the cafeteria. Every time I caught sight of him, my heart sped up.

I thought about approaching him, planned on it, but when I had the chance, I chickened out. My mystery man was older than the rest of us, at least by a few years. He had a detached air about him that was intimidating, even to me.

I'm not easily intimidated. Not by most people. I'm

Annalise Winters. Yes, one of those Winters. The Winters family of Winters Incorporated, heir to a company whose value dwarfed most country's GDPs. I'd been born a billionaire.

Most people thought that made me lucky. In some ways it did. I didn't have to worry about tuition. I'd never had to worry about paying bills or going hungry. I had a beautiful home and a sweet, tricked-out SUV my oldest cousin had gotten me for my high school graduation.

But I don't know that 'lucky' was a good description of my life. I also had two dead parents, victims of a murder/suicide that had drawn relentless media coverage, a clusterfuck that had only gotten worse when the aunt and uncle who raised me died in an almost identical crime when I was seventeen.

The scandal had been irresistible. The legitimate news, gossip columns, people I'd grown up thinking were my friends—they were all obsessed with the downfall of the Winters family.

Money could insulate you from a lot of problems, but it couldn't fix everything. Not the stuff that really mattered. By the time I started high school, I knew how to keep my guard up, knew how to be cautious. I'd learned the hard way not to trust easily. Threats could hide anywhere. Even in the hazel eyes of a cute boy in class.

So, I'd watched him, and I'd let my heart beat too fast when he winked at me, but that was it. I wasn't looking for a boyfriend. I was just trying to be normal for a while. Normal never lasted long for me.

A few weeks after that first wink, I'd turned around and bumped right into him, almost spilling my coffee all over another one of those faded, well-fitting t-shirts.

"Whoah," he'd said, reaching out to steady my arm. His strong fingers closed over my elbow, and my heart fluttered.

"Sorry, sorry, I didn't see you there," I babbled.

His fingers firmly gripping my arm, he led me away from the line at the coffee shop. "It's my fault. I was standing too close. To tell you the truth, I was trying to figure out what perfume you're wearing."

Up close, I could see that his hazel eyes were flecked with specks of green and gold. My brain struggling to catch up, I said, "It's not perfume, it's lotion."

"Good to know," he said, the side of his mouth quirking up in a half smile that made my knees weak. "I'd offer to buy you a coffee but—" he gestured to my coffee with his own. "Looks like you've already got that covered. How about a walk?"

"Okay," I said, my head spinning a little as I let him lead me out of the coffee shop and into the street. We'd fallen into step together, exchanging names, though I only gave my first. I didn't want to tell him who I was.

Not yet.

I had my own reasons for being gun-shy about relationships, reasons that had nothing to do with my family. But I didn't want to tell Riley who I was until I decided if he'd be worth the trouble.

It didn't take long to figure out that Riley Flynn was worth the trouble, and I ended up spilling more than I meant to about my personal life by our third date.

I found out that he looked older than the rest of us because he was. He'd taken off after high school and backpacked around Europe before settling down for college. He'd taken the news about my family in stride, seeming disinterested, though he'd shied away from meeting them. I didn't care.

I was living on campus for the second year in a row, and I was more than happy to keep Riley all to myself. My oldest cousin, Aiden, was technically head of the family now that his parents were dead, and he'd come home to take the reins of Winters Inc. My oldest brother Gage had joined the Army the year before, only a few days after our aunt and uncle had been killed.

My twin brother, Vance, was also in his sophomore year at Emory. I guessed everyone figured he was keeping an eye on me.

Not exactly.

Vance was keeping an eye on coeds and parties. His sister? Not so much.

That was fine with me. I was tired of living behind gates. I wanted to pretend to be a normal college student, with a normal life. I wanted to get serious about my photography and study art. So far, everything had been working out perfectly. I should have known it wouldn't last.

I watched Riley sleep in the hospital bed and tried to tell myself that people got into car accidents. It wasn't good, but it was normal. It happened. It didn't mean Riley was going to die. If it were that serious, they wouldn't let me in his room. The nurse would've seemed more on edge. Everything was fine.

I must have squeezed Riley's hand too hard because his fingers flexed over mine and he let out a low groan. Those thick eyelashes fluttered against his cheeks, and his eyes opened, bloodshot and swollen, but the familiar green-flecked hazel soothed my worries. I felt my own eyes flood with tears, and Riley smiled weakly.

"Hey, hey, it's okay," he said. "I'm okay."

"You wouldn't wake up," I said.

Riley squeezed my hand again. He knew me, knew

what I was thinking. Knew how I feared more loss. More death.

"I'm awake now, and I'm fine."

I swiped a tear from my eye and nodded. He squeezed my hand again.

"Lise, look at me," he ordered. I did. His pupils were uneven, and his words were a little slurred, but he was still Riley. "I'm okay," he said. "Everything is okay. I'm not going to die on you."

"Promise?" I couldn't help asking.

"Promise." His eyes slid shut, and he murmured, "Just need to close my eyes."

I pressed the button to call for the nurse. By the time someone showed up, and I let her know Riley had woken, he was fast asleep again. The nurse was unconcerned, both that he'd woken and that he was back to sleep.

I tried to reassure myself that this was another sign everything was okay. She adjusted something in the IV attached to his arm, murmured to herself, and left the room. I settled back into my chair by his side to wait.

Alarm bells woke me from a light doze. Running foot-steps, flashing lights, and I was pulled from his bedside, his hand torn from mine. I knew better than to interrupt. People in scrubs leaned over him, their voices urgent, the words coming fast and unintelligible.

I didn't know what was happening; I only knew that it was bad.

I did what I always did when things were bad. What all of us did when things were bad.

I called Aiden.

He was there twenty minutes later, bullying the nurses with his implacable authority, insisting I be allowed to stay by Riley's side, demanding to know what was happening.

He shoved a paper cup of tea into my hand and made me sit in a chair in the waiting room on Riley's floor.

"As soon as he's stabilized, they'll let you back in, though they're not happy about it," he said.

"What happened? He was fine. He was sleeping and then—"

"A mixup with the drugs," Aiden said, shaking his head. "The nurse misread the dose on his morphine. They don't know where she is, but they'll question her as soon as they find her. What's important is that they caught it in time and he's going to be fine."

"They messed up his medicine? How does that happen? I thought he would be safe in the hospital—"

When I heard the alarms, saw the flashing lights and the rushing nurses, I'd assumed it was something to do with his concussion. It never occurred to me that they might accidentally kill him.

I wanted to bundle Riley up and take him home to Winters House. Except Winters House had never been particularly safe either. There was nowhere in my life that was safe. Nowhere death couldn't follow.

"After all this, are you going to bring him home for dinner?" Aiden asked, nudging my shoulder with his. My cheeks flushed. I hadn't dated a lot in high school. Between my family's notoriety, my aunt and uncle's deaths my junior year, and other stuff, I just wasn't that interested.

Riley was the first boy—man—to catch my eye. What we had was so perfect I hadn't been willing to bring it into the mess that was the rest of my life. But maybe it was time.

"Is it all right if he comes home to Winters House when they let him out? He has an apartment off campus but—"

Aiden wrapped his arm around me and pulled me into a hug. "Of course it's okay. Now that I know what's really going on with you two, I'd rather have him where I can keep an eye on him."

I made a disgruntled sound low in my throat and rested my cheek against his chest. Aiden was overprotective. If I thought he was bad with me, I just had to see him with my little cousin Charlie. She was twelve, still shaken from losing her parents, and Aiden hovered over her as much as his responsibilities would allow.

He was only twenty-two, barely two years older than me, but he was the one who held us together. He'd left college after his parents died, finishing school in Atlanta and taking his father's place at the company and at home.

He read to Charlie at night and made sure Vance and I got our college applications in on time. He'd been the one to insist I live in student housing when I suggested I should stay home and help him with the kids. He'd given up everything so we could have normal lives.

I'd tried to argue, but no one argued with Aiden. He just stared you down and steam-rolled over you.

I hadn't fought him that hard. Both Vance and I felt guilty about running off and leaving Aiden with the kids, but as much as we'd wanted to help, we'd wanted to get away even more. And it wasn't like we'd gone far. All the Winters went to Emory, right in Atlanta, so we were close if he needed us. Only Aiden had gone out of state to school, but he'd ended up leaving Harvard and finishing at our fathers' alma mater in the end.

We'd gratefully acceded to his demand that we be normal college students. Or as normal as we could be. But now, seeing Riley in a hospital bed, all I wanted was home.

It felt like hours before they let me back into Riley's room. I imagined he looked paler, more worn. Aiden left to make whatever arrangements he was going to make, after reassuring me that Riley would be released in a day or two.

I took my place beside Riley's bed, twining my fingers with his, rubbing absently against his callused thumb, and waited patiently for him to wake.

I opened my eyes the next morning to see a nurse enter the room, her face blocked by a huge arrangement of mismatched flowers. My stomach tightened at the sight of the flowers, and I asked, "Where did those come from?"

"They were left at the desk," she said, setting them on the table across the room. "Odd arrangement. I don't like it much, but I'm sure whoever sent it meant well."

I was sure they didn't.

I waited until the nurse left the room after reassuring me that Riley would wake soon. I had a sick feeling that it no longer mattered. Not for me. Trapped in a nightmare I thought I'd escaped, I pulled my fingers from Riley's and stood.

The few steps across the room seemed to take forever.

The nurse had called the arrangement odd. It was a generous description. The flowers clashed, discordant and ugly together, but the sender hadn't been going for pretty. The flowers were a message, one he knew I could decode.

My mother had loved flowers, had taught me their language, but experience had forced me to understand what they really meant. The clash of yellow and pink blooms told me exactly what had happened to Riley.

Yellow Hyacinth for jealousy.

Rhododendron for danger.

And most terrifying, the deep pink blooms of Begonia—a warning of future misfortune.

The car crash was no accident. Neither was the overdose that had almost killed Riley.

The flowers were a threat and a warning.

Numb, I picked up the arrangement and carried it from the room. I didn't look at the card until I was in my car. It had been a year since I'd seen those precise block letters. A year since he'd sent me flowers.

I'd convinced myself it was over. Convinced myself he'd moved on, or forgotten about me, or died. I'd been so sure I was free.

Safe.

I never would have let myself fall in love with Riley if I thought he was still out there.

Still watching.

I turned the card over in my fingers, knowing I had to read it. Knowing that once I did, my path was set. I'd have to write a note of my own to Riley, one that would make him hate me.

Hate would keep him far from me.

Hate would keep him safe.

A hot tear slid down my cheek as I tugged at the seal of the small white envelope. I'd been arrogant. I wanted Riley so badly I'd convinced myself I could have him. That arrogance had almost gotten Riley killed.

I understood what the flowers were saying; Walk away from Riley, or the next time he'll be dead.

I didn't need to read the card.

I opened it anyway, my fingers shaking.

TELL HIM GOODBYE, OR I'LL DO IT FOR YOU

CHAPTER ONE

ANNALISE

"Miss, can I get more cream for this coffee?"

I took the customer's mug and topped it off with another slug of half-and-half, handing it back with a polite smile. Working as a barista in a small café in Austin, Texas wasn't the best paying job I'd ever had, but it was fun. Mostly.

I'd needed somewhere to go, and my friend Kat had stepped in with a job offer. She'd even hung my photographs on the walls, and in the few months I'd been in Austin I'd sold enough to pay for the repairs I needed on my beat up Jeep.

It wasn't the life I'd imagined for myself, but it was what I had. I grabbed a rag and started wiping down empty tables.

I'm terrible at sitting still, and the café was quiet in mid-afternoon. Kat was in the back doing paperwork. My only customer was quietly drinking his coffee and reading the newspaper.

I preferred the job I'd had waiting tables in New

Mexico—more money and no downtime during work hours —but it was fun seeing Kat again.

We met six years before when I was in Austin for a photography conference. I tried to stay off the radar, and the conference had been big enough I thought I'd disappear into the crowd. I'd stopped in the café for a hit of caffeine, commented to the barista how much I liked the place, and we hit it off.

I wasn't always great at keeping up long-distance friendships. Part of the point of moving around was so that no one knew where I was. But I'd liked Kat, and the loneliness of five years away from home had been wearing on me. I'd wanted to make a friend.

Now, more than ever, I was glad I had. Kat had stepped in just when I'd needed her. I'd left New Mexico in the middle of the night, panicked. No, not panicked. Terrified. He'd found me again so quickly. The flowers had shown up at my door, sitting at the top of the steps to the garage apartment I rented under an assumed name, the velvet-white petals and glossy green leaves of gardenia striking fear into my heart.

Gardenia. The flower of secret love.

The same arrangement he sent to my brother's house only a few weeks later. I wished his love were a little less secret so we could find him and end this thing once and for all. Eleven years I'd been running from him, and nothing had changed.

I had tiny snatches of a life. A few months here. Half a year there. Friends who got to know me just a little before I disappeared. I had a laptop full of photographs that had never been shown, people I'd never called back, a life interrupted over and over by fear.

I was starting to wonder what was worse—the constant running or standing still and facing what might come?

It had started in high school. Notes left in places only I would find them, mostly innocent, almost sweet. Then small gifts and flowers. I didn't understand the flowers at first, didn't get the language, the way he was speaking to me.

My mother had taught me the language of flowers when I was a child, but I'd mostly forgotten it. People didn't pay attention to those things these days.

At first, I'd written notes back, leaving them in our secret hiding places. Under a rock in the woods behind the house. In the notch of a tree.

Looking back, it was hard to imagine I'd been so foolish, but fifteen-year-old girls aren't known for being sensible where love is concerned. I didn't realize the danger, the threat, until the boy who took me to homecoming that year ended up with a broken arm.

Two days later there was a note.

STAY AWAY FROM HIM. YOU'RE MINE.

Of course, I'd gone to my cousin, Aiden. He'd pulled in the Sinclairs and their company, Sinclair Security. Despite their combined power and influence, no one had been able to find my secret admirer turned stalker.

There were periods of quiet, stretches of weeks and months when I felt safe. Then it would start up again. The notes. The flowers. I thought I could handle it until Riley.

I shut down that train of thought before it could go any further.

I didn't think of Riley anymore.

I couldn't.

As far as I knew, he was off somewhere living his life. I'd written him the worst Dear John letter I could come up with, a bunch of bullshit about him being beneath me and reconnecting with my high school boyfriend. Then I'd taken off.

I'd packed my camera, my laptop, and a duffel bag of clothes in my SUV and driven away. My family hadn't been happy. They wanted me to stay. To fight. I would've felt the same in their shoes.

But they didn't have to watch the man they loved almost die, twice, and know it was their fault. If I had stayed, I would've been putting Riley's life at risk.

I couldn't do that.

And who was to say the stalker would have confined himself to Riley? We didn't know who he was, or why I'd caught his eye. If it was about the family, what if he looked to Charlie next?

I couldn't stand the thought of bringing more danger to the people I loved. If he was going to come after me, I'd make him work for it.

And I had. The first few years I skipped around every couple of months, taking odd jobs for cash and renting rooms in private homes to keep my Social Security number off any easily searched records.

He found me anyway.

Not every time, in every city, but often enough.

Usually, where I was working. That was why the flowers in New Mexico scared me so badly. They hadn't arrived at my job; they'd been sitting right in front of my door.

He knew where I slept at night.

I'd thrown away the flowers, sent the note to the Sinclairs, and run. It wasn't right. I'd had a gallery showing set up. People had been depending on me, and I'd let them down, but I'd run anyway.

It was sheer luck that Kat had called the next day, luck

that I'd been only a few hours from Austin. I'd needed a safe place to take stock. To reevaluate my strategy.

The running had started as a short-term plan. I'd wanted to put some space between me and Atlanta. Between me and the stalker. But space was an illusion. He followed me wherever I went. And I missed my family. I missed having a life.

I'd gone home for Charlie's wedding and stayed for Tate's. My little brother was married, and baby Charlotte was all grown up. Holden, Tate's partner in crime and my younger cousin, was also engaged, as was his older brother, Jacob, and my older brother Gage.

They were all moving on. Living their lives. And I was happy for them. I was, truly, honestly happy for them. And more than a little jealous.

I wanted a life.

I'd wanted to fall in love. To get married. To be a photographer and a mom. My college dreams were an unformed jumble, never realized because I'd run away.

I'd taken off and never stopped. Life had left me behind, and as long as I kept running, I'd never catch up.

I finished wiping down the tables in the café and moved behind the counter to make an Americano for a customer, but my mind wasn't on coffee, it was on Charlie.

I'd watched my baby cousin get married, and all I could think was—Charlie wouldn't have run. Charlie was a fighter.

I knew I was right because Charlie had been there. A former business partner of Winters Inc. had taken exception to Charlie turning him in for fraud. He'd threatened her and vandalized her house, but Charlie hadn't run. Charlie had fought back and managed to win herself a hot guy in the process.

She'd inspired me. For about five minutes. Then, a few days after the wedding, an arrangement of gardenias had been delivered to Winters House.

I ran.

Again.

My family, especially Gage and Aiden, had tried to persuade me to stay. They promised that this time we would catch him. This time it would end.

I sat there, the evidence of two blissful weddings still littering the house, and I'd thought about it. Thought about staying. Fighting back. Thought about how little I had to lose.

How much my family had to risk. Vance had a daughter. My twin brother had a baby girl and a wife. A beautiful little family. What right did I have to put them in danger?

We'd lost too much already. I couldn't be the reason we lost more. That was what I told myself. Mostly, I believed it.

Sometimes over the years, when I was packing my car and moving on again, I wondered if I was protecting my family, or protecting myself.

I'd been a mess when I'd almost lost Riley. Seeing him in the hospital bed, watching the lines go flat on his monitor, had almost killed me.

I'd run forever to avoid feeling that kind of pain again.

Kat came down the hall from her back office, rubbing her temple with one hand, her messy, pixie-cut, dark hair falling in her eyes.

"Still slow?" she asked, perching on a stool on the other side of the counter.

"So far," I said. "Skinny cinnamon latte?"

"Please. My head is killing me. I hate doing the books."

"You should wear your glasses," I chided.

"I am not wearing reading glasses," Kat said, not for the

first time. "I'm only thirty-six. I refuse to need reading glasses."

"You can refuse all you want, but the computer screen is still going to be blurry."

Kat just grunted and took the latte I handed her, sipping gratefully. I made one for myself. I was working a double, and I needed the caffeine.

We drank our coffee in quiet harmony for a few minutes before Kat set hers on the counter and said, "I sold two of your photographs this morning. I really think you should talk to some of the gallery owners. Put together a show."

"Not after New Mexico," I said. I still felt awful about leaving them in the lurch. I'd reimbursed their expenses, but that wasn't the point.

Kat leveled a long look at me. "You're sure?"

I nodded. She knew my situation, though she didn't know my real last name. Since I'd left home, I'd been using Marlow, my mother's maiden name, instead of Winters. "Too much planning goes into a show," I explained. "Too much publicity."

"I know," Kat said, quietly. "It's just that you could be selling for a lot more, making a name for yourself. This is just—" She glanced around the café, taking in my photographs decorating the walls and gave a helpless shrug. "It feels like giving up."

I didn't say what I was thinking. That my whole life felt like giving up.

"You want to split a day-old cookie?" Kat asked, brightly, with a gentle touch to the back of my hand. I hadn't held onto many friends over the last decade, but I was glad Kat was one of them.

When I got home, after working a double and closing up the cafe, I called Aiden. He was at work, as usual, which was a little late since I was a few hours earlier than he was. My ten o'clock call put him in the office at eleven. When I told him he needed a life, he just laughed.

"With all of you to keep an eye on, work is relaxing. Charlie and Lucas bought a new flip-house. The place is such a mess I'm having nightmares of it falling on her head."

"I'm sure Lucas wouldn't let her in an unsafe building," I said, in the understatement of the century. Lucas was Charlie's new husband, and he most definitely would not have bought an unsafe building if he thought Charlie would be in danger.

"That's not the point," Aiden grumbled.

I knew what he meant. Charlie might have a new husband to look after her, but she was still Aiden's baby sister. That her husband was former special forces, and currently working with the Sinclairs in their cybersecurity division, didn't make any difference to Aiden.

We didn't talk long. I didn't have much to say. We ended our call the way we always did, with Aiden saying, "We miss you. I wish you'd think about coming home," and me responding, "Maybe."

It was the first time in years I actually meant it.

Maybe.

I didn't know how quickly that *maybe* would turn to *yes*.

The next day I was stocking shelves in the back room during the morning lull when I heard Kat's voice calling my name. I stood too fast, knocking the back of my head against a shelf, but something in the tone of her voice put me on alert.

Rubbing the tender spot on my scalp, I walked down the hall.

Ice ran down my spine the second I saw it. Red and blue spikes of flowers arranged with sprigs of delicate white blossoms. Salvia and lily of the valley, two plants more commonly used in landscaped beds than in flower arrangements.

I didn't need to search my memory for their meaning. I knew them both by heart.

Blue Salvia—*I think of you.*

Red Salvia—*Forever mine.*

Both set off by Lily of the Valley, the flower for those born in May.

I'd been hiding who I was for so long I'd forgotten my own birthday. For the first time in years, I felt more than fear. Hot fury surged in my chest. I'd only been here a few months. I didn't want to leave.

Trying to control my emotions, I said, "Did you see who delivered it?"

"No, I'm sorry," Kat said. "I left the front for a minute to get another carton of milk, and it was sitting here when I came back. There's a note."

She gestured to the white square envelope nestled among the Red Salvia.

I didn't touch the flowers. Didn't touch the note. Going behind the counter, I grabbed a plastic storage bag and pulled it over my hand, inside out. Carefully, I picked up the envelope and pulled the plastic bag over the note. Using the plastic to shield my fingers, I teased the note from the envelope and read the familiar block letters through the protective bag.

I MISS YOU, MY LOVE.

HAPPY BIRTHDAY

"That's twisted," Kat said, reading over my shoulder. "You really don't know who it is?"

I stiffened. I'd heard that before, had let those questions steep me in guilt when I'd been a young teenager and felt responsible for the way I'd played along at the start.

Trying to keep the resentment out of my voice, I said, "No, I don't."

I pressed the air from the plastic bag and sealed it closed. I'd sent every single note I'd received in the last eleven years to the Sinclairs to examine for evidence. None of them had revealed a single clue.

"If I had any idea who was doing this—" I shook my head. It had been going on so long I couldn't imagine a life without the threat of my unknown admirer.

"I'm sorry," Kat said. "I didn't mean it like that."

"I know you didn't," I said. I wasn't really paying attention. My mind was racing as I stared at those stalks of red and blue flowers.

Was I going to run?

That was my usual modus operandi.

He finds me, and I run.

For eleven years, he would find me, and I would run.

If this was a game, I wasn't winning.

He was eating up my life in tiny chunks of fear and threat.

I wasn't living. I was surviving. Sometimes, survival is enough. And sometimes, you either have to choose life or just give up.

I wasn't ready to give up.

Chapter Two

Annalise

I stared at the carefully sealed note in a daze. I was going to leave, but I wasn't running away.

Not this time.

Looking up, I met Kat's curious eyes and said, "I have to leave—"

"Lise, you don't have to leave," Kat protested.

I shook my head.

"I'm not running this time. I'm going home."

I pulled my phone from my pocket and flipped it open. The encrypted device wasn't flashy, but it was secure. A gift from the Sinclairs.

Aiden answered on the second ring, worry heavy in his voice. "Lise, what is it?"

"There's been another delivery," I said, flatly. Afraid to hope, afraid to hear myself speak the words aloud, I said, "I want to come home."

Aiden said, simply, "I'll send the plane."

There were benefits to being a Winters.

I packed my meager belongings and headed back to the

café. Kat had offered to let me leave my Jeep in the alley behind the building. We were silent as she drove me to the private airstrip west of downtown.

Uniformed attendants appeared as we pulled up beside the sleek private jet. I pointed them in the direction of my luggage and gave up on avoiding Kat's curious gaze. She watched as the attendants emptied the car and loaded the plane, taking in the size of the jet before she looked back at me.

"There's a lot you're not telling me, isn't there?"

I shrugged one shoulder and smiled. "Nothing that really matters."

"Having a private jet at your disposal doesn't really matter?" Kat asked, laughter in her voice.

No longer joking, I shook my head. "No, a private jet doesn't really matter. Friends matter." The tears that flooded my eyes took me by surprise. With a little hitch in my voice, I said, "I'm sorry I'm leaving you short a barista with no notice."

Kat pulled me into a surprisingly tight hug and said, "We'll manage. You need to do this. Go home, Lise, and stay safe."

I'd never been in this plane before, but it felt oddly familiar. When you get down to it, one private plane is a lot like another. Custom wood-work, butter-soft leather upholstery, hovering staff.

I'd been living a different kind of life for the past decade, but it wouldn't be hard to get used to the perks of being a Winters.

I hefted my backpack over one shoulder and looked around, taking in the polished table, tobacco-colored leather chairs and matching couch long enough for a Winters male's long frame.

I could imagine Aiden or Gage stretched out on that couch, reviewing paperwork or talking on the phone, barking orders at an assistant as they traveled the country running the family business.

With that picture in my head, I set my backpack on the couch and prepared to lay down. A flight attendant entered the cabin, looked at me regretfully and said, "Miss Winters, you'll have to buckle in for takeoff, but as soon as we're clear I'll let you know."

"Do you make Aiden buckle in for takeoff?" I couldn't help asking.

The flight attendant's sheepish expression answered my question for me. Her lips curved into a gentle smile as she said, "Mr. Winters requested that you arrive home safely. Please take a seat, and we'll get you up in the air as soon as possible. Would you like a drink or something to eat?"

"No, thank you," I said, leaving the comfort of the couch for a seat near the window. I fastened my seatbelt and pulled out the bag Kat had handed me before we got out of the car.

A small thermos of coffee and a sandwich, plus two cookies and a muffin. She was a good friend. I'd had a lot of good friends in my life. I wondered how many would be left when this was all over.

The flight from Austin to Atlanta was only two hours. Just long enough to eat my dinner, open my laptop, and start scanning through the photographs I'd taken on my last day off. I'd only gotten through the first set before the polite flight attendant returned to evict me from the couch and send me back to the seatbelt.

My stomach rolled with nerves as the plane descended. Coming home felt like the right thing to do. Finally.

That didn't mean I wasn't scared to death.

The door to the plane opened, and Aiden was there. Before I could get my bearings, he pulled me into a tight hug. "We're going to fix this, sweetheart. I promise."

Aiden looked like his father. And mine. Tall, well-built, with dark hair. He had Uncle Hugh's deep brown eyes, while my side of the family shared my father's vibrant blue. My older brother Gage looked enough like Aiden to be his twin, eye color aside, as did my youngest brother, Tate.

Vance and I looked more like our mother. Leanly built, with long golden blonde hair streaked platinum from the sun and identical sky-blue eyes, though I was taller than she'd been and my hair was darker, my features bolder.

At my age, Anna Winters had been a physician, a mother of four, and a wife. I was an accomplished waitress, I could sling a mean cup of coffee, and I was barely more than an amateur photographer.

My mother had died at thirty-four, so it was probably a good thing she'd packed so much life into what she'd been given.

The flight attendants loaded Aiden's luxury sedan with my things as I let Aiden help me into the car. He waited to speak until we were pulling out of the airport. The sun was setting, casting a dreamy glow over the trees and sky. Fatigue pulled at me.

I'd been running on adrenaline and determination since the moment I decided to stop running. Now that I was home, I was ready to crawl into bed and fall asleep.

"I called Cooper," Aiden said, referring to Cooper Sinclair, the eldest Sinclair brother and the one nominally in charge of Sinclair Security. "I met with him, Evers, and Knox this afternoon. We have a plan, and we'd like you to hear us out."

I wasn't sure if I was relieved or annoyed. I shouldn't have been surprised the boys would try to take over. It was what they did. Always had been. And Aiden couldn't resist meddling. He didn't even try.

With a sigh, I asked, "What is it?"

He shot me a sidelong glance and said, "It's aggressive. You've given up enough of your life to this creep. Now that you've decided to come home, we took that to mean you're ready to go on the offensive."

"I am," I said. My voice was firm, decisive, but the hollow feeling in my chest wouldn't go away.

I had to face this down. I knew it. I was still terrified.

"We're meeting with them first thing in the morning. I don't want you leaving the house until we work out the details."

"Fine with me," I said. Being home would be overwhelming enough. "Is the security still on high?"

The last time I'd been home, for the weddings over the holidays, there'd been a break-in at Winters House, and Aiden had the security cranked tight.

"Not like it was," he admitted. "We've still been using the motion sensors at night, and we're watching the hidden access in the basement in case the intruder uses it again, but we don't have as many guards on the property. We can reevaluate at the meeting tomorrow, but you don't need to worry about your safety tonight."

"I wasn't worried, Aiden. I know you wouldn't let anything happen to me."

He reached across the space between us and took my hand in his. What he didn't understand, what none of them understood, was that I wasn't scared about what might happen to *me*.

I'd never forgotten the agony of watching Riley almost die in front of me. Aiden would do anything to keep me safe, even give his life for mine. Any of them would. That was the one thing I couldn't live with.

We paused at the first gate, then pulled into the long drive up to Winters House, lined by oak trees and lit by the last fading streams of sunset. I'd been away for so many years, visiting only here and there, but I'd missed this place.

I'd missed home. As we drove up to the inner gate, Aiden stopped and looked at me. "There was a fight about who could meet you at the airport. I won, but they're all inside, and planning an impromptu birthday celebration for you and Vance. We were going to have a dinner party this weekend—still are—but everyone wanted to see you right away. I know you're tired but—"

"I want to see them too," I said. "All of them?"

"Pretty much," Aiden said with a grin.

He pretended we drove him nuts, but I knew he was secretly happy to have everyone under the same roof. Now that we were pairing off, the accumulated Winters made for a big crowd.

We watched the inner gates swing open and drove into the courtyard of Winters House. Built in a Mediterranean-style, with creamy walls and a red tile roof, the house was designed in a square around a center courtyard. When I was a child, the gate to that courtyard was never closed. Since our parents had died, we'd felt safer with bars between us and the rest of the world.

The tall wooden front door swung open, and light spilled into the courtyard. My twin brother Vance, his blonde hair pulled back into a low ponytail and a roguish grin on his face, jumped down the steps and swung me into his arms. "Happy birthday, little sister."

"Happy birthday, annoying brother," I said back, the way we had since we could talk. "Did you bring Maggie and Rosie?"

He slung his arm around my shoulders and squeezed me close, saying, "Of course I did. I don't go anywhere without my girls."

Then Gage was there, pulling me away from Vance and into another tight hug. "You're supposed to get presents on your birthday, not give them."

At my look of confusion, he said, "Are you really home to stay?" I nodded. "Then that's the best gift I could imagine."

He kissed my forehead, letting me have a second to hide my tears. Gage had only recently come home himself. A few days after Uncle Hugh and Aunt Olivia died he'd joined the Army and never looked back.

Gage knew all about running.

Unlike me, he also knew how to come home.

"You're just saving yourself a trip, anyway," he said, stepping back to pull his girlfriend, Sophie, to his side. Sophie was our great-aunt Amelia's nurse. Gage had come home, taken one look at Sophie, and fallen head over heels.

Tugging Sophie closer, he lifted her hand and raised it in front of my face. I'd have to be blind to miss the sparkle of the rock on her finger. I recognized the ring immediately. It had been my mother's, and now Gage had given it to Sophie.

This time I didn't even try to hide my tears. I grabbed Sophie and hugged her tight. I'd met her for the first time when I'd come home for the weddings over the holidays, but I'd instantly adored her. She was patient and funny, took wonderful care of our great-aunt, and loved Gage to distraction.

Sophie returned my hug with a fierce squeeze of her own and whispered, "You don't mind that he gave me her ring?"

I hugged her tighter and shook my head against her shoulder. Straightening, I kissed her cheek and said, "I can't think of anything more perfect. It looks beautiful. Have you set a date?"

My cousin Charlie cut in, "Following our recent tradition they've given everyone a whopping three weeks' notice."

"But at least it's here, and it's small," Gage shot back.

"My wedding was here," Charlie protested.

"But it wasn't small," Gage said.

Charlie shrugged and grinned. "It was small-*ish*. Anyway, next to what Jacob and Abigail are planning, any wedding is small."

I heard Abigail's perfectly modulated, elegant voice cut in, "It's not going to be *that* big."

I looked to my cousin Jacob, standing beside her, and from the amused light in his eyes, I had a feeling their wedding would be huge. The last time I'd been home, they still hadn't set a date.

Jacob's cool silver eyes landed on me and warmed. I was in his arms a second later. He gave me a quick, hard squeeze and murmured, "We're going to do it right this time, Lise, I promise. No more running."

I was turning into a watering pot from all these hugs. I hadn't expected such a heartfelt welcome. It was reassuring, but it also made me feel a little guilty.

When Gage had come home a few months before I knew he hadn't had the same reception. It had taken him months to win over Aiden and make a new place for himself in our family.

My warm welcome wasn't fair, but that didn't mean I wasn't grateful. Seeing my family all together, their girlfriends, spouses, even baby Rosalie, I remembered again how much love I had behind me.

And how much I had left to lose.

CHAPTER THREE

ANNALISE

Breakfast at Winters House was a lot more entertaining than I remembered. Sophie and Aunt Amelia bickered through the meal, Amelia trying to get Sophie to give her a muffin and Sophie reminding her that muffins weren't on her low sugar diet.

Gage leaned toward me and whispered, "They do this every morning. Amelia refuses to give up on the muffin."

"How would you know?" Amelia cut in. She might be in her eighties, but she was sharp as a tack. "You're usually at the office by the time we eat breakfast."

"I know everything," Gage answered smoothly.

Sophie smothered a giggle as Amelia harrumphed in response. "He's spending too much time with Aiden. Thinks he's king of the universe."

Gage slanted Sophie a look that had her flushing a deep pink. She bit her lower lip and looked away, much to Amelia's amusement.

Amelia winked at me and said, "They haven't even gotten married, and already they're acting like newlyweds."

Mrs. Williamson came in, carrying a platter of fresh fruit, her hair in its customary twist, her dress neatly starched. Mrs. W had come to Winters House at eighteen, not long after my parents had died, and she'd been keeping us in line ever since. With our parents gone, she was the closest thing to a mother any of us had left.

She set the fruit tray down in front of Amelia, distracting my great-aunt from her quest for a muffin, and stopped beside me. In an uncharacteristic gesture of affection, she gave my shoulder a hard squeeze and leaned down to place a quick kiss on my temple. Tears flooded my eyes at the kiss, so unlike her, as she whispered, "It's good to have you home."

Blinking quickly to chase the moisture from my eyes, I reached up to squeeze her hand before she could step away and, in an effort to lighten the moment, said, "Have you had enough of weddings yet? Two over the holidays and another in a few weeks—if you ever leave us you could make a career as an event planner."

Mrs. W smiled and shook her head. "I'll never have enough of weddings in this house. With all you children moved out and Aiden working so much it was far too quiet around here. Now, all we need is for Gage and Sophie to give us some babies. You don't remember Winters House filled with babies. This house needs children."

With a wink at Aunt Amelia, Mrs. W picked up the empty carafe of coffee and left. Gage and Sophie watched her go, their jaws dropped and eyes wide.

Amelia sat back, picked up her coffee, and said, "Mrs. W is getting saucy."

"I think it's Abel's influence," Sophie said, quietly. Abel was the cook. He'd been with us since I was in high school, but I'd never had any hint there might be something going on between him and Mrs. W.

I leaned forward and looked across the table at Sophie. "What do you know?" I asked, my voice low. Mrs. W had eyes in the back of her head and ears like a hawk.

Proving that she was no fool, Sophie glanced over her shoulder at the empty butler's pantry before she said, in an equally low tone, "I went to the kitchen weeks ago to make another pot of coffee—bad night of sleep—and they were in the corner, whispering. Abel was holding her hand."

"That's it?" Amelia said, not bothering to keep her voice low. "I can't believe you didn't tell me. Not that that's much to tell. Hand-holding." She shook her head in dismissal.

Sophie rolled her eyes at Aunt Amelia. "Maybe for you hand-holding is nothing. For Mrs. W, that's a lot."

Gage pinned our great-aunt with a firm look. "Don't you dare start any trouble for her, Amelia. If she and Abel have something going on, leave them alone to work it out."

Aunt Amelia made a dismissive sound in her throat, and I shook my head, keeping my eyes on my empty plate and trying to hide my smile. Aunt Amelia was a born troublemaker.

Technically Sophie was her nurse, but Aunt Amelia didn't need much nursing. Mostly what she needed was a companion, and someone to keep her from burning the house down.

Amelia lived to pull pranks.

Sophie spent most of her time either assisting in Amelia's schemes or talking her out of them. If Amelia set her mind to causing trouble, we were all in for it.

Amelia sent Gage a grin and said, "Who? Me? I wouldn't dream of interfering with Mrs. W."

I let out a snort of laughter. Sophie just narrowed her eyes. "Seriously, Amelia. Stay out of it."

"Oh, I'll stay out of it. Scout's honor."

Under his breath, Gage muttered, "Like you were ever a Scout."

Aunt Amelia just sent him a devilish smile. Male voices filtered in from the hall and I felt myself tense. Aiden, and, I thought, Cooper Sinclair. They entered the room, and I saw that I'd been correct.

Finished with my breakfast, I rose. Cooper pulled me into a bear hug. I'd known all the Sinclairs since birth. They were less friends and more like extended family, though the last thing I needed was more overprotective older brothers.

"Mrs. W is bringing coffee to the living room," Aiden said. "I think we'll have more space to spread out there."

He turned to lead the way across the hall to the formal living room. Cooper and I followed, Gage rising behind us to join in.

The living room of Winters House was almost as big as the dining room. It was a formal space, filled with expensive Persian carpets and silk upholstered couches, but not fussy or overly feminine. The high windows let in plenty of light, and the view of the gardens complemented the pale creamy walls and glossy white trim. It had been my Aunt Olivia's favorite room in Winters House, as well as my mother's.

Aiden had an office just down the hall, by the library and wine room. It was more than big enough for the four of us. I hovered in the doorway of the living room and studied Aiden, who stared out the window at the gardens behind the house and didn't meet my eyes.

"We won't all fit in your office?" I asked, carefully.

Cooper cut in. "Evers and Knox are coming," he explained. "And they're bringing someone from our team we think can help. The gate already called up. They should be here any minute."

The boys had a plan.

I knew better than to interfere before I'd let them have their say. Anyway, nothing I'd done had worked—clearly running away wasn't the answer. I might as well see what the guys had cooked up.

If I didn't like it, I didn't have to go along.

Facing down the combined will of Aiden, Gage, and three of the Sinclair brothers wouldn't be easy, but I could do it.

Mrs. W came in, carrying a tray with the coffee pot, cups and saucers, and a plate of shortbread. Giving me a supportive smile, she said to Aiden, "A car just pulled up in front of the house."

I sat and poured myself a cup of coffee. I didn't need more caffeine, but I did need something to occupy myself. I'd been in charge of my own life for a long time, and I had no intention of letting anyone run it for me.

The best way to keep control of the meeting was to keep my mouth shut until I knew what I wanted to say. The front door opened and Mrs. W voiced a greeting. I recognized Evers saying hello and, based on Mrs. W's light laugh, probably flirting a little.

I took a sip of coffee and waited, determined not to let the guys take over. Not to be the victim. I was here to take my life back, and I wasn't going to be bulldozed by this crew of overprotective males.

Every speck of my resolve flew out the window when *he* walked in.

Riley.

Riley Flynn.

Carefully, I set my coffee cup back on the tray, aware

my hands had started to shake. I stood abruptly, composure gone, and met Riley's hazel eyes.

He stared back, expression blank, distantly polite. For a terrifying second, I wondered if he even recognized me.

I tossed that idea away the moment after it flashed through my mind. Of course, he recognized me. But what the hell was he doing here? All of a sudden, nothing made sense.

My plan to keep my mouth shut flew right out the window and I demanded, "What are you doing here?"

Before Riley could answer, Cooper looked between us and said, "Oh, yeah, I forgot you didn't know. Riley's on our team now. He's been with us for a while. When we were considering different options to track down your stalker, Evers remembered that you two knew each other and thought he might be the best man for the job."

I searched Riley's face for some hint of emotion, some acknowledgment that there was more between us than just two people who used to know each other. I got nothing. It had been eleven years, and the sight of him was a knife to my heart, reminding me how barren, how lonely the last decade had been without him.

He lifted his chin in my direction, flicked his eyes over me and said, "It's good to see you again."

"Yes," I said, inanely, "you look well."

"So do you," he said politely, lying.

I didn't look well. I was too thin, and I had circles under my eyes from stress. I looked like crap, especially compared to the twenty-year-old Riley had known.

I wanted to cry. I wanted to run through the door, lock myself in my room, and weep for everything I'd lost.

We'd been so in love.

Now, all we had was a polite, dry, exchange of greetings. It was less than nothing.

I was not going to cry.

I was not going to fall apart.

My first love was here, and he was supposed to help with this plan to draw out and catch my stalker. Fine. If it would get my life back, I would handle it.

Drawing on a trick I'd taught Charlie when we were children and trying not to cry in front of the cameras at her parent's funeral, I stabbed my fingernails into my palm hard enough to cut skin. Hard enough for the pain to drive away my tears.

When I thought I had myself under control, I sat down, picked up my cup of coffee, and said, "So, gentlemen, you have a plan? Because I've got nothing and I'm tired of running."

At my cue, everyone took a seat, Gage beside me. He took my hand in his, squeezing tightly before letting go and leaning forward to snag a square of shortbread off the tray.

In a low voice meant just for me, he said, "Did you know Abel makes these because they're Mrs. W's favorite?"

I hadn't known. I was betting Sophie had figured it out and told Gage. I liked her even more for that and loved my big brother for trying to distract me when he knew I was upset.

I faked a smile and said back, "Snag me a piece, will you?"

He did, and I took a bite, the sweet, buttery, slightly salty crunch of the shortbread reminding me of all the best parts of home. I did my best not to look at Riley, who made it difficult by choosing a seat on the opposite couch.

From the corner of my eye, I noted that he hadn't changed

much. He looked a little thicker around the shoulders and arms as if he'd put on muscle, and his hair was shorter. Otherwise, he looked exactly like the boy I'd loved. The boy I'd left lying in a hospital bed, a brutal goodbye letter tucked under his pillow.

How easy it was to forget that I was the one who'd walked out.

I'd left him when he was at his most vulnerable, doing my best to shatter his heart on my way out the door.

It was no wonder he could barely spare me a polite smile. I never thought I'd see him again. I'd never *wanted* to see him again. The whole plan was to keep him away from me. To keep him safe. To keep him alive.

Riley never would have let me leave him if he'd suspected I was trying to protect him. I'd had to make it real. I'd had to make him hate me. Now he did. It was a lot harder to live with that when he was sitting right in front of me.

A wave of despair swamped me. I'd given up the only man I've ever loved to keep him safe, and here he was jumping right in the middle of the whole fucking mess. I finished my piece of shortbread and fisted my hand at my side, driving my nails into a fresh spot on my palm, using the pain to clear my mind.

I loved Aiden and Gage, loved the Sinclairs, but if they thought I couldn't handle this, they'd take over in a heartbeat. I didn't want that. This was my life.

Cooper leaned forward and said, "Gage said you had a new note for us to look at."

"Yes, he sent it with red and blue salvia and lily of the valley."

"Thinking of you, happy birthday, and forever mine," Cooper said. He knew his flowers, too. A decade of following my case could teach any man everything he needed to know about the language of flowers. "What did the note say?"

"I miss you, my love. Happy birthday," I said, flatly. "I have it in my room. I'll give it to you before you go."

"And no one saw who delivered it?" Knox asked, speaking for the first time. The middle Sinclair brother only used words when he had to. His dark eyes locked on mine, their expression grave. My tension eased a little.

Knox was quiet, but he was focused and tenacious. He was two years older than me, but as kids, we'd been close. In the midst of two very loud families, Knox and I both liked the quiet.

"No," I answered. "It was business as usual. The mysterious arrangement, the flowers with meanings, the block letters on the note."

"He found you fast this time," Cooper said.

"Too fast. I'd only been there a few months. And he knew when I was home for the wedding. Those gardenias —" I trailed off, shaking my head.

I hated gardenias. They were one of his favorites.

Secret love.

Maybe on his side. On my side, there was only hate and fear.

"There are a few ways we can go with this, Lise," Cooper said. "We can stick you in the house, keep you under guard, and keep investigating. Eventually, this guy is going to make a mistake."

"Eventually," I said, picking up on the operative word in Cooper's statement.

He nodded in acknowledgment. "He's been sending you flowers, gifts, and notes since you were a teenager. So far we don't have much. We don't even know definitely that he's a he. Whoever it is, they're smart and careful."

"What's the other option?" I asked. Living under house arrest was worse than living on the run.

"We draw him out."

I looked around the room at six sets of eyes, focused on me. I had a bad feeling I knew what that meant, but I had to ask, "Draw him out how, exactly?"

"Using me," Riley said.

I couldn't hide my flinch. I didn't really try. Deliberately, I leaned forward and placed my coffee cup back on the tray. I didn't think I could look at Riley and keep myself under control, so I looked at Cooper and said, "No. Absolutely not."

Aiden interrupted. "Lise, think carefully. If we use Flynn, have him act like you two are together, this guy will get reckless. If he gets reckless, we can catch him."

"By putting people in danger?" I protested.

Evers leaned forward, shooting a glance back at Riley before looking at me. "I knew you wouldn't like it, but Lise, honey, this guy has a pattern. He broke the arm of your high school boy-friend, Riley ended up in the hospital, and what about that guy you were seeing in Oklahoma? Another car accident? Or was that the weird one?"

My stomach rolled with nausea at the easy way Evers listed my stalker's casualties. I knew Evers, knew he was trying to keep things light, but I couldn't match his tone.

In an emotionless voice, I said, "No. Oklahoma was a fall off a ladder. The car accident was Denver. The weird one was the snow bank in Minneapolis. I stopped trying after that."

We called that the weird one because the reality was too horrible. Derek had survived being duct taped and buried in a snow bank in the dead of winter, but it had been a near miss. I'd fled Minneapolis as soon as I was sure he'd live. I'd never come close to getting involved with another man. That had been four years ago.

Pressing my fingernails back into my palms, I forced myself to stay collected when I looked at Riley and said, "And you're okay with this? Being a target? The last time you almost died. Twice."

His expression was contained, his eyes impenetrable when he said, "I can handle it. This is my job. What happened before—we were kids. It's ancient history. This is business. My business. Going undercover, drawing out a suspect—I've done it before. I'm good at it. If you want to end this, I can get the job done."

"He's the best we have for this," Knox said in a quiet voice.

Backing up his brother, Evers said, "Look, Lise, I know it's weird since you two used to date, but Riley's right, it's ancient history. He's an absolute professional, and he really is the best guy we have for this. He's a genius at undercover, and he's got excellent instincts. He's not going down on the job. You don't have to worry about him getting hurt, do you understand? He can keep both of you safe while he plays the loving fiancé and we get this guy to come out into the open."

I couldn't stand the pressure of all those eyes on me. I stood and paced to the windows, looking out over the gardens behind Winters House to the pool and the woods beyond. If you walked that way, you'd find a path on the edge of the woods that would lead you a quarter-mile through the trees to the house where I'd grown up.

After my parents had been murdered Uncle Hugh had closed the house, bringing Gage, Vance, Tate, and I to live in Winters House. Our home sat empty now. Abandoned.

I'd learned young that there was no going back. Life happened, and the only choice was to move forward.

Right now, my gut was telling me that my only choice was to run. To get in the car and take off. This was too much risk. Risk to me, but more importantly risk to everyone around me. I'd sacrificed everything to keep them safe, and now their plan was to wave a red flag in front of my stalker and drive him to violence.

"And what if he doesn't come after me? Or Riley? What if this time he goes after someone else?" I demanded.

"We can take care of ourselves," Gage said.

"What about Sophie? Aunt Amelia? Mrs. W? And Charlie? Holden and Jacob are both engaged, and Tate just married Emily. Vance has Rosie and Maggie now. You want to put all of them at risk too?"

Aiden shook his head. "He's never gone after anyone except men you've dated. I'm sure Cooper will love invoicing us for extra security, but we'll make sure everyone else is covered. This is the way, Lise."

I crossed my arms over my chest and glared at all of them. They were so sure they were right. Maybe they were, but if they weren't, we wouldn't know until it was too late.

"Isn't that what escalation means?" I pressed. "You're trying to get him to escalate, but I've read enough to know - it's not always a straight line. Sometimes they change. Are you willing to risk the rest of the family? If we're going to do something like this, we should leave, go away from everyone else, try to isolate his targets." The idea grew in my mind. "We don't even need Riley for that. Why don't I just go away somewhere by myself? Have somebody watch me and then catch him when he sends more flowers."

Cooper was already shaking his head. "Lise, no. That's what we've been doing for eleven years. He doesn't deliver the flowers himself. We don't even know that he's writing the notes. We could stick you in a cabin somewhere under constant surveillance, and you'd be there another decade. Waiting. We have to push him off balance enough to get sloppy. You hitting Atlanta with a brand-new fiancé is exactly what we need. I appreciate that you're looking out for everyone else, but now it's time to look out for yourself."

CHAPTER FOUR
RILEY

Annalise stood with her back to the windows, looking hunted. She was thinking of running again. I could tell. Annalise had made a career out of running. I should know, I'd been keeping track of her for years.

She should have been an award-winning photographer. She had an eye for it, and she'd loved her camera almost as much as she'd claimed to love me. Instead, she was a pro at staying on the run. Annalise knew how to get a fake ID, how to find jobs that would pay under the table, how to disappear in the dead of night.

Nothing the oldest daughter of the infamous Winters family should have known. If she wasn't a famous photographer, she should have been married to a country club boy, having kids and organizing luncheons, or helping her brothers run the family company. Not living like a fugitive.

These days Annalise Winters was nothing more to me than a case file. There was nothing between us. Maybe there never had been. But I wasn't going to let her live like this anymore. I'd help catch the creep who'd been stalking her since she was a teenager, and then I'd walk away.

The plan had sounded good on paper. Now, seeing her up close for the first time in years, I wondered if I could do it. There was a part of me, deeply buried and mostly ignored, that hated this woman.

She was just a girl I dated for a few months a decade ago. No big deal. But I could still remember the feel of her hand in mine as I lay half-conscious in the hospital, my head in agony. I'd never forgotten the letter she'd left behind, dismissing me. Dismissing us.

Annalise Winters was a loose end in my life. I'd taken the job to tie it up. Clean and simple. *Do this*, I reminded myself, *and you'll be finished with her for good*.

I watched her, seeing the way her crossed arms didn't just shut us out. She was protecting herself. She was scared. I had to stop thinking of her as the enemy and remember that she was the client.

Sometimes the client didn't know what was good for her. It was my job to make her face reality.

I stood and shoved my hands in my pockets, trying to look as nonthreatening yet competent as I could manage.

"Why don't you guys give me a minute alone with Annalise. She might find it easier to make a decision when we're not all ganging up on her."

Aiden Winters gave me an assessing look that, I'll be honest, made me a little uncomfortable. There was something about him that left me feeling as if he could see all the way to my soul.

We'd only met once before when he'd delivered Annalise's letter. When Annalise and I had dated, I hadn't rated an introduction to her family. I turned to see her older brother Gage giving me the same penetrating look. Fuck, the two oldest Winters men were like twins—tall, broad, and ready to tear the world apart to protect one of their own.

At the moment, I wasn't liking the part of my plan that had me living in the same house with the two of them. They'd do anything for Annalise, and I was disposable. Collateral damage if necessary. It was part of the job, and it had never bothered me before.

Aiden and Gage exchanged a look and rose, nodding at Cooper. Evers and Knox followed along as they filed out of the room. A moment later Annalise and I were alone. I decided to jump right in. This was going to be hard enough. Annalise didn't need me to baby her.

"What part of this has you hesitating?" I asked, sure she was going to say it was me. I should have expected her to surprise me. Lise was always good at surprising me.

"I'm afraid someone's going to get hurt," she said, quietly, her back to me as she studied the gardens of Winters House.

"Someone? Or you?" I took a few steps closer until I stood beside her at the window, only an arm's reach away. She took a tiny step to the side, brushing the heavy silk curtain. Interesting.

"Not me. Someone else. I'm sure you've noticed I have a big family."

"Hard to miss anything about your family," I commented, wryly. There wasn't a single person in the country who didn't know about the Winters family, and in Atlanta, they might as well have been royalty.

Wealthy, powerful, and scandalous. I knew more than I wanted to about the Winters, thanks to my work at Sinclair Security.

Annalise went on, "Then you know we've expanded in

the last few years. Charlie and Tate and Vance are all married, and Vance has a daughter. It's too many people to keep track of. Too many targets if this guy changes his pattern. What if he goes after Rosie? Or Aunt Amelia? She went through enough when Sophie's husband came back. And Sophie—she's been through so much. I can't ask her to live with this kind of risk when her life is just calming down. She and Gage are planning their wedding. I don't want the house put on lockdown again, everyone afraid to go out by themselves. It's not fair."

"I don't think they'd see it that way," I said, gently. Annalise shook her head.

"If we're going to do this, I still like the cabin in the woods idea. No one else around who can get hurt. Just me."

"We've already gone over why that won't work, Annalise. Not visible enough. I've seen this guy's pattern. I think his wet dream is you, isolated, waiting for him to make contact. If we put you in some mountain cabin by yourself, you might never leave. I thought you wanted to end this. I thought you were ready to stop running."

"I am."

Her eyes flicked to mine and then away, too quickly for me to read anything in them. She turned from the window and went back to the sofa, sitting gracefully and pouring herself another cup of coffee. She picked up a shortbread biscuit and took a delicate, precise bite.

I could play along. She wanted distance. She wanted this meeting back on a professional footing. Annalise didn't want to get personal.

That was fine, neither did I. Still, it had to be said.

I took a seat on the sofa opposite hers and poured my own coffee. Meeting her eyes, I asked bluntly, "Is this about me? Would you rather Cooper find another operative? We talked about using Evers. You two have always gotten along. It wouldn't be hard to convince the rest of the world that you're together."

Her blue eyes studied me for a long moment before she shook her head. "Evers has a... thing. A fake fiancée would get in the way."

Curious, I couldn't help asking, "What kind of thing? I know for a fact he's not dating anyone."

A tiny grin worked the side of her mouth, and she shook her head again. "A *none of your business* kind of thing. I haven't talked to him in a while, so maybe it's not even a thing anymore, but either way, I don't want to mess up his life like that."

She took a sip of coffee and another of those delicate bites of the shortbread before she said, "And you're okay with this? It's not going to be weird? You're making yourself a target, and we have no idea how far this will go. You know that, right?"

She had an unsettlingly realistic view of her situation. Usually, we tried to make sure the client was aware of their danger enough to keep them cautious, but not so much that we scared the shit out of them. It looked like I didn't have to worry about that with Annalise. There was a lot in her simple statement. I'd tackle the hard part first.

"Look, we dated for a few months over a decade ago. It's ancient history. We've both moved on since then. The reality is, this is exactly the kind of job I'm best at, and our past history makes me the ideal candidate to play your fiancé. The smart thing to do is put the past behind us and get the job done. We'll play the loving couple, your stalker goes nuts, and we catch him."

"That simple?" she asked, her eyes on the wall behind my head, something in them flat.

She sounded almost hurt. Not for the first time, I wondered about that letter, about her leaving. She was so worried about keeping everyone safe—and again, I dismissed the idea.

If she'd really had feelings for me, she never would've been able to write that letter. She wouldn't have been able to leave the way she had.

Just because she cared about her friends and family didn't mean she hadn't meant every word when she'd dumped me.

"That simple," I said, firmly. "What did you mean about having no idea how far this would go?"

I knew what it meant, but I needed to know if she did.

"I mean that my parents were murdered when I was eight, in their house a quarter of a mile away. Eight years later my aunt and uncle were killed in an almost identical crime right down the hall. By then, the notes and gifts and flowers had already started. They probably aren't related. We're very visible as a family, and we weren't careful enough about the way we handled the press when my parents died.

"There were too many pictures of us, too much attention as we got older. It's entirely possible that some random creep saw a picture of me online or in the paper and got fixated. But I also think it's careless to assume that four unsolved murders are completely unrelated to whoever's been stalking me since I was sixteen. The truth is, we don't know. And if it is related, we're dealing with someone who's killed four people and never been caught."

"And knowing that, you want us to stick you in a cabin in the woods by yourself? Maybe we should leave the door wide open at night, just to make it a little easier for him to get to you. If you really think there's a chance the murders and your stalker are connected then what the fuck were you thinking taking off eleven years ago?"

The door to the living room swung open, and Evers pinned me with a glare, his usual easy-going expression wiped away. "Everything okay in here?"

"Yeah, we're fine," I said, shortly, surprised to find myself on my feet, looming over Annalise. She glared back at me and calmly took another sip of her coffee.

"Lise?" Evers asked, ignoring me.

"I'm fine," she said, in an even, composed voice. "Riley and I are just... having a discussion."

Without another word, Evers closed the door. I knew I should sit, pick up my coffee, and pretend to be a professional. I *was* a professional, god-dammit.

"If we're going to do this," I said, "you have to have a better sense of self-preservation than this."

"I have an excellent sense of self-preservation," she said, coolly. "It's the rest of you who are throwing yourselves into danger."

"Look, you've had eleven years to end this, and you're still running. The longest you stayed anywhere since you left Atlanta is eight months. Lately, it's been more like three or four. You've lost years to this guy. Years. We know what we're doing. This is not our first stalker case. It's not *my* first stalker case. There's always risk, and everyone around you is aware of that. We're telling you, this is the best way to get the job done. So are you in, or are you out?"

"I'm in," she said, setting her empty coffee cup on the tray. "Tell me how this works."

CHAPTER FIVE
RILEY

I wasn't prepared for the relief that washed through me at her words. I hadn't realized how close she'd been to running, again. I should have. After eleven years, running was ingrained. Annalise was threatened, and she bolted, like a wild animal facing a predator.

I'd offered Evers, or another operative, to take my part. It was sensible. I was the best, but I wasn't the only one we could use. I hadn't expected how wrong that would feel. I knew Annalise hadn't been a nun in the last decade. I hadn't exactly been sleeping alone either, but the idea of helping to set up some other guy as her fiancé—no fucking way.

I sat back into the couch and laid it out for her. "I move in here. Tomorrow night, the birthday dinner planned for you and Vance becomes an engagement party. Mostly family, some close friends. Definitely a few we know are good at spreading gossip. We put an announcement in the paper. Then we go about living our lives."

"And who are you supposed to be? Am I calling you Riley? What's your cover story?"

I would've thought she was laughing at me, but there

was no hint of amusement in her face. Still, my gut told me she was teasing, just a little. That was good. Teasing was better than dismissal or reluctance. I could work with teasing.

I propped my ankle on my knee, leaned back into the plush silk cushions of the sofa and stretched my arms over the back. With a grin, I said, "I'm just me, for this one. Riley Flynn, your long-lost college boyfriend and an executive with Sinclair Security."

A ghost of a smile flitted across her face, and she said, "An executive? Impressive. Executive of what?"

Now I knew she was teasing me. Technically, I was an executive, though since my promotion I'd been resisting time behind a desk. I preferred being in the field. "VP in charge of client relations," I said, truthfully.

"I'm guessing that's not as innocent as it sounds," she said.

"It means I coordinate and implement jobs like this one."

"So who's going to do your job while you're here, pretending to be my fiancé? I didn't think executives left their offices to go undercover."

"Normally, we don't. But this is different. The Sinclairs consider you family. And I can do my job remotely. As long as I have my laptop and my phone, I can keep in touch with my teams."

I stood and looked down at her. We'd have plenty of time to talk once we got this whole thing rolling, but if we were going to pull off this fiction of an engagement, I had to get to work.

"I'll be back for dinner," I said. I was halfway to the door before she realized I was leaving and stood to follow me. I didn't stop, just in case she was thinking of a last-minute objection. Over my shoulder, I said, "Make room in the closet for me," and escaped.

Evers met me in the front hall. After scanning me with an assessing look, he said, "We're on?"

"We're on. She's not happy about it, but we can handle that."

"Meet me in the car. I'll get Knox. Cooper is going to review the security changes with Aiden and Gage before he heads back."

I was fine with skipping that meeting. I had a feeling I'd get enough of Aiden and Gage after I moved into their house.

Somehow, I knew they were not crazy about the idea of me sharing a bedroom with Annalise, even if nothing was going on. I ignored the fact that I'd had a similar reaction to the idea of someone else taking my spot on the job. I was supposed to feel protective.

She was vulnerable. She was the client, and the client was always vulnerable because the client was always in trouble. If they weren't, they wouldn't have called us. It was normal to be concerned about anyone taking advantage. It wasn't personal.

I was sitting in the backseat of the standard Sinclair black SUV, making a list on my phone, when Evers and Knox got in. I had to wrap up some details in the office, give my project leads some last-minute instructions, answer a few client emails, and handle some paperwork before I headed out to pack for an indefinite stay at Winters House.

Oh, and I had to buy a ring.

"How'd you talk her into it?" Evers asked, meeting my eyes in the rearview mirror. On the surface, Evers was the most easy-going of the Sinclair brothers, but he had a soft spot for a damsel in distress, and he'd been friends with Annalise since they were in the cradle.

"I tried to pawn you off on her, but she wasn't interested. Said something about no one believing she'd ever go out with you."

Evers narrowed his eyes at me before looking back at the road, but he laughed. "If I thought we could pull it off, I wouldn't let you within fifty feet of Lise, but she's like my baby sister. She's hot, but I can't go there with her and whoever plays her fiancé has to be convincing."

I didn't comment. I didn't like hearing him call Annalise hot, more so because it was true. She was older, and she looked tired, but the added fragility didn't make her any less beautiful.

Evers was trying to goad me into insisting I could be convincing, but I wasn't taking the bait. I already knew I could play the part. Once upon a time, I'd wanted to play it in real life.

"Are you going to tell her?" Knox asked, in his calm, quiet voice. Trust Knox to get right to the heart of it.

I didn't even have to think about my answer. "Hell, no."

"Is that smart?" Knox pressed.

"What do you think?" I challenged. "Would you tell her?" I already knew the answer, but I wanted to hear Knox say it.

"I think," he said, slowly, "that she deserves the truth. I also think she'd fucking kill you. She'd definitely take off again."

"Yeah, exactly," I said.

"But that's not why you won't tell her," Knox said. His dark eyes met mine in the rearview. I looked away.

"Does it matter why?" I asked.

Knox shrugged. "If she's just a job, then I guess it doesn't."

They both shut up after that, which was fine with me. It didn't matter because she *was* just a job. Making things more complicated would only put the operation at risk.

Things at the office took longer than planned—they always did—and it was late afternoon by the time I walked through the doors of the jewelry store. It wasn't the most exclusive jewelry store in Atlanta, but it was close, and Sinclair Security had an arrangement with them.

There were times—this job was a perfect example—when we needed access to expensive jewelry that we didn't want to own. The store wasn't in the habit of leasing jewelry, but they made an exception for Sinclair, and we made it our business to always return the pieces we borrowed in perfect condition. We made sure of it because none of us wanted to be saddled with a forty-thousand dollar engagement ring.

There was no question of giving Annalise a fake. The best way for this whole thing to fall apart would be for some society matron to spot a fake diamond on the hand of Annalise Winters. No, if we were going to pull this off, we had to do it right.

I pushed away any lingering memories of a time when I thought about doing this for real and made my way to the counter. The impeccably dressed young woman waiting there looked up.

"How may I help you today?" She asked in a perfectly modulated voice.

"I'm looking for an engagement ring. Riley Flynn? I have an account."

I spotted the jewelry case with the engagement rings and moved to take a closer look. The salesclerk discreetly checked the computer, and her smile widened. Not only did I have an account set up, it had a very generous limit. This wasn't the average engagement ring. If we were going to make a show of this, it had to be spectacular.

Fortunately, spectacular and Annalise Winters went together well. She'd never been showy about her money. In college, she'd gone out of her way to blend in with everyone else. Since then she'd turned blending in into an art form. Still, you couldn't hide when you looked like Annalise.

The sky blue eyes and long, platinum streaked blonde hair, on a tall, lean frame with just the right curves. She wasn't big into jewelry, but she could carry off a lot of ring, and that's what I was going to give her.

The clerk brought out a tray. I wasn't surprised to see it was the one featuring the biggest rings. I scanned them dispassionately. I'd know the right ring when I saw it.

A little voice in the back of my head reminded me that it didn't really matter. I'd be returning it in a matter of weeks because it wasn't really an engagement ring. It was a costume, albeit a ridiculously expensive one.

Whatever. If I had to play the part, it started with the right engagement ring.

As soon as I laid eyes on it, I knew. This was the ring Lise would want. A square, princess cut stone. Big enough to catch the eye, but not so big it would look ostentatious on her long, narrow fingers. The band was split into two intertwined strands, one unadorned platinum and the other studded with small diamonds. It was delicate and feminine with just enough sparkle to make an impression.

"That one," I said, pointing at the ring and trying to ignore the squeeze in my chest as the salesclerk picked it up and murmured, "A fine choice."

Luck was with me, and the ring was Annalise's size. I

signed some papers, the Sinclair security account took a temporary hit, and I walked out with an engagement ring in my pocket.

Packing was a hell of a lot easier than buying the ring. Especially since, if I forgot anything, I could always come back. I got to Winters House just in time for dinner. This first night, it was just family. Unfortunately, with the Winters, *just family* could still be a crowd. We ate in the dining room, a space more appropriate for a state dinner than spaghetti and meatballs.

The Winters took it all in stride. They were used to this kind of luxury: priceless Persian carpets, the endless length of the polished dining room table, the crystal chandelier, the soaring ceilings, complete with a secret library tucked into the second level.

Everything about Winters House was over the top. I'd worked with a lot of wealthy clients since I joined up with Sinclair Security. We only had wealthy clients. If you weren't wealthy, you couldn't afford us.

It was different, though, seeing Annalise here, realizing she'd grown up with this. For just a second, I could understand why she'd kept me away from her family in college.

We got through dinner with a minimum of conflict, mostly because Sophie and Amelia's bickering provided a distraction, especially when the housekeeper set a bowl of fruit in front of Amelia and gave the rest of us slices of chocolate cake.

The older woman glared up at the housekeeper, who responded with a neutral smile, saying only, "Don't look at me. Sophie sets your menu."

Beside Amelia, Sophie just shook her head at the housekeeper and said, "Would you mind bringing out a scoop of that sugar-free ice cream Abel made?"

The housekeeper, Mrs. W they called her, murmured, "Of course," and disappeared back through the butler's pantry. Aunt Amelia scowled at Sophie and said, "I'm not eating it. Sugar-free is never as good as the real thing. I want chocolate cake."

"Well, you can't have it," Sophie said, crisply. "You snuck shortbread today."

At Aunt Amelia's mutinous expression, Annalise burst out laughing, her blue eyes sparkling when she said, "How do you always know? Your kids are never going to get away with anything."

"I know, I tell her that all the time. Sophie has eyes in the back of her head," Gage said.

Amelia let out a disgruntled harrumph. She might not have been happy about that sugar-free ice cream, but when Mrs. W placed the bowl in front of her, she ate it. Every bite.

I was happy to get chocolate cake. Food wasn't always a focus for me. Depending on the job I was on, meals could be infrequent and too much take out got to be an easy habit. Living at Winters House, that was not going to be a problem. Three meals a day prepared by a personal chef who knew what he was doing in the kitchen.

I hoped they had a gym somewhere around here or I was going to get soft.

Annalise stood after dinner and announced that she was tired and just wanted to read in bed. She didn't realize I was following her down the hall until we passed the kitchen and family room and were almost in the corner of the house occupied by her suite and her cousin Jacob's.

Jacob owned a mixed-use residential/commercial building in midtown and had modified the top floor into a spacious penthouse that he occupied with his fiancée. We'd be the only ones living in this corner of Winters House. I saw her shoulders tense as I followed her past the door to Jacob's suite. When she reached her own door, she turned to face me.

"Where are you going?"

"To bed. You said we were turning in for the night," I said.

She crossed her arms over her chest and set her feet, clearly not prepared to move. I did the same.

"You are not staying here with me. This is a huge house. If you need to be close, Jacob's suite is right there." She threw out her arm and pointed at Jacob's closed door.

"No," I said. "That doesn't work." Lowering my voice, I took two steps closer, until we were almost touching and said, "I have two jobs here. The first is to play your fiancé to draw out your stalker so we can catch him. The second is to keep you safe. This guy may not be dangerous, but if he is, we're poking at a tiger. I am not sleeping fifty feet away with two closed doors and a hall in between us. It's not going to happen."

Annalise stared me down, eyes narrowed, before she let out a huff of breath, dropped her arms and turned on her heel. She opened the door and swung it wide. "Fine. You can have the couch. And it doesn't fold out."

I took one look at the couch in her sitting room and let out a sigh. I was six three, with broad shoulders. That couch would've been perfect for cuddling in front of the TV, but it was more love seat than couch. It sure as hell wasn't going to fit me. Not if I wanted a good night sleep.

Annalise stalked into her bedroom and returned a moment later with a pillow and a blanket. She tossed them on the couch, sent me another glare, and disappeared into her bedroom.

At least I had a TV. I left her suite to collect my bags and came back to find the door to her bedroom shut. A little poking around and I discovered the other door off the sitting room led to a full bath, which in turn opened into her closet, and from there to her bedroom. She'd left both doors shut. I changed into something more comfortable and stretched out, as much as I could, on the short couch.

I woke the next morning with a stiff neck and an aching back. I'd left the couch sometime in the middle of the night and made up a bed on the floor. I'd slept in worse places, but the floor still wasn't comfortable. No way was I doing that again. Not when Annalise had a king-size bed.

CHAPTER SIX
RILEY

Annalise avoided me most of the following day. The quiet family dinner celebrating Vance's birthday had turned in to a party for two when they'd learned Annalise would be back, and from there into an engagement party. Nothing big, but more than just a family dinner.

After warning Annalise not to leave the house without me, I'd made use of the desk in her sitting room to get some work done. She ignored my orders and roped her younger cousin Charlie, and Charlie's husband Lucas, into going shopping for the party.

I was not invited.

Under any other circumstances that would've been a no-go, but Lucas Jackson was former special forces, former president of a biker gang, and currently the head of Sinclair Securities cyber division. He was a hacker with a talent for combat, and I had no question he could keep Annalise safe.

I also knew he had better things to do than take his wife and her cousin shopping, but I didn't push. Lise would have to get used to having me around, and she would, but if I pushed too hard, she'd bolt.

She came home late in the afternoon and disappeared into the bathroom of the suite, stopping only to say, "Do you need to get in here?"

I'd barely said 'No' before the door shut with a click. I didn't see her again until just before the first guest was scheduled to arrive. I was already in my suit and was fastening my cufflinks when the door to her bedroom swung open.

My breath caught in my lungs at the sight of her. It had always been like that with Annalise. She'd walk into a room, and I'd lose my breath at how beautiful she was. She was older but no less perfect than she'd been at twenty.

She should have been. Objectively, I knew she was too thin and had circles under her eyes, fine lines around her mouth. Dealing with this stalker might take care of the signs of stress, but she wasn't twenty anymore. It didn't matter. Annalise was breathtaking.

She wore a deep navy wrap dress with a slit up the side and a deep V neckline. It covered everything it was supposed to, and then some, but when she turned to close her bedroom door I saw that it flirted and teased when she moved, the skirt floating up to show a hint of the top of her thigh before settling back into place. Her feet were encased in matching navy spike heels with hot pink soles that looked dangerously uncomfortable.

She crossed the room on steady feet, her eyes taking in my navy suit. We'd look like we'd dressed to match, though I hadn't asked her what she'd be wearing, mostly because she didn't know until she bought it that afternoon. I supposed she could've seen my suit hanging in the other side of her closet. I wasn't going to ask.

Instead, I reached for the black velvet box on the desk and said, "Wait a second, you're missing something."

"What?" She scanned herself, saw nothing amiss, and met my eyes, her brows pulled together in confusion. She'd left her hair down and done something to it, so it curled in loose waves, past her shoulder blades. Pieces were pulled back and secured with sparkling pins, the only jewelry she wore aside from a pair of sapphire and diamond studs.

I took her left hand in mine and held up the box. "You can't go to your engagement party without a ring."

"Oh," she said, the sound a sigh. "I didn't think of that."

"It's my job," I said, gruffly, opening the box and taking out the ring. It caught the light, and I thought I heard her breath hitch at the sparkle of the stones.

I slid the ring on her finger and stopped for just a second, admiring how perfect it looked there. She made a fist and pulled her hand back, dropping it to her side.

"Thank you," she said, quietly.

Half of the guests were there when we made it down the stairs, mostly because they were family or Sinclairs. Aiden was at the door, playing the official host. Lise took me around and introduced me to the family members I didn't know well, mainly her younger brother Tate, his new wife Emily, her cousin Holden, and his fiancée Josephine.

I didn't know the older Winters that well, but because of their friendship with the Sinclairs, and with Lucas Jackson working with us, we'd run into each other often enough that introductions weren't necessary.

The beginning of the party was easy enough. Everyone there knew what was going on. It wasn't until the other guests arrived that Lise stiffened up on me. The first through the door were the Stevens, Sloane, and Rupert. Sloane was Vance's gallery manager, a beautiful woman in her early 40s married to a man old enough to be her father, who indulged her rampant cheating and social climbing in exchange for having her on his arm.

Vance and his wife Maggie both despised her, but Vance insisted he put up with her because she was too good at her job to fire. Normally, they wouldn't rate an invite to a family dinner, but Sloane was one of the biggest gossips in town, and since Vance had a show coming up it wasn't completely odd to invite her to the party.

She fawned over Annalise, saying, "Darling, you're such a surprise. Gone all these years and then, poof! Back and reunited with your first love. Such a sweet story. You must come into the gallery. Vance was showing me some of your work. I'd love to talk to you about it. Love it."

She air-kissed Annalise on both cheeks, scanned me with hot eyes I imagined could somehow see straight through my suit, and swanned off leaving a cloud of heavy perfume in her wake. Like a shark scenting blood, she headed straight for Aiden. Annalise shook her head in wry amusement.

"And there she goes, straight for the only unattached Winters male. Aiden can't stand her. She's exactly like his first wife. And she has no shame. Her husband is right over there."

I slid my arm around her waist, and she stiffened. I dropped my head and said in a low voice, "Relax, Lise."

She started to pull free, and I tightened my fingers on her hip. My lips at her ear, I whispered, "Lise, this isn't going to work if you keep pulling away from me."

Annalise drew in a deep breath, and let it out slowly, her muscles unwinding, her hip brushing mine as she eased closer.

"Good girl," I whispered, trying to ignore the scent of

her skin. We were sharing a bathroom, so I already knew she still didn't wear perfume. This wasn't the same lotion she'd worn in college, it'd been so long that one probably wasn't even made anymore, but she'd always favored the same scents.

Light, fresh, with just a hint of sweetness. This one smelled like the beach and summer fruit. It took an effort of will to suppress the urge to take a bite out of the side of her neck.

We needed to sell our engagement, but that didn't include groping her in the middle of the party. Even if I wanted to.

Fuck.

I needed a second of air. A minute away from the summer scent of Annalise, from the memory of how soft her skin was.

"Do you want a glass of wine?" I asked.

"Please," she said. "White."

I couldn't resist dropping a kiss on her cheek before I crossed the room to the linen-draped table where Mrs. W had set up the drinks. Standing at the makeshift bar, I said to the bartender, "Club soda with a lime and a glass of white wine."

Griffin Sawyer, one of our best operatives, nodded and turned to make the drinks. Wearing glasses, his hair darkened a few shades; he blended into the background. All of the support staff came from Sinclair.

Normally, Mrs. W would have called in temporary help to serve and assist in the kitchen, but we didn't want any strangers in the house, and it never hurt to have extra eyes on the guests.

I glanced across the room to see Annalise standing stiffly, talking to an older man who appeared to be lecturing her. He wasn't much taller than her, with an average build, medium brown hair, and nondescript brown eyes. Overall, an unremarkable man, especially next to the brightly dressed woman hanging on his arm, her diamonds flashing, eyes narrowed as they flicked from Annalise to her companion.

William Davis and Melanie Monroe. Davis was a very old family friend. He'd been tight with the older generation of Winters and until recently had acted as a sort of stand-in father.

I knew from the Sinclairs that he'd been less welcome since he'd tried to stop Jacob from falling for his fiancée, Abigail. It hadn't helped that Davis had tried the same thing with Charlie and Lucas. Apparently, he had very old-school ideas about who made an appropriate spouse for the Winters children.

If Abigail Jordan and Lucas Jackson hadn't passed muster, it was a pretty good bet that I wouldn't either. I didn't have to guess what he was saying to Annalise. Little did he know, if he'd just shut up for a few weeks, I'd be out of the picture and Annalise would be free to find a more suitable mate.

I crossed the room, startled to see Annalise shoot me a desperate glance. Hoping I was reading her right, I stepped into their circle of conversation, handed her the glass of wine and wrapped my arm around her shoulders, pulling her to my side.

She leaned into me and said quietly, "Thank you."

I didn't know if she was thanking me for the wine, or for interrupting Davis's lecture. I'd heard the tail end, something about making sure she stayed home and found someone who could take care of her properly.

Annalise narrowed her eyes at Davis and said, "Uncle

William, I haven't seen you in so long. I'd appreciate it if you could just be happy for me. That's all I'm asking. You know, my mother wasn't quite appropriate for a Winters. She came from a small town in South Georgia. She wasn't even planning to get married. She just wanted to go to medical school and be a doctor."

"And then she met your father, and everything changed." His voice was heavy with emotion, and I remembered that we were talking about two of his oldest friends, dead now for over twenty years.

His eyes touched on me briefly, coldly dismissing me, before he gave Annalise a gentle, affectionate look and said, "Your mother was an exception. Exceptional. James was lucky to have her." The softness left his voice, and he went on, "That doesn't change the fact that none of you children seem to understand your position and your obligations."

I expected Annalise to get angry, but instead, she laughed and patted Davis on the arm. "Uncle William, I know Charlie tells you all the time, but you're a dinosaur. The world doesn't work that way anymore. And the only thing I owe the Winters name is my happiness. That's what my parents would've wanted."

Davis shook his head sadly and reached out to squeeze her shoulder with a quick touch. "Our world will always work that way, Annalise. Don't make a mistake you'll regret once you figure that out."

Annalise shrugged off his hand and leaned up to give him a quick kiss on the cheek. "Uncle William, I love you, but you're wrong. And if Aiden hears you saying stuff like this, he's going to get upset."

Davis made a sound in his throat and said, "I can handle Aiden."

An amused voice cut in as Vance said, "I'd love to see

that, Uncle William. None of us can handle Aiden. We just let him steamroll through life and try to stay out of the way."

Smoothly, he slid in next to his twin sister and tugged her from my side. I was oddly reluctant to let her go, though I knew she was safe enough with Vance.

"Will you excuse us for a few minutes Uncle William?" Vance asked. "I need to talk a little business with my baby sister."

Davis made that sound in his throat again, nodded to Annalise, and walked away, towing his date behind him. I'd noticed that Melanie Monroe hadn't spoken a word, but she'd taken in every nuance of the conversation.

Another of the biggest gossips in town, every detail would be relayed to her cronies at lunch the next day, if not over morning coffee. That was the plan; it was exactly what we wanted, so why did it bother me?

I looked at Vance and said, "I'm sticking with Annalise."

CHAPTER SEVEN

RILEY

Vance shot me a grin and said, "You're not the one I was trying to get rid of. But, I did want to talk a little business." Looking down at Annalise, he said, "Sloane said she talked to you about your work."

"She did," Annalise said, slowly. "Did you show her my photographs?"

Vance hedged, "Well, the thing is—"

His wife Maggie slipped her arm through his and said, "Annalise, I'm sorry, it was actually my fault."

Vance turned to look down at the curvy redhead and his eyes, so like Annalise's, went hot. He wound his arm around her waist and tucked her into his side, murmuring into her hair, "Nothing is your fault, sugar."

She rolled her eyes and laughed. "Don't I wish that were true. But really, Vance had some of your work laid out in his studio. We were trying to decide where to hang it, and Sloane stopped by. She loves to do that—I think she's trying to catch Vance alone."

Vance let out a growl of frustration. "Remind me again why we're not firing her?"

"Because neither of us has the time to manage your career as well as she does. Especially not right now when we still haven't found someone to fill in for Ella."

She gave a quick glance over her shoulder to make sure the subject of the conversation couldn't overhear and said, "Sloane is an interfering pain in the ass, but she does a great job selling art. Especially yours because she loves to suck up, and she's still hoping to get you in bed."

Vance's shudder was genuine. Maggie looked at us and said, "I do my best to protect him. She's good at selling art, but she's not subtle. Anyway, did she say she wanted to talk to you about your work?"

Annalise nodded. "She did, but I figured it was just cocktail party talk."

Maggie shook her head. "It's not. When you've got the time, let me know, and I'll set up a meeting. She didn't know who shot the photographs when she saw them, and she was very interested. When she found out they were yours, and that you weren't represented, she got a little rabid about it. We told her to back off and give you space to settle in, which is the only reason she didn't try to drag you down the hall and make you sign a contract."

Annalise stared at Maggie and Vance, lips parted, eyes wide. She blinked, slowly. "Are you serious?"

"Of course she's serious, Lise," Vance said. "You know you're good."

Annalise shook her head in denial, still looking stunned. I didn't know a lot about art, but I knew a good bit about the Winters family, and by extension, Vance's career. Sloane's gallery was no joke. She might've been a social climber with a predilection for sexually harassing her artists, but she moved a lot of art through that gallery, and none of it was cheap.

Maggie put a hand on Lise's arm and said, "Look, I know you've heard a lot of bad things about Sloane because she drives Vance and me nuts."

"Didn't she try to break you two up?" Annalise asked.

Maggie waved her hand in the air, dismissing the past. "She made up for it when she helped orchestrate Vance's proposal."

"It was either that or get fired," Vance cut in.

"That's my point," Maggie said. "She has a lot of irritating qualities, no question. But she wouldn't be interested in talking to you if she didn't think she could sell your work. Sloane does not take on deadweight. Now, if Riley here were the artist..."

She scanned me with a hilariously lascivious look that had her husband elbowing her in the side, "Then I might caution him not to meet with her alone. But she's not into girls, and since she married Rupert, she doesn't need you socially. She's interested because she thinks she can make money off of you, which means she'd also make money *for* you. Once you're ready to settle down, if you want to make a real go of your photography, I'd say it's worth talking to Sloane. If you want, I can act as your go-between at first."

"I'd appreciate that," Lise said, still sounding shocked. "I've sold things here and there, mostly by myself, from hanging them in cafés, salons, stuff like that, but I haven't really had a proper show. I was supposed to in New Mexico but..."

"Maybe it's for the best, then," Maggie said, briskly.

She was sharp and knew enough of the situation to understand it was better to steer Annalise away from any discussion of why she left home or why she was back.

The whole point of the party was to spread the right gossip, not just any gossip. The family had kept her stalker under wraps for all these years. The last thing we needed was for it to get out now.

Maggie went on, "If you're planning to set up a base in Atlanta, Sloane is a good place to start. Vance and I can help you, and Vance uses Dave Price to check the contracts, so we can do the same for you. I know you just got home, and you have other concerns right now, but when you're ready, we'll set something up."

I heard a beep and Maggie pulled her phone out of the tiny purse hanging on her wrist. "It's the sitter." Vance plucked the phone from her hand and answered it, pacing to the corner of the room and talking in low but insistent tones.

To us, Maggie said, "Rosie had a fever when we left. Probably normal. Her nose was running, but we overreact. We asked the sitter to call and report in after she put Rosie down. That's probably all it is." She glanced back at Vance, a tiny frown line between her eyes.

Lise looked at her brother as he paced in the corner of the room. "I never imagined I'd see Vance like this," she said.

Maggie let out a laugh that almost hid her worry over their daughter. "I know, right? If you'd told me when we met that he would be such a good dad, not to mention an amazing husband, I would've laughed you out of town. But people change. Sometimes, all you need is a little push."

Vance ended the call and returned to his wife, handing her the phone. "She's fine. Didn't eat much dinner, but her fever broke just after she fell asleep. The sitter said her nose is running less and she's sleeping just fine."

Maggie let out a long breath. "I wish Ella were here." Explaining, she said, "Our nanny, Ella, is a grad student at Tech. Jo and Emily found her for us. She's amazing with Rosie, but unfortunately, between her studies and a fiancé in California, she's not available as much as she used to be. We're supposed to be finding someone new, but it's not as easy as you'd think."

"Especially when you're interfering and overprotective," Vance said.

Maggie poked him in the stomach and said, "Are you talking about you or me?"

He leaned down and kissed her, murmuring against her lips, "Both."

Vance tugged his wife off to the side, sending a wink as he eased her towards the door to the hallway. A new voice, one I knew well, said, "There they go. I wouldn't open any closed doors for a little while."

I looked over to see Jacob Winters beside us, holding the hand of an elegant woman with dark hair and eyes, dressed in a deep red sheath with matching shoes, her ears, neck, and left hand sparkling with diamonds.

I'd never met Abigail Jordan in person, but seeing her side-by-side with Jacob, I completely understood that these two belonged together.

A quiet smile spread across her face, and Abigail said, "I think it's sweet." Holding out her hand to me she said, "It's good to meet you, Riley. We've been so excited that Annalise is coming home and so happy for both of you."

I took her hand in mine, surprised at the firmness of her grip. I shouldn't have been. She may have looked the part of a young society matron, perfectly dressed with appropriate manners, but no woman could be a pushover and handle Jacob Winters. And Jacob Winters wouldn't have fallen in love with a woman he could boss around.

"Annalise," Jacob said, sending a speaking glance at his younger cousin, "Abigail thought she'd take you around and introduce you to some of the guests you need to meet."

"That's why I hate this kind of thing," Annalise said under her breath.

In an equally quiet voice, Jacob said, "I know, sweetheart. But that's the point of the party. Let Abigail take you around. She's brilliant at this, and you'll barely have to say a word."

He took her arm, tugging her gently from my side, and handed her off to Abigail after dropping a quick kiss on her forehead. We watched the two women cross the room, Abigail deftly leading Annalise to an older couple, the woman decked in jewels, the man glancing wistfully toward the bar.

His eyes on his fiancée and younger cousin, Jacob said to me, "She'll be fine with Abigail. Lise has always hated parties like this, but Abigail loves them, and she's making a career out of wrapping these people around her finger. She went to work handling events at the family's charitable foundation, and she's raking it in. Despite the fact that she's gorgeous, the matrons love her, and the old men can't say no to her."

The pride in his smile was obvious, as was the love. Jacob was another one of the Winters men I would have bet would never fall in love. He was notorious for dating women and walking away without a second look. He didn't do girlfriends. He didn't do relationships.

Then, suddenly, Abigail Jordan was living with him and a heartbeat later they were engaged. I knew more about Abigail's past than most people, considering I'd been part of the team assigned to protect her when her former father-in-law had threatened to kidnap her. She'd run to Jacob for help, and he'd called Sinclair Security.

Abigail's first marriage had been a nightmare, and Jacob was the last man I would've put her with. I knew for a fact

Evers had tried to save her from Jacob, imagining Jacob was going to use her and throw her away like he had every other woman. Instead, Jacob had fallen hard.

We stood in silence, nursing our drinks and watching our women until the bell rang announcing dinner. I reclaimed Annalise with relief. She wasn't in danger at our engagement party, but I was ill at ease without her by my side. The point of the party was to make our new relationship visible, but until we knew who the threat was, she was in danger.

Dinner was easy. The food was good, as always, and with me on one side and Gage on the other, Lise could relax.

She stayed that way as long as I kept my distance. The first time I reached out to take her hand, she stiffened, grabbing her wine and taking a long sip. Leaning closer, I murmured, "This won't work if you cringe when I touch you."

She let out a huff of breath, turning her face to mine. Her lips almost grazed my cheek as she whispered, "I know. I'm sorry. This is weird, that's all."

"Weird because it's me? Or just weird?" I couldn't help asking, my voice so low it was barely audible, even to me.

"Both," she admitted. So quietly I wondered if I'd imagined the words, she said, "I'm not used to being touched. You keep surprising me."

"You'll have to get used to it," I said, pressing a light kiss to her cheek and taking hold of her hand. I held it, in full view of the rest of the table, as she went back to her conversation with Gage, a pink flush high on her cheeks.

I didn't want to be affected by something as simple as holding her hand. It was an act. That's all. Just part of the job. Her long fingers twined with mine didn't mean anything. Part of the show, nothing more.

Then why did her confession leave a hollow feeling in my gut? The Annalise I'd known had been affectionate. Touchy. At least she had been with me. We hadn't been able to keep our hands off each other. Had she been so isolated over the past few years that a simple touch put her on alert?

I'd kept track of her movements over the years at Aiden Winters's request, but I hadn't watched her directly. Aiden had learned the hard way that following Annalise too closely would only send her into hiding.

The first year she'd been gone Cooper had sent a newer operative to keep an eye on her, and she'd realized she was being watched. Not knowing who it was, Lise had assumed the worst, and she'd taken off, dropping completely out of sight for over a year. After that, Aiden asked Cooper to put someone on her, but give her plenty of space. We knew where she was living, when she moved, when her stalker found her. We didn't know the details of her day-to-day.

After the way she flinched every time I touched her, I was beginning to wonder exactly how isolated she'd been lately. Fear could be a trap. It could box you in, make you see threats everywhere. I didn't like to think of Lise like that —alone and afraid, not letting anyone close.

She'd have to let down her guard with me. We wouldn't be able to pull off this engagement if she treated me like a stranger. It wasn't the ring that would push her stalker to act. It was intimacy. Connection. Right now, it looked like we had none. Holding hands wasn't enough.

The staff cleared the dessert plates, and a few guests rose from the table. I joined them, taking Lise with me, leading her out of the dining room and into the hall. At the foot of the staircase, in view of the rest of the guests, I took her in my arms.

I brushed my lips across her cheek, and she whispered, "What are you doing?"

"If I have to explain, obviously I'm not doing it right," I said, tasting the line of her jaw.

It was part of the act. After the way Vance and Maggie had disappeared, and all of the blatant PDA between the other Winters couples, it would've looked off if Annalise and I hadn't even kissed.

It had nothing to do with the tension stringing my muscles tight, the ocean and fruit scent of her teasing me all through dinner. The sound of her laugh, the way the light hit her golden hair, sparkled in the ring on her finger.

"Why—"

I cut her off before she could finish the thought. "We have to sell it, remember?"

Before she could come up with another objection, I kissed her.

Her body went stiff in my arms. I pulled her closer, sealing my mouth over hers and tasting her. How could it be the same after so many years?

I fell into the kiss, claiming her, leaning her back over my arm and taking her mouth with mine. She let out a low moan, her tension draining away as she softened in my arms, setting off something inside me.

I forgot where we were. I forgot why I was kissing her.

I just wanted more.

More of her taste, more of the tug of her fingers in my hair as she pulled me closer. More of her tongue stroking mine, more of her breath in my lungs. Just more.

I wanted everything.

A throat cleared behind us and Annalise turned to

stone in my arms. Fear flashed in her eyes as I reluctantly lifted my head and looked back to see William Davis glaring at us, his eyes hot and furious. His date's eyes were avidly curious, and I knew three things.

One—Aiden could expect a visit from William Davis, the topic yet another inappropriate Winters engagement.

Two—Melanie Monroe was going to wear out her phone spreading the news of Annalise's engagement and our hot and heavy kiss in front of all the guests.

And three—I couldn't kiss Annalise again. Ever. Not if I wanted to keep my head on the job.

CHAPTER EIGHT
RILEY

My eyes opened at the first pale streaks of dawn filtering through the closed curtains in Annalise's bedroom. I'd had another miserable night of sleep, though I couldn't blame this one on the floor or the too short couch in her sitting room.

After that ill-advised kiss, a kiss that had left me aching, hard, and determined never to touch her again, Annalise had stayed by my side until the last guest departed. The second the door shut behind them, she fled for the safety of her bedroom.

I gave her enough time to change before knocking on her bedroom door and swinging it open.

I found her tucked into bed reading, a tablet propped on her lap. I still don't know if I was disappointed or relieved to see her wearing a sleep shirt with matching pajama pants.

The last thing I needed after that kiss was Annalise in lingerie. Not that the sleep shirt and cotton pants were a turnoff. I was trying to put the kiss out of my mind, but it refused to go. I could still taste her.

"I'm taking the other half of the bed," I announced.

"That couch is about two feet too short for me, and I'm not sleeping on the floor again." Gesturing to her bed, an antique style brass bed covered with ribbon trimmed pillows and a pink and white quilt, I said, "This thing is plenty big enough for the two of us. You won't even know I'm there."

Annalise's blue eyes narrowed on me. I imagined I could see the wheels turning in her brain. She must have decided to save her energy for a fight worth winning because she flung out her hand toward the opposite side of the bed and said, "Keep your hands to yourself, and we won't have a problem."

She then proceeded to ignore me completely. I did the same.

I had no interest in sleeping on the floor, but the last thing we needed was an intimate chat while we shared the same blankets. I was here to do a job, and it was bad business to fuck the client.

I pretended to go to sleep, long before she turned out the light. The bed was huge, and we were separated by feet of mattress, but I could feel her there, hear the soft cadence of her breath in sleep, the scent of ocean and fresh fruit drifting from her side of the bed. Behind my closed lids, I saw her in that elegant navy dress, teasing the barest hint of cleavage and long leg. I saw the desire in her eyes after I kissed her, the swollen pink lips and flags of color in her cheekbones.

I saw her need, and her shock, and her fear. It was the last part I couldn't quite figure out. Need was easy. As hot as that kiss had been, both of us were close to desperate by the time we broke away.

Shock was also easily explained, considering she hadn't expected me to kiss her, though logically, she should have.

But the fear... It was almost like she was afraid I'd hurt her. Like she had to protect herself from me. The distance she tried to put between us. The way she slid her chair away from mine. She had to know she was safe with me.

That was the reason I was here—to keep her safe.

What was she afraid of?

In the night, I grabbed one of the pink-ribboned pillows and shoved it between us, needing the barrier after I'd woken for the third time to find myself reaching for her. It was one thing to sleep in half of her bed, and another to wake with her in my arms.

I watched the light through the curtains grow brighter and knew I wasn't going back to sleep. Carefully, so I didn't wake Annalise, I got out of bed and headed for the bath-room, passing through the closet on my way and grabbing my workout gear. If I couldn't sleep, at least I could burn off some of this tension while Annalise was safely contained in her bedroom.

Winters House was massive, but the layout was a simple square around the center courtyard. Once I'd walked through it, it was easy to find my way around.

I headed for the lower level, skipping the regular entrance by the kitchen in favor of the secret staircase hidden in the library. Aiden had shown me the latch, deep in a groove in the underside of the mantle. I slid my fingers in and pushed. The door swung open, appearing out of the wood paneling as if by magic, revealing a narrow, spiral staircase lit by flickering lights.

The staircase from the library opened into a wide, tall, brightly lit hallway that ran the length of the house. The first room to the left was the theater, though it held more than an oversized movie screen and reclining leather chairs.

The Winters had stocked it with a full bar and a pool

table, along with a random assortment of old school arcade games and pinball machines. The next door opened into an expansive home gym, complete with multiple treadmills, a rowing machine, every weight I could possibly need, even ropes fastened to the ceiling for climbing and wall ladders for agility. The ropes and ladders looked ancient, and I doubted anyone had used them in decades.

The walls were tiled in shiny rectangles, subway tiles, that had come back into style in the last few years. These were vintage. I could see echoes of the past century in the unused exposed pipes still fastened to the ceiling and the antique leather medicine balls piled seemingly haphazardly in the corner.

I hit the treadmill and settled in for a run at a good pace. I'd grown up in a normal house in the suburbs, my parents both professionals who drove newish cars and took us on fun vacations. None of that even remotely equipped me to handle a family like this.

I couldn't imagine the weight of history, of the past, that came with being one of them. What was it like for Aiden to come down here and work out in a room his grandfather had built? What was it like to carry that legacy?

I was glad I'd never know. I liked my independence. I didn't want the past to dictate my future. I finished my workout on the treadmill, hit the weights for a while, and used one of the private showers connected to the gym, planning to change into fresh clothes I'd brought just for that purpose.

Sharing the suite with Annalise was hard enough, I didn't want to walk in on her in the bathroom. Just the thought of her in the shower, the scent of her soap, her shiny wet skin—I squeezed my eyes shut and banished the image from my mind.

Annalise is a job, I reminded myself. *You're not going there again.*

Even if I could forget the fact that she dumped me while I lay in a hospital bed, breaking my heart and never looking back, she wasn't my ex-girlfriend here.

She was a client.

She was the job.

Hadn't I just been thinking I didn't want the past to dictate my future? Just because we'd fucked back in the day didn't mean it was going to happen now.

My head was on board, but my cock wasn't getting the message. Every time I thought about Annalise. In that dress, sleeping in her modest pajama set, naked in the shower—it didn't seem to matter.

Annalise popped into my head, and my cock came to life.

Since he wasn't running this job, he was going to have to wait. When it was over, I'd call one of my regular hookups, and he could work out his issues. That idea should have held appeal, but when I tried to conjure up a mental image of the last woman I'd slept with, I got nothing.

Bracing one hand against the tiled shower wall, I leaned forward and wrapped my soapy fingers around my cock, stroking and trying to think of anything but Annalise.

I just needed to work out a little tension, that was all, and I didn't need her to do it. I was halfway there, caught up in a fantasy of a faceless woman with big tits when Annalise invaded my mind. The mystery woman and her big tits were gone, and I was in Annalise's bed, reaching for her in the night.

This time, I didn't put a pillow between us. This time my fingers met bare skin, and she rolled into me, raising her arms and murmuring my name. This time, when I kissed her she wasn't surprised, she was ready. Sinking her fingers into my hair and rolling to hook her legs over my hips, the heat of her body against mine drawing a groan from my throat.

I didn't even get to the fucking part of the fantasy before my balls drew tight, my hand stroked faster, and I came against the shower wall, gasping for breath.

Fuck.

That hadn't gone the way I'd planned.

Then again, not much had since Annalise Winters had walked back into my life.

Just my luck, everyone was at the breakfast table when I arrived, freshly showered, and not at all relaxed. Especially not with Lise sitting there beside Sophie, her long blonde hair in a messy knot, her face bare of makeup, wearing a faded T-shirt and a loose pair of jeans.

How the fuck could she be that gorgeous first thing in the morning?

I grabbed a plate and helped myself to the buffet set out on the sideboard. The cook, Abel, didn't go halfway with breakfast. There were Belgian waffles, fluffy scrambled eggs, grits, and a linen-covered basket of biscuits. A separate steamer held fat sausages and crispy bacon. I piled my plate high, glad I'd put in extra time on my workout.

The seat next to Lise was empty, and I took it, filling my coffee cup from the carafe. "Sleep well?" I asked her, the question coming out more abrupt than I'd intended. My session in the shower clearly hadn't taken off the edge.

Annalise's face was a polite mask as she said, "Yes, very well. You?"

Across the table her great-aunt Amelia snorted with barely suppressed laughter, her sharp Winters blue eyes bouncing from me to Annalise and back to me.

Annalise dropped the mask to scowl at Amelia. "Do you have something to say?"

Amelia shrugged in badly feigned innocence. "Me? Oh, no. I could, but I think I'm going to let you two make a mess of this all on your own." Sending a conspiratorial glance at Sophie, she said, "It's more fun for us that way."

Sophie just shook her head and concentrated on her breakfast. Both Gage and Aiden ignored Amelia's comment, though a tiny smile played at the corner of Aiden's mouth. Covering his amusement, he said, "Does anyone have any interesting plans for the day?"

Annalise said, "I was thinking about taking my camera and getting out. I don't know where; it just feels like forever since I've shot anything new." Looking at me, she said, "If Riley thinks it's okay."

A part of me wanted to lock her in a closet until we caught her stalker, but that wasn't the point of the job. She was supposed to get out there, her brand-new fiancé in tow, and hitting the town with her camera was the ideal excuse, mostly because it wasn't an excuse at all.

"I think we'll be fine."

Annalise shot me a grateful look, as Sophie sat up straighter and brightened. "You should come with Amelia and me," she said. "Aiden and Gage have to do some work, and Amelia and I were going to head over to the Botanical Gardens. They're beautiful, and we love to walk over there, especially this time of year when everything is in bloom."

A smile spread across Annalise's face, and her eyes drifted to the ceiling. I imagine she was lost in thought over all of the opportunities in the Botanical Gardens if she had her camera.

I remembered that look. Before I could think twice, I

said, "That works for me. Is that the kind of thing you're looking for?"

For the first time, Annalise's smile was entirely genuine, bright and wide, lighting up her face.

She opened her mouth to say something when Aiden's phone beeped. The expression drained from her face as his eyebrows drew together in consternation.

Gage murmured, "Is that the gate?"

Aiden nodded and tapped the screen of his phone, then raised it to his ear. "Yes, Did you ID the deliveryman? I see. I see. Check it, and if it's clean, bring it to the house. Yes. I understand."

Aiden lay the phone on the table and said to Annalise, "You have a flower delivery." His eyes moved to me, and he said, "They weren't delivered by a florist, but by someone who works for a jobs-for-hire website. They're holding him for the moment, but it's unlikely he knows anything about who hired him. He said he picked up the flowers and delivered them to this address as instructed. Someone will be by to bring them to Sinclair Security, but I thought we should take a look first."

"Is that the best idea? Does she have to see them?" I challenged Aiden.

Annalise's face had drained of blood, eyes wide with panic. Her voice was tight when she said, "They're my flowers. I have a right to see them. I need to know what he's saying."

Aiden gave me a look that said, *Better to let her see the flowers than fight about it.*

He wasn't wrong, trying to shield her would only end in an argument, but I saw the fine tremble in her fingers as she picked up her coffee cup and it turned my stomach.

No one spoke as we waited for the knock on the front

door. When it came, Aiden rose to his feet, saying, "I'll bring them in here."

Annalise gave a short nod beside me. Every muscle in her body was drawn tight. I could hear the shortness of her breath, could see her pulse pound in the vein in her neck.

Anyone who didn't know her would see a casually dressed, composed woman, enjoying the remains of her breakfast. But every single person in the room *did* know her, and we could feel her fear permeating the room.

Aiden returned with a beautiful arrangement of flowers in bright colors, set off by a plant with narrow, glossy green leaves. I hadn't thought it possible for Annalise to wind any tighter, but she went rock solid beside me, her eyes fixed on the blooms in Aiden's hands.

Across the table, Amelia said, "That's just wrong."

Sophie looked at Amelia and said quietly, "You know what they mean?"

Amelia took in the sight of her great-niece, frozen in her chair, eyes fixed on the flowers and said gently, "It's Mother's Day. Most of those are day lilies. Orange and red. Anna's favorite. James and the children gave them to her every year. Day lilies mean motherhood. They were planted all around the house."

"And the others?" Aiden asked, his voice rough and heavy. He set the arrangement in the center of the table, and leaning closer I could see that the day lilies stood alone, surrounded by stems topped with yellow balls of petals, intertwined with the glossy green leaves, here and there sprinkled with violet flowers. The colors didn't quite go, but apparently, the colors weren't the point.

From beside me, Annalise's voice cut in, thin and strained. "The yellow are Tansy. Hostility. They're twisted up with Myrtle for a happy marriage."

"News gets around fast," Gage said, under his breath.

The whole point of the engagement party, of inviting some of the biggest gossips in town, had been to provoke a reaction. When we planned it, it had been with the detachment of strategy. We had a goal in mind and were determined to accomplish it.

I hadn't expected the wrench of regret in my chest when Annalise shoved back her chair and rose to unsteady feet, blinking hard once before whirling and running from the room.

Gage pushed back his chair to follow her, and I stood, blocking him. This was my fault. Provoking her stalker had been my idea. I hadn't anticipated how it would feel to be responsible for that look on Annalise's face. When I reached her room, she stood in front of the windows of the sitting room, arms crossed tightly over her chest, looking out into the courtyard of Winters House. The fountain in the center was turned on, the water sparkling cheerfully in the spring sunshine.

Annalise was shaking, her shoulders hunched, arms crossed tightly over her chest. Her eyes were wide and dry, her breath coming in short gasps. If she wasn't having a panic attack, she was close. I dealt with a lot of clients under extreme stress. I'd seen this before, but it had never been like this. Not for me.

I tried to summon my customary professional distance, and it wouldn't come. This wasn't some client. This was Annalise. My Lise. The first woman I'd ever loved. The only woman who had broken my heart.

Without thinking of the consequences, I pulled her into my arms, holding her tight against me, absorbing her trembles, and then her tears as she broke down and sobbed against my chest.

She didn't cry for long, only a few minutes, and when her tears stopped, I expected her to pull away. Instead, she said, "I didn't think he'd find me so fast. I know that was the plan but—" Her breath hitched in her chest and another sob escaped. "Those were my mother's flowers. He took my mother's flowers, and he made them something ugly. I don't understand. I've never understood. I just want this to be over. Why can't it be over?"

She exhaled a long sigh and pressed her cheek to my chest. I didn't realize she was weeping again until I felt the heat of her tears soaking through my shirt. I tightened my arms around her, pressing my thumb to her spine and stroking up and down, slowly, gradually relaxing her tense muscles. I thought of a thousand things to say, generic platitudes I'd spouted to other clients on other jobs.

We're going to fix this.

Everything's going to be okay.

Don't worry; we'll keep you safe.

I couldn't force the words from my mouth. They were all true. We were going to fix this. None of us were walking away until we caught her stalker and ended the threat. And there was no question that I would keep Annalise safe. Nothing would happen to her on my watch.

None of those promises could take away her fear.

I hadn't understood before. Not really. I'd thought I had, but I'd been wrong.

Something inside me changed. Shifted. I pressed my lips to Annalise's soft hair and murmured, inarticulate sounds, soft and gentle. Soothing. My hand stroked her back, and we stood there for what felt like hours, her heart beating against mine, her breath gradually easing.

I couldn't do it. I thought I could see her as just a client, but I couldn't do it. Just a few days before, the past had seemed so important. Because of my job, Annalise had never been completely out of my life, but I'd convinced myself that my feelings for her were dead. I'd told myself she'd used me, and thrown me away. I blamed her for leaving, for not loving me enough to stay and fight.

In the face of her fear, my grudge didn't hold up. She'd already admitted that she'd run to protect her family. I'd been in the hospital, had almost died twice. I had to at least acknowledge the possibility that she hadn't left because she didn't love me, she'd left to protect me.

The woman in my arms, weeping over her mother's favorite flowers and the sick twisted fuck who'd sent them to her—this woman wasn't coldhearted. This woman wouldn't abandon the man who loved her because she was tired of him. Because he wasn't good enough for her.

It's not that I forgave her. Leaving had been the wrong choice, and the fact that she did it, the way she did it, was fucked up. But I was done blaming her. She didn't need that shit from me. She needed help. She needed support. She didn't need me to treat her like the enemy.

There was only one enemy in the situation, and he was drawing closer. If we couldn't find him, there was a very good chance I wouldn't lose Annalise to a breakup; I'd lose her forever.

CHAPTER NINE

ANNALISE

The day went sideways after the flower delivery. The sight of those flowers, my mother's flowers, used by this asshole to hurt me—it poked at a place inside of me I thought had healed over. Something raw and open, a part of me that was still a child. Still hoped my parents would one day come home.

After I wept all over Riley, I pretended to pull myself together, but my heart throbbed in my chest like a rotten tooth. I'd forgotten it was Mother's Day until I saw those lilies. I wanted my mother. I wanted to go to her grave or walk through the woods to the house where we'd lived, but both were off-limits for the time being.

Riley canceled our outing to the Botanical Gardens, saying he wanted me to stick close until the Sinclairs had a chance to take a look at the flowers. The kid who dropped them off hadn't known anything, and though the flowers in the arrangement had been unusual—at least the Myrtle and Tansy—so far they hadn't figured out where they'd come from.

There hadn't been a note with the arrangement this

time. Riley and the Sinclairs didn't know what to make of that, but I had a sinking feeling there was no note because my stalker had been too angry to write one. The few times I'd had a boyfriend, he hadn't responded well. A fiancé was guaranteed to enrage him.

I reminded myself that enraging the stalker, throwing him off balance, was the whole point of this charade with Riley. That didn't mean I liked it. I hated pretending Riley and I were engaged at least as much as I hated painting a target on his back.

It didn't matter that this was Riley's job. I didn't care that he could defend himself, that he'd done things like this before. I'd left him once to keep him safe, shattering my own heart in the process, and now I'd thrown him right in the line of fire.

For what?

To save myself? What kind of selfish bitch was I?

Every time Riley faked being my fiancé, every time he took my hand or kissed my cheek, little pieces of my heart were torn away. Once, I'd wanted this more than anything. Pretending it was real was torture.

So was sleeping beside him in my big, brass bed. There was plenty of room. The bed had belonged to my parents, a gift from my father to my mother, who'd loved the look of antique brass beds, and often lamented that they didn't come in a modern king-size.

Aunt Olivia and Uncle Hugh had moved the bed to my room in Winters House after they died, hoping it would bring me comfort. It had, and all the years I'd been away, I'd missed it.

Sharing it with Riley felt disturbingly normal. When he'd climbed in bed with me, that second night in Winters House, I thought it would be impossible to sleep with him only a foot away. I'd been right and wrong. I was aware of him beside me, more aware than I wanted to be.

For the first time in years, I felt safe. Whole. Like I could relax because everything was finally going to be okay.

It was stupid. My lizard brain responded to Riley's presence like he was the answer to all my problems, but the rational part of my mind knew that was the furthest thing from the truth. I had enough to worry about with this plan to draw out and catch my stalker. I didn't need to get any ridiculous ideas about Riley.

He'd made it clear that the past was the past and after this job, there was no future. Not for us.

He kept us cooped up in Winters House for two days. The day the flowers were delivered, even the day after, I could understand. The delivery was on a Sunday, and no one was working. Not in the lab or in research. And I could see not getting all the information they needed in one business day, but by Tuesday I'd expected Riley to relax. He hadn't.

I was getting tired of staying in the house. The whole point of Riley as my fiancé was to provoke my stalker, not hide from him. I hated hiding. I hated waiting. Hated being passive.

All those years ago I'd known I had two choices - let Aiden lock me behind the walls of Winters House or run. Neither was much of a life, but I'd chosen to run. At least I was in control. Now I was little more than a child, sitting around waiting to be told when I could leave the house.

I resisted the urge to throw a tantrum when Aunt Amelia and Sophie went out to Annabelle's coffee shop to try her new sugar-free hot cocoa. Their promise to bring some back didn't make me feel better. I ground my teeth and paced down the hall to my rooms where Riley was working at the sitting room desk.

Planting my hands on my hips, I felt like a shrew when I demanded, "This is the last day we're stuck in the house. I don't care what kind of evidence they're waiting for. This is driving me nuts."

Riley leveled a calm look at me and said, "Agreed. So far, they're not finding anything new. This guy never leaves any trace, and he covers his tracks. Always." He ran his fingers through his short hair, ruffling it, and said, "Most criminals are stupid. The smart ones are a total pain in the ass."

"So tomorrow we can go out?" I pressed. I already knew my stalker was smart. If he hadn't been, we would've caught him years ago.

"Tomorrow. For now, I'm about done with this," he said, gesturing to his laptop. "How about we hit the pool table or watch a movie?"

I nodded and said, "I'll meet you down there."

I didn't really want to play pool or watch a movie, not after we'd done the same the day before, but it was better than nothing. I had the balls racked by the time Riley made it to the lower level. We played pool until he got bored, then settled into the plush, reclining, theater seats and put on a movie.

Sitting in the dark beside Riley was harder than sleeping next to him. He was awake, for one thing. So was I. Very awake. And very aware of his arm resting only inches away from mine.

The temptation to slide my hand just a few inches to the left, to reach out my pinky and touch his, was almost too much. Eventually, I reclined my chair all the way and rolled on my side, turning my back to Riley and propping a throw pillow under my head. A few minutes later, I was asleep.

Riley didn't wake me until dinner time, and I sat up in the oversize chair slowly, struggling to lower the footrest. Napping during the day always leaves me feeling off, as if I can't quite get my brain back in gear.

Dinner passed in a dream. I ate mechanically, only half following the conversation and not protesting when Riley refilled my wine glass. After dessert, everyone piled into the couches in the family room to watch a Braves game. I snagged my tablet from my room, using my late arrival as an excuse to choose a seat away from Riley.

We ended up sitting in armchairs, side-by-side, anyway. Closer than I would've liked, but at least we weren't scrunched on the love seat. I'd had too much wine at dinner, and combined with my afternoon nap and the mocha Sophie brought me from Annabelle's, I was wired and nowhere near sleep by the time the game was over.

Riley was in bed when I came out of the closet in my pajamas. My cotton tank top and matching pajama bottoms were not sexy in the slightest, but the thin fabric was too flimsy against my skin. I needed more of a barrier against Riley.

A robe or a sweatshirt. A suit of armor would've been good. Riley wore a T-shirt and loose pajama bottoms. Looking at him, my mouth went dry.

It wasn't just the way the T-shirt stretched across his muscled chest, or the sight of his bare toes against my pink and white comforter, so familiar and yet completely out of place.

No, the thing that got me was the glasses. My Riley, college Riley, did not wear glasses. But this Riley, eleven years older, was mildly farsighted and needed glasses to read.

Not just glasses.

Sexy glasses.

Dark brown horn rims that perfectly complemented his light hazel eyes and dark hair.

Glasses that made him look like a naughty professor and —No. No thinking about naughty professors and bad girl students. This was Riley, and he was off-limits.

But those glasses were killing me.

I'd always loved his eyes—the light hazel flecked with gold and green surrounded by thick, dark lashes—they were enough to make any woman melt. When you added in the dark brown horn rims...

I sighed.

Riley's eyes met mine as he said, "You okay?"

How to answer that question?

Not with the truth.

I imagined myself saying, *I'm fine, you just look unbelievably fucking hot in those glasses, and I'm thinking about stripping off my pajamas and jumping you.*

Not going to happen.

If I said it he'd either reject me—which might kill me with humiliation—or he'd take me up on it, and we'd be in even more of a mess than we already were.

"I'm fine," I said. "Just restless. That nap, and too much coffee."

I wandered into the sitting room and came back with my camera. Perching on the end of the bed, catty-corner from Riley, I took off the lens and focused on my comforter, drawing the light pink blossoms into high detail and snapping a picture. I wouldn't do anything with it, but I missed the feel of the camera in my hands, the sound of the shutter clicking, the way everything looked right with my eye to the viewfinder.

I hadn't thought much about Sloane's offer for getting my work into her gallery. I'd deal with that later. But photography had never been a career thing for me. It was my heart. My release. My freedom.

Rising and crossing the room, I lifted the camera and aimed it through the window, into the courtyard where the fountain still ran, lit by spotlights hidden underwater. I lost myself in adjusting the focus, the light meter, getting exactly the look I wanted in the contrast between the glowing water and the shadows around the fountain.

I pressed the shutter button again and again, falling into a familiar rhythm of taking pictures, adjusting settings, and shooting again. Lowering the camera, I flipped open the screen to review my shots.

"Let me see," Riley interrupted, leaning forward and reaching out a hand for my camera.

I stepped back, holding it out of reach, and flipped the screen shut, raising it to my eye and clicking the shutter button rapidly. Riley fell back against his pillows and shook his head at me.

"No pictures of me," he said, halfheartedly.

I didn't need any more pictures of Riley, that was certain. In the few months we'd been together, I must have taken a million. Just like this, goofing around before bed, I'd lift my camera and click the shutter button, and once I started, I'd keep going.

The camera loved Riley. The planes of his cheekbones, that shiny, thick hair. Taking a quick check of the last few shots, I groaned. And the glasses. The camera fucking loved the glasses.

If I were smart, I'd go put the camera away, climb into

bed and pretend to sleep. That's what I'd do if I were smart. If I were stupid, I'd lift it to my eye and take another picture. And another, capturing the quirk of his grin, the way his glasses almost exactly matched the warm brown of his hair. The smooth satin of his skin where it met the faded green cotton of the T-shirt he wore to bed.

Riley was just as stupid as I was. He pretended to ignore me, but he was paying attention. I knew by the way he lifted his chin and turned his face in my direction. He might not even have realized he was doing it. If I was flooded with memories of all the times we'd done this in the past, he must have been too.

I stood and moved to the end of the bed, going for a different angle, catching the way the light fell across his forearm. It was a nice forearm, lean but corded with muscle, his tattoos inky black against his tanned skin. College Riley had a few tattoos, but not this many.

I liked them. I liked everything about him, but then, I always had.

Some things didn't change.

"You done taking pictures yet?" Riley asked, his voice low and rough.

I shook my head and lifted the camera to my face, hiding behind it as I opened my mouth and heard myself say, "Take off your shirt."

Lust and embarrassment hit me in equal measures, sending a hot flush into my cheeks, leaving me almost dizzy. It got worse when, after sending me a long, level look, Riley put down his tablet, sat up, and peeled off his T-shirt.

It took everything I had to pretend to be unaffected. He settled back against the pillows, his eyes on mine. I didn't move except to press my finger to the shutter release button again and again.

Riley with a shirt on was temptation enough. Bare-chested Riley, still in those fucking glasses, had me drooling. Not literally, but I could feel the hot flush burning my cheeks, my heart pounding, my nipples beading tight beneath my thin tank top. Heat gathered between my legs, and I resisted the urge to rub my thighs together.

There was a dare in his hazel eyes as he watched me. His tattoos spread across his chest, a stylized, almost abstract Eagle, wings and a medallion. I let the camera trail down his muscled chest, documenting the ridges of his abdomen, the tight skin by his hipbone leading to the V of muscle that pointed straight to his cock.

The thin cotton of his pajama bottoms did nothing to hide the long bar of his erection. My pussy pulsed in sympathy.

I had the crazy thought that our bodies were having a silent conversation, both wondering what the hell was wrong with our brains.

Why were we across the room from one another when we could be fucking right now?

Because doing anything with my slick pussy and his hard cock would be pretty much the dumbest move either of us could make.

My body didn't think much of that argument.

I wasn't sure my brain did either, but I was frozen.

Frozen with lust, half terrified by the strange familiarity of being like this—Riley half naked and aroused, me with the camera in my hands. We'd done this before, at his apartment, in my dorm room. Almost every time we'd ended up stripping off our clothes and jumping each other.

Not this time.

My breath strangled in my chest as I took a step back and pressed the shutter release button. Once, then twice.

Over and over, still hiding behind the pretense that this was about taking pictures, that I wasn't drowning in desire.

Two flags of color bloomed in Riley's cheekbones. His eyes were molten gold and fixed to my hard nipples poking through the ribbed cotton of my tank top.

Abruptly, he rolled to his feet. I almost dropped my camera. He strode to the end of the bed and stopped in front of me, looking down into my eyes. Carefully, he pulled the camera from my hands and set it on the end of the bed.

His fingers held my jaw on both sides, tilting my face to his. When his lips touched me, I went still. A heartbeat later his mouth opened over mine, his tongue driving deep, the kiss liquid and hot.

His lips were hard. Demanding. His kiss a claiming I did nothing to stop. I swayed into him, my bones turning to jelly, my mouth hungry for his. I was reaching for him when he tore his mouth from mine and stepped back.

I was still rocking on my heels, trying to get my balance, as he moved around me and disappeared into the bathroom.

Knees shaking a little, I sank to the edge of the bed, picking up my camera out of reflex and pressing the power button to turn it off. The last thing I needed was more pictures of Riley.

The shower turned on, and I closed my eyes, squeezing them shut, trying not to think about exactly what Riley was doing in that shower. I would not imagine him fisting his hard cock while thinking of me.

I wouldn't.

For a fleeting moment, I considered sliding my hand between my legs and relieving some of the tension, but the thought of Riley walking out of the bathroom to see me touching myself was both deeply arousing and more embarrassing than I could stand.

Instead, I put my camera away and crawled into bed, turning off the lights as I did. I curled up on my side and stared at the wall and the bathroom door. The shower cut off, and I closed my eyes, trying to breathe evenly as if I were asleep.

Light flashed and cut off as Riley opened the door to the bathroom. He climbed into bed, hugging his side as I hugged mine, leaving as much space as possible between us.

Both of us pretended to sleep.

I have a feeling I wasn't the only one who stared into the darkness well past midnight.

CHAPTER TEN
ANNALISE

Riley was gone when I woke up. I blinked my eyes, trying to clear the grit, and rolled out of bed, heading straight for a hot shower. I hadn't slept well. No surprise. I'd lain awake long into the night, listening to Riley breathe and wondering if he was awake.

Wondering if he was thinking about the same thing I was—rolling over and touching my fingers to his skin, sliding those fingers down beneath the waistband of his pajamas and wrapping them around the thick, hard cock waiting there.

If his thoughts were anywhere close to mine, he probably hadn't slept any better than I had. I washed my hair, shaved my legs, and gave myself a firm lecture.

Riley is here for a job.

That's all you are to him.

A job.

If you sleep with him, you'll get your heart all tangled up again. And when he leaves, you'll be destroyed.

What had he told me that first day? It was time to look

out for myself. Sleeping with Riley was not looking out for myself.

I knew all of that was true. I did. Really. And it wasn't just lust. It wasn't just that he was hot. He was Riley. My Riley. I'd fallen so hard for him and missed him so much when I'd left. Having him this close after all these years was like being on a diet surrounded by chocolate.

I needed to keep focused. I needed to remember who he was.

Not mine.

That's all I really needed to know.

Riley was not mine.

And if he wasn't, there was no need to bother with makeup or doing my hair. I wasn't trying to impress him, right? I pulled a comb through my wet hair without drying it, but I did stop for a minute to put on eyeliner and mascara. I looked tired enough without foregoing makeup completely. My favorite pair of jeans and a T-shirt later, I was ready for breakfast.

Aiden and Gage were long gone, but Sophie and Amelia looked like they had just sat down at the table when I arrived. I grabbed a seat opposite them and reached for the coffee decanter.

I needed coffee. A lot of coffee.

If we got the go-ahead to leave the house, I planned to talk Riley into taking me to Annabelle's. I needed another one of those mochas, and Annabelle had a way with chocolate.

I looked up from my steaming mug to see Riley in the doorway of the dining room, his dark hair wet. He must have been in the gym and used the shower down there. I caught sight of his arms, the swell of a vein running along his bicep, and tried not to think about Riley working out. Riley sweating. Riley taking off his shirt.

Down, girl. No Riley, remember?

I usually had more self-control than this, but the instinct to touch Riley was ingrained long ago. Overriding it was proving harder than I'd expected.

Mrs. W came in, her usual starched white apron tied over a dark dress, and stopped beside me, patting the back of the chair next to me for Riley. He slid into it and grinned at me. If he'd been up half the night, it didn't show.

"Are you two all right with the buffet or would you like Abel to make you something?"

"The buffet is great, thanks," I said, reaching for my coffee again. As long as the coffee kept flowing, I didn't really care what I ate. Everything Abel made was good.

"I'm good too," Riley said. Then, sniffing lightly, he said, "What smells like chicken soup?"

A low growl sounded above me. Mrs. W's teeth were gritted, her eyes narrowed as she shot a deadly glare across the table, right at Aunt Amelia. I looked between them, surprised to see Aunt Amelia's guilty expression as she dropped her eyes to the floor.

What was going on?

Riley, always good at picking up subtext, caught the tension immediately and dropped the subject, saying, "I'm starved."

We both got up and went to the buffet, aware of Mrs. W leaving the dining room as quietly as she'd come in. I scooped scrambled eggs on my plate as Sophie said from behind me, "You are in so much trouble."

I grabbed some bacon and a biscuit and made my way back to my seat, more interested in the drama than the food.

Picking up a piece of bacon and crunching in I said to Sophie, "Why? What did she do?"

Amelia took a sip of tea and ignored me, studying the Persian carpet with far more attention than it called for, especially considering it had been here when she'd been a girl. By now, she should have the pattern memorized.

Sophie leaned forward and said, "She saw this prank on-line where you put a piece of bullion in someone's shower head. I told her I wouldn't help her with it. I have no idea how she managed to get in and out of Mrs. W's place and mess with the shower head without anyone knowing, but she did. Mrs. W is not happy."

"I may have gone just a little bit too far," Amelia admitted. She nibbled a piece of bacon and shrugged one shoulder. I couldn't remember the last time she'd looked embarrassed or apologetic.

Amelia made her choices and stood by them. Regret was not in her vocabulary. "It seemed like it would be so much funnier than it is. But the bullion soaked into her hair, and it seems that it's very hard to wash out."

Amelia sank her teeth into her bottom lip, and I had the troubling thought that she was fighting a smile.

"If Mrs. W catches you laughing, you may not get a decent meal for the rest of your life," Sophie hissed under her breath. "And you have a few decades on Mrs. W. She *will* outlive you."

"Aiden won't let her starve me," Amelia said, with less confidence than I would've expected.

"I wouldn't be so sure about that," Sophie said, darkly. "Aiden adores you, but he also adores Mrs. W., and you know it. If I were you, I'd consider a heartfelt apology."

Amelia harrumphed and chewed her bacon. I shook my head. Mrs. W and Amelia had never gotten along, but

I had to agree with Sophie. Dousing Mrs. W in chicken soup was going too far. And despite Amelia's protests, no one in this house would hold Mrs. W back if she wanted revenge.

Thinking to change the subject I said, "Is everything set for the wedding? Do you need help? We haven't gotten cleared to leave the house, but I can pitch in around here," I offered.

Sophie and Gage's wedding was on Saturday, only a few days away. It was small, but I couldn't imagine they were ready.

Sophie shrugged one shoulder and smiled. "Actually, there really isn't anything to do. Mrs. W said she has everything under control. We got Charlie's wedding planner, and she organized all the details with the music and the pictures."

"You're very relaxed for a woman who's getting married in four days," I said. I had a feeling if it were my wedding I'd be running around with a clipboard double-checking everything.

Sophie gave a small, blissful smile and said, "I'm marrying Gage," as if it were just that simple. And maybe, for her, it was. She went on, "After my first husband, I never thought I'd fall in love. I never imagined a man like Gage. I don't want a big fussy wedding. I just want to marry Gage, in the gardens with the peonies in bloom and our family around us. That's my dream wedding, and fortunately, it's very easy to throw together. A little music, some flowers— Mrs. W assures me it's not much more than a dinner party, really."

"If you're sure," I said, a little deflated at the idea that there wasn't anything to do. Looking beside me to Riley I said, "Can we go out today?"

Shaking his head, he said, "I'm waiting for a call from the office. Maybe after that. Why, you getting restless?"

I nodded. My usual MO was to take off when the stalker knew where I was. Maybe it hadn't worked out very well, but at least it gave me the illusion of action. Packing up my stuff and taking off, finding a new job, a new place to live, put me in control.

I knew I was safe here in Winters House, but I was also bored.

Leaning forward, Amelia said, "I've got a project for you."

I narrowed my eyes at her. "I'm not doing anything that's going to get me in trouble with Mrs. W. I like my food. And I love Mrs. W. You're on your own."

Amelia scowled at me. "I'll apologize, all right? But this isn't a prank. I promise. I want you to help me find the other hiding places in the library."

I'd completely forgotten about those. Earlier in the year, during the winter, there'd been a few break-ins at the house. The intruder hadn't been caught, though the Sinclairs had discovered how they were getting in. They'd set a trap, but the intruder had never returned.

During the last break-in, we'd discovered what they were trying to steal. A box of letters to my mother from an unnamed lover, someone—according to the dates—she'd been with before she'd started dating my father.

Someone she'd been dating not long before she gave up a child for adoption. A boy. My brother. A brother we hadn't been able to find.

The Sinclairs were working on it, but the last I'd heard they were starting to suspect their father had a hand in hiding both the child and the identity of the father. At the very least, it hadn't been a normal adoption, or they would've found my long-lost brother already.

Even weirder, the letters to my mother had been in a box that had belonged to my father, in a secret compartment in the library that was apparently common knowledge in the older generation of Winters. One of those things our parents had probably meant to pass along to us at some point, not realizing they'd never have the chance.

According to family lore, there were three secret hiding places in the library. The intruder had known about one, at least, and during the break in to retrieve the letters had revealed it to us. Amelia vaguely recalled the other two, but she'd left Winters House long ago, and her memory of the secret compartments was foggy at best.

"You haven't found them yet?" I asked. I would've expected Amelia to make it her life's mission to locate the secret compartments once she'd remembered their existence. Especially after we'd realized it was possible they were tied to my mother and missing brother. The letters had been in one compartment, who knew what might be in the others?

"We were looking," Amelia said, "but then there was the whole thing with Sophie's husband, and we got a little distracted."

Understandable. Not long after Sophie and Gage got together, Sophie's dead husband had come back for her and ended up kidnapping Amelia. I could see how that would've been distracting.

"So you really have no idea where they are?" I asked. I could help with that. It was like a treasure hunt. And if it led to answers about my mother, her mysterious lover, and my missing brother—how could I say no?

I expected Riley to leave us to our search in the library

and work at the desk in my sitting room, but he brought his laptop to the library and worked on whatever it was he did while we searched. I snuck glances at him out of the corner of my eye, trying not to drool every time I saw him with those glasses on.

Yum.

Still wearing the T-shirt that stretched around his biceps, with those glasses and the serious expression on his face, Riley was drool-worthy. Painfully so.

When he caught me staring and shot me a wink, I felt my cheeks flush red. Perving over Riley was one thing. Getting caught at it was another.

Looking for secret compartments in the library was a lot less exciting in practice than it had sounded at the breakfast table. The library was lined, floor to ceiling, with book-shelves and cabinets, custom-made in quarter-sawn, dark stained oak.

It made for a gorgeous, cozy room, but all those shelves and cabinets also created a million places someone could have hidden a secret compartment.

Amelia was perched on the couch, close to the unlit fire-place, bossing Sophie around as Sophie searched. Amelia claimed she was too old to be sitting on the floor and Sophie had the patience to put up with it. Probably because Sophie was both patient and sweet, and at almost eighty Amelia *was* too old to be sitting on the floor.

Methodically, Sophie emptied shelves of books and searched for something, anything, that felt out of place. A crack or bump in the wood. A lever or switch.

We found nothing.

I was on a short stepladder, checking the shelves closest to the door. After I finished the first two, I started getting bored. There was no guarantee there actually were two more secret compartments, only Amelia's memories of her childhood. And even if they were there, it didn't mean we'd find anything about my missing brother. Still, I didn't have anything else to do for the moment. I might as well help.

I lifted books, three or four at a time, and felt behind and around where they'd been, then replaced them and moved on to the next section. It was easy, mind-numbingly easy, and provided no distraction from Riley, sitting in an armchair behind me, focused on his laptop.

I was trying to ignore him. I'm pretty sure it looked like I was ignoring him, but I was aware of every shift of his body. The sound of his fingers on the keyboard, the way he cleared his throat.

My eye landed on the engagement ring on my finger, and my heart beat a little harder. There'd been a time when I thought he might give me one of these for real. And I would've accepted him, happily. No, more than happily. I'd been head over heels for Riley Flynn.

And you almost got him killed, I reminded myself. *If you'd stayed, he might not be alive today.* It was true; he might not. I could armchair quarterback the past all I wanted, but the truth was, Riley had been safer with me gone. And until we figured out who was behind all this, no one would be safe while I was home.

The whole thing sucked, and I was in no position to be listening to Riley clear his throat and thinking about kissing him. Not going to happen. We were stuck together, and it wasn't fair to put him in that situation.

Mrs. W came in, interrupting my reverie, carrying a tray of tea and shortbread. I saw the cookies with a new perspective since Gage had told me Abel made them for Mrs. W.

Sneaky, because shortbread was kind of a family thing. My mother had loved it, I loved it, I knew Aiden did, and it was Aunt Amelia's favorite cookie. That was a problem because Aunt Amelia wasn't supposed to eat sweets.

Mrs. W placed the tray on the coffee table, within arm's reach of Amelia. On her way out of the room, she said to me, "Find anything yet?"

"Nope. I've only done three shelves," I said.

Mrs. W looked around the room, then back at me, and shook her head. "You've got your work cut out for you," she said.

"And you're sure you don't know anything?" I asked.

"I promise you I do not."

Mrs. W left, and I couldn't help but notice that Aunt Amelia had slid closer to the tea tray, and the forbidden cookies. Sophie didn't seem to have noticed. That was odd. Not Aunt Amelia going for cookies—Aunt Amelia trying to cage forbidden sweets was pretty much a guarantee in any situation.

But, Sophie not noticing was...suspicious.

As if she knew I was thinking about her, Sophie glanced up and saw me looking at the tea tray and Amelia, a question in my eyes. She shook her head, the movement so slight I almost missed it. Hmm. Interesting.

I picked up another short stack of books and slid my hand against the cool wood of the shelf, fingertips probing for a change in texture. Nothing. I was sliding the stack of books back into place when behind me, Amelia let out a garbled shout.

I shoved the books back on the shelf and turned to see Amelia spitting out the shortbread cookie, the crumbs spewing everywhere—her skirt, the carpet, and some in her hand. Her lips were pursed as if she'd been sucking on a lemon.

To my utter shock, Sophie burst out laughing.

Riley, warned by Amelia's half choking splutters and the crumbs of shortbread flying everywhere, put his laptop aside and poured Amelia a steaming cup of tea. She sipped at it cautiously, then thirstily, trying to wash away the shortbread residue in her mouth.

Riley picked up one of the squares of shortbread and took a small bite off the corner. His face instantly twisted, though he swallowed instead of spitting it out. I climbed down from the ladder and tried a piece myself. Normally, Able's shortbread was buttery and sweet with just a hint of salt, crumbly and rich and perfect.

This piece was crumbly, but not sweet. I couldn't begin to guess what he'd used, but the shortbread looked completely normal and tasted bitterly, pungently sour.

Amelia's nose should have alerted her to the coming assault on her tastebuds, but her sense of smell wasn't what it had been when she was younger, and she'd missed it.

Amelia finished her cup of tea and stood, brushing the crumbs off her skirt onto the carpet. Beside her, Sophie was still giggling, her cheeks pink and her eyes alight with laughter. She was immune to Amelia's glare and completely unafraid of the bony finger pointed at her.

"You knew!" Amelia said, outraged.

Sophie let out another peal of laughter and said, "Of course, I knew. When was the last time you got that close to a cookie without me spotting you? If you hadn't been so greedy, you would've realized something was up."

"You should be ashamed of yourself," Amelia said.

Sophie shook her head and stood, surveying the mess on the carpet. "I'm going to get a vacuum." Looking at Amelia, she said, "You had this coming, and you know it. Pay attention. Don't mess with Mrs. W. You can pull all the pranks you want, but leave her out of it. Sour shortbread was just the beginning."

"I'm going to brush my teeth," Amelia announced and stalked from the room.

Sophie laughed again and picked up the tea tray. "I should probably feel bad, but she really did have it coming. Anyway, she should know better. No one messes with Mrs. W in this house."

Sophie left with the tea tray, and Riley and I were alone. He was grinning, his hazel eyes alight behind his glasses. Remembering the plate of shortbread, I said, "They looked so innocent. I wonder if Abel has any real shortbread in the kitchen."

"You knew something was up," Riley said, quietly.

I shrugged a shoulder. "Sophie has eyes in the back of her head. I had a feeling something was off when she let Amelia get that close to the tray. And Gage told me Abel was sweet on Mrs. W." I said that last part under my breath, just in case.

Riley raised one eyebrow, his grin spreading wider. "Getting revenge for his woman?"

"Something like that," I said, "Though I have no idea what's going on between them."

Riley's eyes were fixed on mine, warm and amused. "I bet I can find out," he said stepping closer, so we wouldn't be overheard.

I leaned in, feeling his body heat radiate through his T-shirt, smelling the woodsy, clean scent of his skin. "How can you find out?" I asked.

"I have my ways," he said, his smile in his voice.

I leaned closer, swaying into him, drawn by his heat and smell and the sound of his voice in my ears. He was only inches away, and for one crazy second, I was absolutely sure I was going to kiss him.

His lips parted, maybe to speak, maybe to close the distance and land on mine.

His phone rang, and we jolted apart. I knew that tone. It was the front gate, and if the front gate was calling, something was up. Stepping back, I crossed my arms over my chest and waited, braced for whatever was coming next.

CHAPTER ELEVEN

ANNALISE

R iley raised the phone to his ear and barked, "Yeah?" His eyes rose to the ceiling, avoiding mine, and he said, "Send them up."

Slowly, he lowered his hand and shoved his phone back in his pocket. He took his time before he looked at me, but I knew. I knew as soon as he said, *send them up*.

"More flowers?" I asked, proud of how even and calm my voice sounded.

Riley was hoarse as he said, "Yeah. I'm going to meet them at the door and bring them in. Why don't you go to the dining room?"

"No," I said. "I'll wait here with you."

"Lise—"

"No, Riley. Please." I didn't want to sit at the big dining room table by myself and wait for him to bring the flowers to me. I didn't want to be alone.

Logically, I knew there was no threat. No immediate physical threat, that is.

The flowers were a threat all on their own.

Riley nodded in grudging agreement. He reached out

and closed his hand around mine, holding it tightly as he led me down the hall toward the front door.

My mind raced as I tried to guess what would be in this arrangement. The last had been daylilies with tansy and myrtle. Motherhood, marriage, and hostility.

Would this one be creepily romantic?

Maybe white clover and gardenia; Think of me and forbidden love.

Or old-fashioned?

Red roses and white jasmine for desire and love.

Riley stopped in front of one of the long narrow windows flanking the door, keeping an eye on the court-yard. He dropped my hand and dug in his pocket for something. Finding it, his eyes still focused out the window, he dropped the small, square package in my hand. I looked down, and my heart stuttered in my chest.

A caramel.

"Where did you get this?" I asked, turning the candy over in my fingers. I hadn't seen one of these in years, hadn't been able to stand the sight of them after I'd left Riley, but I used to love them.

Riley moved one shoulder in an embarrassed shrug. "Do you still like them?"

"I haven't had one in eleven years," I admitted, quietly. Riley's head jerked up, his eyes fixed on me as I carefully unwrapped the candy and popped it into my mouth. Sweet buttery caramel melted across my tongue and I fell back in time.

I'd always hated getting flowers. Obviously. For the first part of my life, I loved flowers. They'd been a connection to my mother, something my aunt and I had shared after she was gone as a way to keep her close. But after the stalker entered my life, I grew to hate them.

On our second date, Riley had shown up with a bouquet of flowers. I'd already had it bad for him and had pretended to love them, but he'd seen right through me. On the next date, he brought me candy.

I hated flowers, but I loved candy. Riley turned it into a game, trying everything to see what I liked best. Milk chocolate, dark chocolate, truffles, hard candies, butterscotch, and mints. Combinations like turtles and chocolate covered pretzels.

He tried it all and discovered that my very favorite treat was a simple cellophane wrapped caramel, the kind that wasn't entirely hard candy and wasn't completely soft, but somewhere in between. He'd hide them in his pockets and slip me one here and there, sometimes secreting them in my backpack or my purse so I'd find them and know he'd been thinking of me.

I sucked on the candy and felt oddly comforted. Riley would never forgive me for leaving him the way I had, even if he finally understood why. The woman who would keep Riley had to be strong. He deserved strength beside him. He deserved someone who would fight for him, not a woman who ran at the first hint of trouble.

I had too much baggage, too much fear. I was a runner. I didn't know how to stick. I couldn't be the woman he deserved. When this was all over, he would move on.

Maybe he'd be glad he'd taken the job because he finally got closure. Maybe he was so over me he didn't need closure.

It didn't really matter. We had a past, but no future. Still, the familiar taste of caramel on my tongue was a comfort.

Together, we watched one of the Sinclair SUVs pass through the inner gates and curve around the fountain in the center of the courtyard, coming to a stop in front of the steps leading up to the front door of Winters House.

My stomach tightened to a knot, and I squeezed my eyes shut. Suddenly, I didn't want to see. I couldn't watch the security guard carry the arrangement to our door in a mockery of someone delivering flowers.

I stepped back, saying, "Can you just bring them to the dining room?"

Riley reached for my hand, but I was already too far away. I could hear the concern in his voice when he said, "Why don't I have them taken to the Sinclair offices? They can send a picture and tell us what's on the card."

I stopped in the center of the front hall and stared at the tall wooden front door, thinking. I didn't want to see those flowers. I didn't want to see the note. If I said yes, Riley would make them go away. But he couldn't make them disappear, and hiding didn't erase the threat. I'd learned that the hard way. I shook my head.

"I'll be in the dining room. I need to see them before they go to the lab."

The doorbell rang, and I flinched. I was so distracted, I almost bumped right into Sophie, crossing the hall, carrying the vacuum. I'd completely forgotten about the shortbread and the crumbs on the carpet. Sophie took one look at my face and stopped cold, reaching out to close a hand over my upper arm.

"Annalise. What happened?"

"Flowers," I said, succinctly.

"Where?" Sophie asked, setting the vacuum down on the hardwood floor and turning me to face her.

"Riley's bringing them to the dining room."

Sophie, the vacuum forgotten, led me to the dining room and sat beside me. She didn't say anything, just gave me the comfort of her presence. We heard the murmur of Riley's voice, the click and low thud of the door closing, and the sound of his feet crossing the front hall.

I thought I was braced for the sight of the flowers. I should be used to them by now. There'd probably been close to fifty since I was a teenager. No reason to get worked up. But this arrangement was a stab to my heart.

"That's hideous," Sophie murmured from beside me.

It was. The frothy blooms of yellow hyacinth beside the crepey, deep pink begonia petals made for a weird, discordant combination. I had the same reaction the first time I'd seen the two flowers together when Riley lay unconscious in a hospital bed.

"What does it mean?" Riley asked.

"Yellow hyacinth for jealousy."

"And the pink one?" Sophie asked, quietly.

I reached out a finger and almost touched one of the vibrant pink petals. "Begonia. It means beware."

Riley narrowed his eyes on the arrangement. "Why does that look familiar? I feel like I've seen it in the file."

I let out a strangled half laugh. I should've known they had a file. They'd been documenting the gifts and flowers since I was a teenager. My voice shaking a little, I said, "It's almost the same arrangement he sent after he put you in the hospital."

"Almost the same?" Riley asked.

"It's missing the rhododendron," I said, trying to put the clues together.

"What does the rhododendron mean?" Sophie asked, staring at the flowers with narrowed eyes.

"Danger."

"How is that different from the Begonia?" She asked.

"Begonia is a warning of something bad to come, but it

hasn't happened yet. Rhododendron indicates a danger that's happening now. When Riley was in the hospital—" I glanced over to see his jaw set tight as he glared at the arrangement. "The yellow hyacinth—jealousy, was the reason. Rhododendron was the car accident and the accidental overdose. Current danger. And the Begonia—"

"The Begonia was why you left," Riley said, his voice so low it was almost a whisper.

Tears pricked the back of my eyes, and I sucked in a short breath. My voice barely audible over the pounding of my heart, I admitted, "Yes. The Begonia was why I left."

Sophie looked between us and said quietly, "I'm going to go take care of that floor before Mrs. W gets to it."

She slipped from the room in silence. Riley never looked away from the flowers.

"There's a note," he said. I reached for it, but he raised his hand to stop me. "Evidence. We'll look at the note and then let the guards take it to the lab for processing. Stay right here and don't touch anything. I'll be back in a second."

I sank into a chair, my eyes fixed on the flower arrangement, my mind racing. I understood why the rhododendron was missing. The danger hadn't happened yet, but the Begonia said it was coming. Not for me. He never hurt me. He came after the people I loved, and I'd lost enough of those already.

I'd wondered over the years if I'd done the right thing in leaving Riley. Especially the way I had, with a letter full of lies. Looking at the arrangement on my dining room table, the twisted jealousy and the threat, I knew I'd been right.

Riley would never have left me to face this alone. His loyalty would have gotten him killed.

It still might. I'd left home to keep my family safe. To keep Riley safe. Was coming back selfish? Aiden and Gage,

Vance and Charlie, Holden and Tate and Jacob had all convinced me that this was the right thing to do.

But there was Rosie, and Jo and Emily and Abigail. I was pretty sure Lucas could take care of himself, but what about Maggie? While I'd been gone my family had grown. The idea of losing a single one of them made me physically ill.

I braced my hands on the cool polished surface of the dining room table, palms flat, fingers spread, and stared blindly at the flower arrangement. At the white square envelope nestled in the deep pink Begonia blossoms. A warning of coming danger surrounding what I was sure were words of threat.

I couldn't do this.

I wanted this to be over. I wanted to catch this guy and end it, once and for all. But there was no subtlety here.

He was coming after my family.

After Riley.

And if we did catch him, but he took one of my own with him, would it be worth it?

Every part of me rejected that idea. No. Never. I'd live my life on the run before I'd let that happen.

Riley's feet beat a cadence on the stairs, and I jerked back to awareness. He knew me too well. I couldn't let him see what I was thinking. That I was doubting the plan.

"You sure you want to read this?" he asked, placing a few plastic bags and two sets of tweezers on the table.

"I'm sure," I said. I didn't want to read it, but I had to.

With a precision that spoke of experience, Riley plucked the envelope from the Begonia blossoms with one set of tweezers and teased open the flap with the other.

"Open the plastic bag, would you? The one on top."

I did as he asked, and he dropped the envelope inside

after carefully extracting the note card. As he read the words on the card, his face turned to granite, his jaw set, teeth clamped together, his beautiful hazel eyes fierce with anger and frustration.

YOU BELONG TO ME.

YOU ALWAYS HAVE.

SOON, WE'LL BE TOGETHER.

"Put it away," I said, my voice choked in my throat. "Put it away. I don't need to see it again."

Riley did as I asked, carefully slipping the note card into a second plastic bag. "I'll have this picked up and brought to the lab. It'll be out of the house in five minutes," he promised.

I gave a short nod, all I could manage, and said, "I'm going to my room for a minute. I just need... I just need a few minutes."

I didn't see Riley's response. I turned on my heel and left the dining room, my stride jerky, every muscle in my body tight with strain. I couldn't do this. I couldn't.

I was trapped in this house—there was no way they'd let me out now—and as long as I was here everyone near me was in danger. Riley most of all.

How could I have thought this would work? What if something happened to him?

I walked into my room and shut the door behind me. Riley was everywhere. His papers on my desk, his shoes by the sofa, a discarded T-shirt hanging over the arm. How could I have let them talk me into this?

I knew the answer. Surrounded by all that male self-assurance, the Sinclair brothers, Gage, Aiden, and Riley all assuring me everything would be okay—I'd folded.

But now, those cheerful yellow hyacinths and deep pink begonia had shot me right back to one of the worst days of my life. I'd lost my parents as a child, my beloved aunt and uncle as a teenager, and standing beside Riley's hospital bed after he'd survived two accidents meant to kill him, I'd known leaving was the only thing I could do.

They all wanted me to stick it out, to trust their judgment, to let Riley risk his life. They wanted me to believe them when they told me everything would be okay. But what if they were wrong? Could I live with it? If something happened to Riley because of me, how could I face myself?

It was clear enough that he was over me. The attraction was still there, but that was just biology. Riley had moved on, and that was okay. It was the way it had to be.

I never would. All these years apart and I still loved him. If anything happened to Riley because of me, I wouldn't survive it. I didn't want that responsibility. For the last few years, my nomadic existence had begun to feel like a trap, like an endless hamster wheel of moving, of superficial friendships, and meaningless jobs. Of missing my family.

After seeing that arrangement, remembering how close I'd come to losing Riley all those years ago, it was this house —this plan—that felt like the trap.

If anything went wrong, Riley would end up dead.

I was packing before I realized it, my suitcase sprawled open on my bed as I shoved clothes inside, not bothering to fold anything, mixing the dirty and clean. I could sort all that out later.

The flash of the diamond on my hand caught my eye, and I closed my fingers over it, hiding the fire in the stone and tugging it against my knuckle.

The damn thing was stuck. I pulled harder, not hearing the door open behind me.

CHAPTER TWELVE
ANNALISE

"Running again?"

Riley shut the door. A moment later the click of the lock filled the room. Riley's body was still on alert, his hazel eyes molten with anger.

One shoulder jerked in a shrug, and he said, "I guess I shouldn't be surprised. This is what you do, right? You run when things get hard."

"That's not fair," I shot back. It was so very unfair I gritted my teeth at the need to yell, to scream out my frustration.

"I'm just calling it how I see it," he said, his voice level and dangerously restrained.

My fist tightened around the T-shirt I held, and I looked down at the suitcase sprawled open on the bed, the haphazard way I'd jammed clothes inside, forgetting completely about my toiletries and my camera equipment.

What was I doing? Was I really going to take off? Again? If I ran this time, I'd never stop.

My fingers relaxed, and I dropped the T-shirt into the suitcase, my shoulders slumping, my head hanging down.

"You don't understand," I said, my throat growing tight. "Why doesn't anybody understand?"

His warm hand flattened between my shoulder blades, and I leaned into him, needing his heat and his strength. Pulling me into his arms, he pressed his lips to my ear and said, "Explain it to me."

"I don't know how I can when I don't understand myself." His hand rubbed up and down my spine and I let out a breath. "I don't want to lose anyone else. I'm not afraid for me. Why doesn't anyone see that? He never hurts *me*."

"You need to let the rest of us take care of ourselves," Riley said, gently.

I shook my head, rolling my forehead against his chest, losing myself a little in the woodsy scent of his skin. "He almost killed you last time. Twice. I can't live with that."

"It's not going to happen again. I promise, Annalise, it's not going to happen again. We're going to get him this time and then it will all be over."

"You don't know that," I said. "You can't promise me that. And what if he doesn't go after you? What if he goes after my family? I can't be responsible for that."

"You're not responsible for that," he said. "That's crazy. Your stalker is responsible. That's who put me in the hospital. That's who almost killed me. Not you. It's not your fault."

"It's not my fault," I agreed, pulling from his arms and stepping back, "but it is my responsibility. I'm the reason. I have no clue why, or what I did to set this guy off, but I'm at the center of it. As long as I'm here, no one is safe."

"Do you think anyone cares about that?" Riley asked, throwing his arms out to his sides in exasperation. "This is your family. They don't want you to live like this anymore. If they're willing to take the risk because they love you, what gives you the right to take that choice away from them?"

"And what about you?" I folded my arms over my chest and took another step back. "Is this just another day for you? One more job where you throw yourself in front of a crazy stalker to protect the client? Do you understand what those flowers meant? If I don't make you leave, he'll get rid of you. Permanently."

Riley crossed his arms over his chest, mirroring my stubborn stance. "This is unfinished business."

I had no idea what the hell he meant by unfinished business. I opened my mouth to ask, then snapped it shut. I didn't want to know. I didn't want to hear him tell me I was just a loose end he was wrapping up.

I looked at my open suitcase and shook my head. I wanted to zip it closed and take off. I'd rather be lonely than risk losing another person I loved.

I understood what Riley was saying. I did. But if this went wrong, he wasn't the one who had to live with it. He'd be dead. And I'd have to wake up every morning knowing I'd gotten him killed.

"I'm going to be really fucking pissed at you if he kills you." I flipped the suitcase upside down, dumping my tangled clothes across the comforter. Riley stepped behind me, his hands closing over my shoulders.

"You guys need to stop making assumptions," he muttered, under his breath.

I turned to stare up at him. "What does that mean?"

His eyes met mine, and he shook his head. "It means that it's been half your life and none of you have any idea who your stalker is. You refer to the stalker as 'he,' but you don't know that it's a man. You assume it's a stranger when the evidence suggests it's not."

"Cooper said—" I began, but Riley interrupted.

"Cooper too. All of you, the Sinclairs, your family—making assumptions is dangerous. Especially in a case like this. The only two people I am absolutely positive are not the stalker are me and you. Everyone else is a suspect."

I burst out laughing. I couldn't help it. Riley's eyes narrowed as I shook my head and grinned up at him. "What about Aiden? Or Cooper? Or maybe their brother Axel is stalking me all the way from Las Vegas because I used to steal his comic books."

Riley was not amused.

"You're the one who keeps telling me how dangerous this is. Act like it. You're all so used to the situation that even when you think you're being careful, you're not."

I stopped laughing. I didn't want to admit it, but Riley was right. I refused to believe it could be anyone in my family or the Sinclairs, but I'd always shied away from thinking it might be someone I knew.

"Okay. You're right. But what am I supposed to do? Suspect everyone?"

"Yes," Riley said, his eyes serious. "Everyone."

"Everyone? Sophie? Mrs. W? Aunt Amelia?" I couldn't keep the incredulity out of my voice on that last one.

Riley didn't think it was a joke. "Everyone. Don't forget Abel, Mr. Henried, your uncle William, Vance's gallery manager. Everyone."

I sighed. Riley was making sense, and I was too smart not to listen, but just the thought of it was exhausting. How was I supposed to suspect every single person I knew? It was easier to assume the stalker was a stranger. How could someone I knew hide this level of crazy? Wouldn't I sense it? Wouldn't they give themselves away?

"Lise, I'm not going to let anything happen to you. You

have to know that," Riley said, closing the distance between us and cupping my chin in his hand.

I stared into his eyes, studying the flecks of green and gold, his concerned expression. "I'm not afraid of something happening to me," I said.

Riley gave an impatient jerk of his head and tightened his fingers on my chin. "You should be, dammit. Stalkers like this always escalate. He's threatening me now but—"

"He almost killed you twice," I said, quietly. "I was there. I'll never forget a single second. Don't tell me I should worry about myself when he's threatening to hurt you again."

"It was my fault he got to me back then," Riley said, not making sense. "It's not going to happen this time. You have to trust me."

I tried to take a step back, but he wrapped an arm around me and pulled me tight to his body. Under my breath, I said, "It's not you I don't trust, Riley. It's the psycho who's threatening to kill you."

A laugh huffed out of his chest, and he said, "Fair enough," just before he kissed me.

Every time I kissed Riley, it was like coming home. Forget this house, and my family, and sleeping in my childhood bed. Riley's mouth on mine, his arms around me, were all the home I'd ever needed.

Reason went out the window at the first touch of his mouth to mine, and I never stopped to think. I had a thousand reasons why kissing Riley was a terrible idea, and none of them mattered.

My lips parted beneath his, and my tongue slipped out, tracing his mouth and sliding against his tongue. The hum of pleasure resonated in his chest, so strong I felt it against my breasts down to my core. He moved away just long enough to murmur, "You taste like caramel," before taking my mouth with his again, looking at me, tasting me, until I was drowning in him.

I could've kissed Riley all day. His arms tightened around my back, and he lifted me, moving us to the side of the bed that wasn't covered with my clothes and tipping me back, coming down on top of me.

I spread my legs, my knees rising to clamp to his hips. It was muscle memory and history and me just wanting to be back like this with Riley, no matter how stupid it was.

I sank my fingers into his thick, soft hair and kissed him harder. I didn't want this to be a mistake. I didn't want to regret it later. I just wanted more of Riley.

When his hand left my face to slide down my body and find the hem of my shirt, I didn't stop him. I arched my back to take my weight off the fabric so he could slide his hand beneath and cup my breast. He found my nipple through my bra and swirled his thumb over the hard peak in the same light, feathery motion that had always sent sharp spikes of pleasure straight to my clit.

He did it again, and I groaned, pressing my breast harder into his hand and rocking my hips up into him. I could feel his cock against me, through the layers of fabric between us. I was wet and ready, just from kissing him and those light, sweet touches on my breast.

It had been years, but Riley hadn't forgotten a thing he'd learned about turning me on. All it took was his mouth on mine and his hands on my body, and I was melting.

I couldn't think. I didn't want to think. I just wanted to touch him. I slid my hands under his T-shirt, taking my time, absorbing the heat of his skin through my fingertips, the steel of the muscles in his back, the flex of his shoulders as he rose over me.

He took my nipple between two fingers and pinched.

I let out a gasp of shocked pleasure.

After the feather-light, teasing graze of his thumb, the firm pinch sent a bolt of heat through my body. I sank my fingers into his shoulders and cried out when he did it again. His mouth drank up the sounds.

I was losing myself in him, tugging at his shirt, pulling it up, wanting to strip off my own and be skin to skin, to finally feel him against me when he murmured, "Fuck, baby. You haven't changed. So fucking hot for it."

I went still under him, his words a bucket of ice water. I was hot for it with Riley. I always had been. I'd loved that about us. The way he could turn me on so easily, the way I always came with Riley.

But now, with the words *unfinished business* still rattling in my head, it didn't feel like a compliment when he said I was *hot for it*. It felt like I was disposable. Easy.

With any other man, that might have been okay. I was under plenty of stress. A recreational orgasm might be nice. Not with Riley. Nothing about Riley was simple. Sex least of all.

It only took a second for him to realize I wasn't into it anymore. Lifting up to meet my eyes, he said, "Baby, what's wrong? Just let yourself go. It's okay. I'll take care of you."

I squeezed my eyes shut, fighting the tears that pricked behind my eyelids, and rolled away. Riley let me go, sitting up and letting out a huff of breath that could've meant anything. Frustration. Annoyance.

"This isn't a good idea," I mumbled, escaping to the privacy of the bathroom. I tugged down the hem of my T-shirt and sat on the closed lid of the toilet, bracing my forehead on the heel of my palm.

I didn't want him to call me 'baby.' I didn't want him to tell me he'd take care of me. Riley was talking about the job. I was a client. I was trying, but I couldn't see him that way.

Since the day I'd left him, he'd been out there living his life. I'd been frozen in time, living on the run.

I'd never gotten over him.

Riley Flynn was still the only man I'd ever loved. I was already in too deep. If I slept with him, it would only be worse. He was going to leave me, one way or another, and when he walked away, I'd never be able to put the pieces of my broken heart back together.

CHAPTER THIRTEEN
RILEY

I wasn't usually a big fan of weddings. When you work security and private investigations you see way too much of the dark side of marriage. Cheating. Lying. Divorce cases are the bread and butter of our business. I preferred corporate espionage and stalkers. At the sight of white tulle and wedding cakes, my first thought was to wonder how long it would be until they were hiring lawyers.

Call me cynical, but I've seen too much not to be.

Still, Sophie glowed with happiness as she beamed at Gage Winters. He beamed right back. I wanted to believe these two were going to make it. Fuck it; I did believe these two would make it. They'd been through way too much to screw it up now.

The wedding was small, and security was high, but I hadn't left Annalise's side. Sticking close was no hardship. I rested my hand on her back, her skin sleek and as soft as silk.

She wore a blush pink dress with a halter top and long full skirt that showed only a hint of cleavage but left her back bare. The deep pink suited her tanned skin and long blonde waves. She'd left her hair loose, pulled back from her face with only a few sparkly pins. On her feet, she wore hot pink sandals instead of more formal heels.

Every time I looked at her I wanted to drag her off somewhere private and finish what we'd started in her bedroom a few days before.

I'd thought she was gorgeous when she was a college student, but the younger Annalise had nothing on the woman standing beside me. It wasn't just physical. Her body had changed in the last eleven years, and if you asked her she'd probably say something about the lines around her eyes, but all I saw was *more*.

She'd had a promise to her beauty at twenty, and that promise had been fulfilled. Her curves were fuller, her breasts bigger, that tight ass a little more of a handful leading to a waist that was still trim. It wasn't just her body, though. She'd been smart, and funny, easily affectionate and hot as hell in bed.

This new Annalise was still the girl I remembered, but she'd grown into herself. She was comfortable with her intelligence, and her sense of humor was as sharp as ever. She'd proved she was still hot as hell in bed, though I'd barely gotten my hands on her. Her easy affection was nowhere in sight.

She took a step to her right, discreetly moving out of reach, my fingers sliding across her skin and the smooth fabric of her dress, leaving me grasping at air.

I gritted my teeth and gave her the space she wanted. She'd been doing this all day—trying to put distance between us. Avoiding touching me.

She couldn't have made it clearer that she didn't want to mix work and pleasure. Normally, I'd be right there with her. We didn't have a strict company policy at Sinclair, but it was generally understood you didn't fuck the client.

I always kept it professional. Always. Most of the time that was easy. Our clients tended toward the corporate, and old, rich, white guys weren't my thing. Of our private clients, the young ones tended to be celebrities, with their heads so far up their own asses I didn't want to fuck them no matter how good they looked.

Everything that was normal had gone out the window the second I'd seen Annalise again. She wasn't a client. She was Lise. Her case had been mine for years, and my periodic checks on her should have been enough to tell me that I'd gotten our breakup all wrong.

I should have known that Dear John letter was bullshit. Nothing I'd seen of her over the years gave any indication that she was the kind of cold-hearted bitch to tell a guy she loved him and then turn around and dump him because he was boring and she'd been cheating.

The lies in her letter seemed so obvious now. But fuck, it had burned when I'd read it. I'd been in the hospital, feeling like shit, and my girl had walked out on me. I'd been low enough to believe everything she'd written, and when she never came home, never called or wrote or tried to see me again, I'd assumed it was all true.

Why wouldn't I?

If I'd had doubts, they'd been put to rest by Aiden, after I'd read the letter. He'd sat beside my hospital bed, his dark eyes grave, and told me that she was taking some time off school to travel with her new boyfriend, an old flame, and friend of the family.

He'd apologized for her behavior and the cowardly way she'd left, gently suggesting that I was better off without her and reminding me that I was too old for her anyway. Too old, not enough money, no background. Not the right man for Annalise Winters.

Aiden's list of reasons was bullshit and impossible to argue with. He'd patted my shoulder and walked out, taking my last wisp of hope with him. Love turned to hate, and I'd forced any thought of Annalise Winters from my mind.

A few years later when her case hit my desk, I took it. Why not? I was over her. Ancient history. Except that I'd never gotten over her. And the love I'd thought became hate had never really died.

I should have known Aiden was lying.

Standing beside her, the distance she wanted between us a chasm she hoped I wouldn't bridge, I was painfully aware that I'd been a fucking idiot.

What if I'd tracked her down all those years ago? What if I'd forced the kind of confrontation we'd had over her suitcase? Would we have been together all this time? Would we have a family? Kids? How much time had we lost because we were both too scared to be honest with each other?

I'd never know. Life is too short for *what if's*. I did know that I wasn't wasting any more fucking time. I took a step to my right and wound my arm around Annalise's waist, pulling her into my side.

She stiffened, almost imperceptibly, but didn't fight when I took hold of her left hand and raised it to my mouth, kissing her finger just below the engagement ring.

The couple she was talking to gave us an indulgent smile and said something about young lovers. A gorgeous blush spread across Annalise's cheeks, and, as the couple moved on, she turned to face me.

"Was that necessary?" she demanded under her breath, the smile on her face hiding the challenge in her words.

Fighting in front of the wedding guests wasn't good for our charade.

I lowered my head and kissed her jaw, just below her ear, and whispered, "Absolutely necessary. Have you seen how beautiful you are? If you wanted me to keep my hands off you, you shouldn't have worn this dress."

I'd known the comment would make her bristle, and it did. Her eyes flashed, and her spine went straight, but, before she could launch into a lecture about how what she wore didn't give me the right to grope her, I cut in and said, "Then again, I'm pretty sure you could wear a potato sack, and I'd still want to get my hands under it. It's not the clothes. It's you."

Her eyelids fluttered shut, and she let out a breath. "Riley, don't do this. Don't make it so hard. I can pretend, but not when you make it so hard."

"What if I don't want to pretend, Lise?" I asked.

Her breath caught in her throat and she leaned back to look up at me, hope and fear and need swirling in the deep blue of her eyes.

Her lips parted to speak, and every cell in my body strained toward her, desperate to hear what she would say.

A hearty male voice interrupted. "May I steal your date for a dance?"

I hadn't noticed the music starting up. The wedding was small, but Sophie had wanted dancing. They'd hired a string quartet, and Mrs. W had ordered the carpets rolled up in the front hall during the ceremony, so when we'd reentered the house for the reception, the front hall had been transformed into a ballroom, albeit a small one.

Annalise smiled up at William Davis and said, "Of course, Uncle William. I'd love to dance with you."

He'd asked if he could steal my date, but William Davis

never looked at me. I already knew he disapproved of the engagement. Aiden had warned me that William Davis had very specific ideas about who the Winters children should marry. A guy like me did not make the list. Not enough money. No pedigree.

Davis's girlfriend, Melanie, took Annalise's place beside me, standing a little too close. In a confidential tone, she said, "Don't mind William. Since they lost their parents, he sees himself as something of a stand-in to all the Winters children. He's very overprotective. I'm sure he'll warm up to you once you two are married."

"As long as Annalise is happy, I don't worry about much," I said, evenly. She walked with me as I moved to the side of the dance floor where I could keep an eye on Annalise.

It was unlikely anything would happen inside Winters House, but security was harder to maintain when there were people coming and going. I had no plans to let Annalise out of sight.

Melanie watched Annalise and William foxtrot, taking in William's paternal smile and Annalise's laugh as he said something amusing. Quietly, she said, "She looks so much like her mother, sometimes it's startling."

"Annalise?" I asked. I'd seen photographs of Lise's parents, but to my eye, both Annalise and Vance looked like a combination of Anna and James Winters.

I knew Melanie was a champion gossip and she didn't disappoint when she said, "Oh yes. Anna's hair was lighter, almost a platinum. I was always so jealous of her. She never touched a dye bottle. Just naturally gorgeous. Annalise has her eyes, same figure, and there's something about the way she holds herself that turns her into a carbon copy of Anna."

"They don't look a lot alike in pictures," I said, hoping that would keep her talking.

Melanie's head tilted to the side as she studied Annalise. "I could see that. Annalise is a little taller, I suppose. The difference in hair color could fool the eye— Anna's platinum was so striking—but trust me, coming from someone who knew Anna well, Annalise looks exactly like her mother."

She shook her head, and I was shocked to see the gleam of tears in her eyes. She gave a sniff and lifted a finger to blot the moisture before it could smear her makeup.

Waving a hand in front of her face she said, "I'm sorry. It's been so many years since we lost them, but seeing Annalise like this, looking so much like her mother and only a few years younger than Anna was when she died, it's just..." She let out a gusty sigh. "It's nice to see the family happy, that's all. William has had plenty to say about the children's choices, Lord knows."

"But you disagree?" I probed.

She shot me a conspiratorial glance and said, "I admit, I do. He's so fussy about who people's people are. It's not that it doesn't matter, because it does, but happiness matters more."

Then, maybe realizing that her comment about people's people mattering only proved William's point about me, she reached out to squeeze my hand and said again, "Happiness matters more."

I couldn't argue with that. Annalise's breakup letter, aside from implying that she was seeing someone else behind my back—which I now realized was an utter load of crap because Lise would never cheat—had also gone on about the differences in our social status. Another thing Lise had never cared about until it had seemed she decided she did.

The more I got to know them, the more I realized that the Winters family truly didn't care about social status. Maybe it was easy not to care when you had more money than God and enough power to get whatever you wanted.

I might not be a suitable choice for the oldest daughter of the Winters family, but if she dragged me with her to the country club that wouldn't stop anyone from kissing both of our asses.

I wasn't worried about that. People like Melanie and William Davis could have their ideas about what was appropriate and proper in their social strata, but it didn't have anything to do with Annalise and me. I wouldn't let it.

We stood there, watching William and Annalise dance, Melanie making a funny humming sound in the back of her throat as William said something with a scowl on his face and Annalise shook her head. Melanie sighed and said, "I don't know why he bothers. They just ignore him and do what they want anyway."

I made a vague sound of agreement. I'd already heard how William Davis had tried to interfere in Jacob and Abigail's relationship, and then again with Lucas and Charlie. All of them were doing just fine, so I wasn't worried about Davis confusing Annalise. Lise knew her own mind. We had a lot of problems, but William Davis wasn't one of them.

I couldn't help but think about what Melanie had said. Just looking at photographs, I hadn't picked up on the strong resemblance between Annalise and her mother. Her mother who had been murdered. No one in the Sinclair or Winters family had mentioned the resemblance, but it was possible they didn't see it the same way an outsider like Melanie did.

The sad fact was, Anna Winters had been dead for over two decades and the oldest of them, Aiden, had only been eleven when she died.

I had to consider that they hadn't mentioned the resemblance because none of them had noticed it. But Melanie had, and maybe the stalker had as well.

At that thought, an icy chill ran through me. I had the sudden urge to stalk onto the small dance floor, grab Annalise's hand, and drag her away from the party. To stash her somewhere safe until we found whoever was sending her flowers.

We already knew her stalker was obsessed. Whoever had killed Anna and James Winters had never been caught. Until Melanie's comments about Lise's mother, I'd thought it a weak connection, at best. Now I wasn't so sure.

While Lise was worried about protecting her loved ones, I was growing more certain she was the one in danger.

CHAPTER FOURTEEN

RILEY

I waited patiently for Annalise to finish her dance with William Davis. Okay, not patiently, but I did wait. Melanie sent me another one of those sidelong looks and murmured, "Young love. I remember how that goes."

I smiled at her, playing the part, but what I was feeling was anything but the horny impatience of young love. It was demanding and a little desperate. William returned Annalise to my side, handing her back to me without meeting my eyes, somehow managing to be both sexist and condescending in one gesture.

Instead of taking her hand, I slid my arm around her shoulders, nodded at Melanie, and turned Annalise to the doorway of the living room, pulling her along with me.

"Where are we going?" she demanded, trying to tug free as discreetly as possible. I was having none of it. I was tired of her distance, tired of her holding herself aloof from me. Her stalker was playing enough games. We didn't need to waste time playing them with each other.

"You can't just drag me from the wedding reception," she hissed as I led her down the hall. There was no way to get back to her suite without crossing through the makeshift ballroom in the front hall. I led her to the opposite corner of the house where I hoped we could get a little privacy in the wine room.

As soon as we were out of sight of most of the guests, Annalise twisted out from under my arm and took a step away. My hand shot out, and I caught her wrist in my fingers. "Stop running from me," I said, keeping my voice low.

"Stop manhandling me."

"I'm not manhandling you. You're my fiancée for fuck's sake," I said, my voice rising.

Annalise stopped on her heel and whirled to face me. In an angry whisper, she said, "I am not your fiancée. Stop toying with me. I know I deserve it after the way I left you, and I know you're over me, and this is no big deal for you. But it is for me. I don't need you making this harder, okay?"

She choked a little on her words and my stomach got tight. Fuck. Why could I never say the right thing to her? Why couldn't I just be fucking honest?

My feelings for Annalise had always been real. Always. But I'd never given her the truth. Not once. She deserved more than that from me. I opened my mouth to speak, to say something, anything. Maybe everything.

I looked around and realized we were standing in the middle of the hallway. The things I had to say were only for Annalise. Wrapping my arm tightly around her shoulders, ignoring her squirms to get away, I reached for the door to the wine room and swung it open.

Annalise let out a shocked gasp, followed by a laugh as she dropped her forehead to my shoulder and I looked up to see Jacob Winters balls deep in his fiancée Abigail. I couldn't see much of Abigail other than her face, which turned bright red as she let out a screech.

Ignoring Jacob's growl, I hastily pulled the door shut saying through the thick wood, "You might want to lock that next time."

Annalise was laughing, her cheeks pink as I pulled her through the library to the hidden staircase in the corner. She'd stopped resisting me, distracted by the sight of her cousin and Abigail.

"I know they both mostly had their clothes on but I really wish I hadn't seen that," she said through a giggle. "Why does no one ever lock that door? There's a deadbolt on the other side. Plus, Jacob has his own room."

"Maybe they couldn't wait," I said in sympathy.

Annalise finally realized I was still dragging her through the house and dug in her heels. "Where are we going?" she demanded.

I pressed the crevice in the mantel to release the secret door, flipped the light switch, and pulled Annalise inside, closing the door behind us. We were encased in shadows, broken only by the orange flickers of light from the wall sconces that lined the staircase as it curled down in a tight spiral.

"I wanted some privacy," I said.

"We're sharing a room. We have enough privacy. I don't think this is a good idea."

"We need to get something straight," I said.

"Fine, what?" she snapped, crossing her arms over her chest.

I wasn't going to mention that when she did that it plumped up her perfect breasts, taking her demure neckline and making it ridiculously tempting.

I did my best to ignore her breasts and met her eyes, hot

and blue even in the dim light. "Did you mean everything you wrote in that letter, or did you leave because you thought you were keeping me safe?"

"Why does it matter now? It was eleven years ago," she evaded, the anger fading from her eyes as she dropped my gaze and looked away.

"It matters."

"No, I didn't mean any of it. I never would've cheated on you, and I don't care about your background or your family or how much money you have. If I'd told you I was leaving would you have let me go?"

"No fucking way," I said. "Did you send Aiden to talk to me?"

Annalise gave a helpless shrug, her eyes sad. "I had to. I had to make you believe."

"Believe a lie," I said, old anger thick in my voice. "Believe that the woman I loved threw me away."

"I didn't know what else to do," she said, her eyes fixed on the wall behind my head, swimming with tears.

"You could have trusted me. We could've figured it out together. Instead, we lost a decade."

Annalise pressed her lips together and shook her head. "I'm sorry I lied to you. It was the only thing I could think of. I was panicked. But he tried to kill you two times, Riley. I watched you almost die from an overdose while you were in the hospital, after sitting by your bedside waiting for you to wake up from a car accident that almost killed you. I didn't want there to be a third time."

"Annalise," I said, stopping her. There was no point in digging up the past, and I couldn't explain why I hadn't needed protection. Not yet. Maybe not ever. Everything that came before was history, and I was done with history. I was a lot more interested in our future.

Biting the bullet, I said, "I never got over you. I don't think I ever will. I don't want to pretend with you when it feels real."

Annalise stared at me, dumbfounded, her pink lips parted in surprise. I knew I should wait for her to say something, but I reached up and slid my fingers along her jaw, stroking her soft skin before burying them in her hair and running my thumb along her cheek.

"Tell me this doesn't feel real," I said, drawing her closer. "Tell me you want me to stop, and I will. We'll go back to pretending, and I won't touch you again."

She swayed into me, silent, her eyes scanning my face, studying me. Her voice a husky whisper, she said, "It *feels* real, but that doesn't mean it *is* real."

"It is if we want it to be," I said. Curling my fingers around the back of her head I drew her close slowly, a millimeter at a time, giving her plenty of chances to draw back. To stop me. To change her mind.

Her breath feathered across my lips, smelling of caramel. I knew exactly how she would taste—hot and sweet. I wanted to kiss her gently, to seduce her and tease her, but this was the first time we'd kissed when it wasn't a game or a dare. I couldn't hold back.

Her mouth opened for me like a flower in bloom, her tongue meeting mine in lush strokes, her lips so soft. I wrapped my other arm around her waist, bringing her body flush against mine and leaned in, pinning her shoulders to the stone wall in the stairwell.

I'd wanted privacy, but the top of the staircase in the dark wasn't going to cut it. The stone was hard and cold against her bare back, and it was too dark.

I wanted to lay her across her bed in the early evening light to see every inch of her beautiful body. I wanted to watch her come for me over and over. I didn't want a furtive coupling in our clothes. I wanted all of her. I wanted everything I'd craved for eleven years.

In a minute. Mindful of the stairs, I turned us, bracing my back against the stone and pulling her into me, kissing her harder, so hungry for her I needed to own every inch of her mouth. Her hand skimmed my body, under my suit jacket, pressing into my thin dress shirt, the heat of her touch setting me on fire.

I broke the kiss. "Not here," I managed to get out. "Come with me to your room. Will you?"

In answer, she took my hand, said, "This way," and led me down the stairs. I followed, watching the golden gleam of her hair in the flickering lights as we descended the spiral staircase to the lower level of Winters House.

I'd always loved that the staircase felt like it belonged in a castle, but I'd never felt so much like I was in a fairytale, following my princess anywhere she wanted to take me.

Especially if it was to bed.

The door at the bottom of the steps opened into the wide hall that spanned the length of the lower level. Now that we were off the precarious staircase, Annalise moved faster, dragging me down the hall behind her.

Instantly, I understood her plan as we passed beneath the living room, then the entry hall—faint strains of the string quartet filtering through the floor—then beneath the dining room and finally to the wider, brighter staircase on the opposite side of the house.

We jogged up the stairs, a little breathless, laughing as we spilled out into the kitchen, weaving our way through the caterers who started in surprise at seeing two wedding guests appear in their midst. The kitchen opened into the family room, and from there it was just a short stretch down the hall to Annalise's suite.

We made it without running into another guest. When we finally crossed the threshold of her sitting room, I stopped and closed the door behind us, flipping the lock. I had no intention of being interrupted. Not after spending too many nights laying in that big brass bed, burning for Annalise and unable to touch her.

She spun to a stop in the center of her sitting room, her hair flying out around her to match the whirl of her skirts. Reaching up beneath her hair, she began to untie the knot at the back of her neck holding up her dress. The shimmering pink fabric began to sag, sliding down her soft, tanned skin, and my mouth went dry.

CHAPTER FIFTEEN
RILEY

T held my breath as I watched Annalise work on the knot holding up her dress, my heart pounding harder as the fabric sagged and slipped, revealing her skin inch by torturous inch.

Finally—thank fuck—finally, she let go. The shimmering pink silk fell to her waist baring her upper body.

She was as beautiful as I remembered. More beautiful because this time the sight of her was precious. After eleven years apart, nothing meant as much as her trust. Pink bloomed in her cheeks as she worked the zipper at her lower back.

With a shimmy to her hips, she pushed the dress all the way off. Yards of pink silk pooled around her feet, and Annalise stood before me in nothing more than a pair of blush lace panties and miles of shining blonde hair.

She looked down at herself and hooked her thumbs in the sides of her panties, then shot me a look through the curtain of her hair that was both teasing and shy. She didn't have anything to be shy about as far as I was concerned.

Everything about her was perfect. Long legs, gently

toned with muscle, gorgeously rounded hips leading up to the most perfect pair of breasts I'd ever seen. Round and full, the perfect weight for my hands, tipped with rosy nipples drawn tight.

My mouth watered, and I was done with waiting.

Striding forward I leaned down, set my shoulder against her stomach and stood, tossing her over my back in a fireman's carry. She let out a sound that was both a laugh and a screech of surprise, then reached down to close her fingers over my ass and squeeze.

I'd always loved that about Annalise. She wasn't just hot in bed; she was fun. We'd laughed together as much as anything else.

I returned the favor, squeezing one globe of her perfect ass just before I slid my fingers between her legs and stroked her pussy. Her laughter cut off with a gasp and I worked my finger under the lace shielding her heat.

She was wet. I needed more.

Leaning down, I flipped her to her back and dropped her on the bed, stripping her panties off and stepping between her legs before she could get her bearings. She looked up at me, her eyes hot, laughter shaking her body.

Just the sight of her breasts jiggling along with her giggles made me hard as a fucking rock. I loved the way her breasts moved—when she was laughing, when I was fucking her, it didn't matter. However it happened, it worked for me.

"Don't move," I warned, stripping off my jacket and tossing it aside before going to work on my cufflinks.

"I could help you with that," she offered, squirming a little under my direct gaze. Her nipples were hard, and between her legs, I caught the gleam of moisture.

I shook my head. "You stay right there. If you had any

idea how many times I've jacked off in the last decade thinking about you, naked and spread out for me..."

I shook my head again. Probably better if she didn't know.

"What was I doing? Just laying there, or something else? Was I doing this?" Annalise reached up and cupped her breasts, rolling her nipples. Her blue eyes went dark and her lids drooped.

My cock jerked in my pants, and I tugged harder at the buttons of my shirt, two of them popping off and bouncing on the carpet.

"Sometimes," I managed to say, tearing at my belt in frustration.

"What about this? Did I ever do this?" Annalise cocked up her left knee and let it fall open, baring her pussy. She slid one long finger between the pink of her lower lips, and it came away shining with moisture.

That was it. I shoved my suit pants down, toeing off my shoes, and lunged forward, grabbing her hand and sucking that shiny finger into my mouth. Fuck, she tasted like heaven, salty and sweet. I ran my tongue over her fingertip before I pulled her legs over my shoulders and dragged her to the edge of the bed.

I needed more of that taste. I needed my mouth on her.

Her fingers sank into my hair, and I raised my head. "No, I'm busy," I said. Taking her wrists, I led her hands to her breasts, forming her palms around them, placing her fingers at her nipples. She took my cue and went back to rolling them, tugging, her teeth sinking into her lower lip at the sensation. "You do that," I ordered. "I'm going to do this."

I dropped back between her legs, bracing my palms on her inner thighs, pushing them wide. She smelled as good as she tasted, her pussy already swollen with arousal. I ran my fingertips over her, stroking the springy golden hair. She rocked her hips up at me, urging me to touch her.

"Impatient," I whispered against her skin, my breath teasing her clit. I flicked out my tongue to taste her, and she tensed, her gasp dissolving into a moan as I closed my mouth over her and sucked hard. She cried out, and I glanced up to see her back arched, her hands gripping her breasts, fingers pinching her nipples.

My cock throbbed, jealous of my mouth. I drove my tongue inside her, the heat of her pussy scalding. I went back to her clit as my fingers took its place in her pussy, first one, then another, filling her, getting her ready.

She thrust hard on my fingers, taking them deep, and when I lifted my mouth, she rode my hand with abandon. I needed to watch her come. I drove my fingers in to the hilt and ground my palm against her swollen clit, rising over her to watch her face.

I needed to absorb every nuance as her eyes widened, her pupils dilated, and her lips fell open. She dragged in ragged breaths, her ribs rising and falling as she trembled below me.

"I want to watch you come," I whispered, my lips feathering against her cheek. "Are you going to come for me?"

The orgasm broke free with a strangled cry as her eyes went wide and blind. Her hands fell to her sides, and she stared at me, lids heavy, as I slowly drew my fingers from the clasping heat of her pussy.

"I feel like I've been waiting for that forever," I said.

"Me, too." Her words came out on a breath, barely audible.

I lifted my fingers to my mouth and licked them clean, watching as her breath hitched and her eyes widened.

"I'm going to do that again later," I promised, leaning

over her, bracing my elbow on the bed as her legs came up around my hips, cradling me, opening for me. She fit me perfectly. She always had.

I meant to take her slowly. That was the plan. But once I was inside her, once I felt her tight pussy close around me, I couldn't hold back. I pulled out, my head spinning at the slide of that tight hot flesh and sank back in, dizzy with the sheer fucking pleasure of being inside Annalise again. I drove into her again and again.

Her fingers sank into my shoulders. Her legs twined around my waist, her heels digging into my ass, urging me to fuck her harder. Her back arched as she lifted her breasts to my mouth and I closed my lips around one nipple, sucking hard. She ran her hands down my back and up again, bucking beneath me, pulling her legs back to give me more. Without warning, her fingers sank into my skin, and she cried out my name, "Riley, fuck, Riley."

Her pussy tightened around my cock like a fist, and I fucked her harder, driving her higher, my own orgasm taking me by surprise, a white-hot rush blanking out my mind as I stiffened between her legs and spilled myself inside her.

I was barely aware enough to roll us over. Annalise went limp on top of me, her legs splayed beside mine, her hand coming up to rest against mine, palm to palm. Our fingers twined, our heart beats slowly calming, breath evening out. She turned her head so her cheek rested against my chest, the flutter of her eyelashes a delicate caress.

My softening cock slipped from her body, cool air chilling my wet skin. I realized with a shock that we'd forgotten a condom. I'd never had sex without a condom. Not since Annalise. And not before. She was the only woman I'd ever fucked bare. Maybe that was why I never stopped to think. I had a box of condoms in my suitcase. Wishful thinking. The second I'd seen her naked, I'd forgotten all about protection.

I felt safe assuming we were both clear of disease. I knew I was, and Annalise hadn't slept with anyone in a while. I shut down that train of thought, my stomach tightening at the knowledge that there'd been men since the last time we had been together. I didn't have a right to be upset about that. My own sex life had been a lot more active than hers in the years we'd been apart.

But what about pregnancy? I turned the thought over in my mind, surprised that I didn't feel the slightest twinge of panic at the thought. If she were pregnant, we'd deal. She'd always talked about having kids.

All those years ago that had been the plan. Finish school, get married, work for a while, and then settle down and start a family. I doubted she'd changed her mind about family. I'd seen how she was with Vance and Maggie's kid. And if she were pregnant, she couldn't run. She'd never do that to a child.

I was just getting used to the idea when she shifted on top of me, propping herself up on her hands and looking down at me. I got distracted by the sway of her breasts, tightening my arm around her waist too late to keep her where she was.

Annalise slid from the bed and disappeared into the bathroom. Water ran in the sink for a minute before she reappeared, a warm wet washcloth in hand. She climbed onto the bed beside me and stretched out, hooking her leg over mine and stroking the washcloth over my cock cleaning me gently, slowly.

She didn't meet my eyes when she said, "We didn't use anything."

I swallowed, bracing and said carefully, "I know. I'm sorry. I've been tested recently. You don't have anything to worry about."

She dragged the warm washcloth down the inside of my thigh and back up again, teasing me, before she tossed it on the floor and stroked her fingers up the length of my hardening cock.

"Me too," she said. "And I have an IUD."

I tried not to think too hard about the stab of disappointment as she shut down the possibility of pregnancy. I should be glad. If we were going to have a baby, we should plan for it. Of course, we should.

I didn't have time to dwell on my weird reaction. Lise moved down the bed just far enough to close her mouth over the head of my cock.

It should have taken me a lot longer to get hard again. It usually did. I'm a regular guy, not a superhero, but it had been a while and Annalise had been driving me crazy for days.

She rubbed her tongue against that spot on the underside of the head of my cock, remembering exactly the pressure that made me lose my mind. I tried to resist the urge to thrust into her mouth and instead reached down and buried my fingers in her long hair, twisting it around my fist, feeling every flex of her jaw and pull of her head as she took my length in her mouth.

I'd be lying if I said I'd forgotten that Annalise Winters gave amazing head. Fucking amazing. For a girl who hadn't had much experience when we'd met, she'd caught on fast. I pressed my skull back into the pillow, gritting my teeth against the need to move, to fuck her wet, hot mouth. My fingers tightened in her hair, not guiding her head so much as hanging on for the ride.

She sucked me until I thought my head was going to explode. Both of them. When she pulled her mouth from my cock, she said, in a raspy, husky tone, "You're okay if we don't use a condom?"

"If you are," I ground out.

"K." That was all I heard before she straddled my hips and nudged the head of my cock against the gate of her pussy. I froze, letting her sink slowly, taking my length and rocking against me, grinding her clit into my abs, bracing herself on her palms and dangling those perfect breasts right in front of my face.

She rode me slowly, letting it build, watching as I sucked at her nipples, going from one to the other until they were shiny and swollen, more red than pink. I dropped a hand to close over the curve of her ass, urging her to fuck me harder. Her hips swiveled in a figure eight, her pussy stroking my cock from a completely different angle, setting off fireworks behind my eyes.

I slid my hand between her legs, finding her clit and squeezing with a pulse of pressure that made her gasp. I wanted to watch her come on my cock. Wanted to know I was the one who gave her that, needing to know that she was mine.

I closed my teeth around one nipple and squeezed her clit again, sucking at her breast as I worked her clit, loving every gasp, the way her rhythm stuttered from the flash of pleasure, the way it took her over, dragging low moans from her chest as her orgasm swept her under.

Her pussy clenched hard on my cock and I let go, following her, giving her everything I had as pleasure took us both.

I managed to carry her to the shower, keeping her hair out of the spray as we let the hot water wash away the sweat and sex. After a lazy swipe with a towel that left both of us still mostly wet, we climbed under the covers and slid easily into sleep, Annalise tucked in my arms, her head on my shoulder, her breath fluttering across my skin. Her hand lay across my chest, the engagement ring I'd given her sparkling on her finger.

It would put a dent in my savings account, but as soon as I could get to my phone, I was wiring the money for the ring to the Sinclair account. I'd picked that ring for Annalise, and it wasn't going back to the store.

We could have a long engagement. I could work with that if it was what she needed, but none of this was pretend. It never had been. I'd been kidding myself before. There wasn't another woman for me. I'd always belonged to Lise.

Even when I hadn't wanted to.

We lay there, Annalise dozing and me lost in thought, in plans for the future, when my stomach rumbled. The sun had long since set and dinner had been hours before. Annalise's hand drifted lower, resting over my abdomen and she murmured, her eyes still closed, "Hungry."

I kissed the top of her head and slid out from beneath her, tucking the comforter around her body. "Stay there. I'll be back with food."

She mumbled something into the pillow, wrapping her arm around it and tugging it close with a little sigh. I checked through the bedroom curtains to see the courtyard empty of cars. There might still be staff in the kitchen, but the guests were gone. I threw on clothes, stopping for a minute to grab my phone and send the money for Annalise's ring from my savings account to Sinclair Security.

I didn't want to wait. I wanted that ring to be mine. To

be hers. Not on loan from the store. Not a tool for a job. I hadn't been thinking about the job when I picked it. I'd been thinking about her.

The confirmation flashed on the screen, and a sense of completion settled in my chest. Years before I'd dreamed of putting my ring on Annalise's finger. Now I'd done it. Not as a ploy or a game. For real. Even if she didn't know it yet.

The door to Jacob and Abigail's suite was firmly closed when I passed. I hoped the family room would be empty, but I was out of luck. The bride and groom were missing, probably locked in Gage's rooms upstairs if they had any sense, but Charlie, Lucas, Aiden, Vance, and Maggie were all in the family room, sprawled on the oversize couches and curled in the armchairs, watching a movie.

"And where have you been?" Charlie asked, her eyes sparkling with laughter.

"Taking a nap," I said with a straight face. Looking at Vance and Maggie, I asked, "Are you two staying here?"

Vance grinned and shook his head. "No. Sophie hasn't officially moved out of my room yet. She's been holding off until she and Gage made it legal."

Maggie poked his arm and explained, "We would've gone home anyway. Rosie's with Ella, our nanny, so we're taking advantage of a grown-ups night out." She yawned, and Vance tightened his arm around her, pressing a kiss to her cheek.

"Some date you are. Hours from midnight and you're ready to turn into a pumpkin," he said.

"It's not my fault. Rosie woke me up at five o'clock this morning," she protested, burrowing her head into his chest and letting out a sigh.

"I know, I was there."

"You were there, but you pretended to be asleep."

Turning her head to look at Charlie she said, "when you two have kids, watch out. Vance pretends he's in a coma every time Rosie needs something in the middle of the night."

"Why do you let him get away with it?" Charlie asked. Maggie's cheeks turned pink, and Charlie burst into giggles. "Oh, yeah. I have that problem too."

Aiden narrowed his eyes at his baby sister and her husband. I grinned when Lucas shifted uncomfortably under Aiden's hard gaze. Lucas and Charlie were married, had been for almost six months, but I got the impression Aiden was still getting used to his baby sister being someone's wife. Especially a guy like Lucas Jackson.

I worked with Lucas at Sinclair Security. Different departments, but we'd gotten to know each other. He was smart as hell, honest, and loyal. He also loved his wife like crazy. Still, taking in the look in Aiden's eyes and seeing the way he could make a guy like Lucas squirm, I thought about what it would be like to have these people as in-laws.

I guessed I'd find out. After I talked Annalise into marrying me. Getting her into bed didn't mean this was a sure thing, but I was one step closer. I shoved a hand in my back pocket and made my way down the hall, ignoring Charlie as she called out, "Where do you think you're going?"

The kitchen was mostly empty except for Mrs. W and Abel, who were standing suspiciously far apart considering Mrs. W's swollen lips and flushed cheeks. Looked like Sophie was right, there was something going on between those two.

"Sorry to interrupt," I said, easily. "I was just going to get something to eat. Lise's taking a nap, but she said she was hungry."

"Good idea. Have a snack now so you won't wake up in the middle of the night starving. I'll make you up a tray."

"You don't have to do that," I said, moving toward the giant stainless steel subzero refrigerator.

Mrs. W intercepted me, shooing me away and said, "Go find whatever you want to drink in the butler's pantry while I make your tray."

The side of Abel's mouth quirked up, and he said, "You might as well let her have her way."

She sent him a look that turned his half smile into a full-on grin, and he sauntered out of the kitchen saying over his shoulder, "I'm just going to head up to my apartment."

I didn't know Mrs. W well enough to tease her, and I wasn't willing to risk pissing her off after witnessing the shortbread incident, so I disappeared into the butler's pantry and tried to decide between beer or wine, while Mrs. W put together our food.

CHAPTER SIXTEEN

ANNALISE

It was official. I wouldn't kick Riley out of bed for eating crackers. Especially when he fed them to me between sips of wine.

He'd tucked me in and gone in search of food, just like he had when we'd exhausted ourselves on my futon all those years ago, making love until we were half-starved and barely able to stay awake.

Curling into my pillow, I drifted in a light sleep, pleasantly sore between my legs and caught in a dream of me and Riley.

Together.

Happy.

It had to be a dream. After so many years I'd never dared hope it could be real.

Then he was back, coming through the door of my bedroom carrying a tray with food and a bottle of wine. I let him feed me, raising crackers layered with cheese to my lips, giving me sips of red wine.

Our stomachs full, he set the tray on the desk in the sitting room and came back, sliding beneath the sheets and pulling me into his arms. He made love to me with a patience I didn't remember.

He was slow. So slow and so careful. He touched me everywhere, as if committing to memory every inch of my skin.

Treasuring me.

Savoring me.

I wanted to return the favor, to stroke and touch and kiss, but he held me back whispering only, "Let me. Please, Lise. Let me."

I did as he asked, trembling and shaking beneath him as he set every nerve in my body on fire. When he finally filled me, made me complete, tears slid down my cheeks even as orgasm swamped my senses.

We slept tangled in each other's arms, my head on his chest, the thud of his heart beneath my ear reassuring me that he was real.

He was real, and he was mine.

I woke slowly, long after sunrise, to the faint sounds of voices. Mrs. W was serving breakfast. I thought about waking Riley. Getting dressed. Going down the hall to the dining room.

We could do that. Or, we could do something else. He'd had his way with me the night before. Now, it was my turn. I slid down his body, leaving butterfly kisses in my wake until I reached my goal. My lips slid over the head of his cock, and I sucked gently, tasting him, loving the way he filled my mouth as he hardened for me.

I'd only ever done this with Riley. There'd been other men in my life. Eleven years was a long time, and there'd been one before him, too. But no one like Riley. No one who had my heart.

His fingers threaded through my hair, and I knew he

was awake. I'd always loved the way he held my hair when I sucked his cock. Never using it to control me, to push me. No, he'd sink his fingers into my long hair, wrap it around his fist, and just hold on. Though, sometimes, he used it to pull me off.

Without a word, he urged my mouth up, releasing my hair and hooking his hands under my arms to haul me up the bed, flipping me over and settling between my spread legs.

His hand dropped between them, fingertips seeking, finding me wet. Ready. His lips took mine as he sank inside. We rocked together, not rushing, feeling everything.

I didn't last long. Not with Riley's mouth moving on mine, possessive and claiming. His body inside me, driving me higher with each thrust of his cock. The pleasure broke over me like a wave, sweet and sharp, stealing my breath. Riley breathed my name as he followed.

As he had the night before, as soon as we had our breath back he rolled, pulling me on top of him, wrapping his arms around me. I needed to go to the bathroom to clean up, but I didn't want to move. I lay there, my head on his chest, listening to his heart, tracing lines on his skin with my fingertip.

I hadn't had time to study all the changes in his body. He'd been in good shape before. No, not in good shape. Ripped. His body had always been a work of art, but now there was something different.

He was harder. And damaged. Scars decorated the skin stretched tightly over his muscles. I traced my finger over the curve of raised white tissue on his bicep and said, "What happened here?"

"Shrapnel. Piece of metal from a car accident." His voice was lazy, half-asleep.

"You were in a car accident?" I asked, stroking my fingers up to his shoulder to outline another scar, this one a lumpy circle.

"Not me," he said. "Client. Confidential."

I let out a low hum of understanding. Most of his work was confidential. I'd known the Sinclairs long enough to know the drill. They didn't keep clients by talking. I traced the circular scar on his shoulder again and asked, "This one?"

Still in that sleepy voice, he answered, "Bullet. Small caliber. No big deal."

I stifled a laugh. Getting shot was a very big deal from my point of view, but I could see how someone doing Riley's job might have to get used to it. I'd think more about that later. I wasn't ready to deal with reality. Not yet.

I liked cuddling with him, drowsy and warm and safe. I trailed my fingers back down his arm, stroking them over his. He'd always had such strong hands. Unbidden, my body shivered at the thought of what he did with those strong hands. The way he'd hauled me up the bed and settled on top of me. The way they cupped my breasts.

I played with his fingers, that callus on the web of his thumb scratching me. Such an odd place to have a callus. "What's this one?"

I ran my fingertips over the thickened skin as he said, "From shooting. Training after Rangers. You shoot so much you get a callus."

His answer settled in my brain just a little bit off. I believed him, but his words felt wrong.

He felt wrong.

I don't know what it was that tipped me off. Was there a new tension in his muscles? Did he start to speak and then think better of it?

Absently, I rubbed at the callus on the base of his thumb, my sleepy mind working.

We lay there in silence for a full minute before I realized what it was.

The scar on his shoulder, the one on his bicep—those were new.

The callus on his thumb was not.

A chill spread through my chest. Before I decided to move, I was rolling away, mumbling under my breath, "Bathroom. I'll be right back."

I heard the rustle of sheets and Riley's voice, oddly urgent. "Lise, wait."

"Be right back," I said again, shutting the bathroom door behind me. Quietly, carefully, I turned the lock.

Putting my brain on hold, afraid to think too much, I turned on the water in the shower, using the toilet while I waited for it to warm up.

Something inside me was frozen, and I had the sinking feeling that if I let myself stop and think, I would shatter.

I heard Riley's voice through the door, the knob rattling under his hand. "Lise, let me in."

My voice cracked as I said, "I'll be out in a minute."

I stepped into the steaming water of the shower, letting it rinse me clean, knowing Riley could pick the lock if he wanted to.

He didn't.

I washed my hair, combed the conditioner through it, rinsed, every movement stiff and jerky. I got out, mechanically putting my hair in a towel, smoothing on lotion. I didn't want to think, and I couldn't stop myself. Tears threatened as I pulled on jeans and a T-shirt. Braided my hair.

The truth took shape in my mind, against my will.

I didn't want the truth.

I wanted to be happy just a little bit longer.

But I was done with running, and I couldn't run from this.

College Riley, my Riley, had been a history major who'd taken a few years after high school to backpack through Europe. That Riley had no reason to train with a weapon. I'd never even seen him with a gun. But he'd had that callus in college.

Memory rushed in, vivid and excruciating. Sitting beside him in the hospital, holding his hand, rubbing my thumb over that callus and praying he'd wake up.

A callus he'd had because he'd trained to shoot for so many hours he bore a permanent mark. I stood there, my hand on the doorknob, wracking my brain for any reason, any excuse that would explain why a history major would've put in hundreds of hours training to use a weapon.

I was jamming the wrong puzzle piece into the picture in my head.

My gut knew the truth. I just needed Riley to confirm it.

I opened the bathroom door to find Riley, fully dressed, sitting on the edge of the unmade bed.

Waiting.

His hazel eyes were cautious. Careful.

"You okay?" he asked, scanning me from head to toe, eyes sharpened with concern.

I shook my head and swallowed hard. "I don't think I am," I said, slowly. Feeling sick, I said, "You had that callus in college. If it's from shooting, from training to shoot a gun, when did you get it? In high school? When you were backpacking through Europe? Were you in the Rangers in junior high?"

I heard the thin edge of hysteria creep into my voice. Riley's eyes widened in alarm. "Lise, it's not a big deal. I can explain—"

I couldn't look at him. "You weren't a college student, were you?" The question sounded absurd the second it left my mouth. He'd been in my classes for months before he talked to me.

"I was enrolled at Emory," he said, carefully.

Frustration slapped into me, and I cried out, "Don't lie to me. You're lying to me right now, and you were lying to me then. Who are you?"

"I'm Riley Flynn. You know who I am." He rose to his feet and took a step toward me.

I backed up, smacking into the door frame. I still couldn't look at him. My eyes skidded around the room, falling on the flip-flops I'd discarded the day before. I crossed the carpet and shoved them on my feet. "I don't know anything. I don't know who you are."

"Lise, calm down. I'll explain everything if you just—"

I whirled and dashed for the door, Riley right behind me. Hot tears spilled down my cheeks.

I didn't want to be alone with him. I wanted to go back to before when Riley was Riley and not a liar. When I was happy. For one goddamn fucking second I was happy, and now it was all gone.

My feet pounded down the hall, Riley just behind me. I skidded to a halt just outside the dining room. Most of the family still sat at the table, finishing their coffee.

The newlyweds were missing, but Jacob, Abigail, Charlie, and Lucas added to our usual crowd. Aiden caught sight of me and rose to his feet, his eyes moving between me and Riley.

Another piece of the puzzle fell into place, and nausea punched me in my stomach.

My eyes on Aiden, I whispered, "You knew. You did this, didn't you?"

"Annalise, come sit down," Aiden said in a commanding tone I was sure worked like a charm in the office. It didn't work on me. Not now.

My vision blurred with tears, I looked at Aiden and said, "How could you do this to me?" Riley's hand closed over my wrist as he tried to turn me to face him. I yanked it away shouting, "Don't touch me. Don't fucking touch me."

I stepped backward, almost tripping over my flip-flops, and wiped at my eyes with the backs of my hands. It didn't do any good. I couldn't stop the flow of tears. I couldn't pull air into my lungs. My stomach rolled, my mouth watering with nausea.

Riley stood only a yard away, his weight balanced on the balls of his feet, ready to move toward me. If he touched me, I was going to lose it.

I looked between him and Aiden, understanding flooding my mind, my brain putting together the pieces of the story my heart didn't want to hear.

I dropped my hands to my sides, my fingers curling into fists, driving my nails into my palms hard enough to draw blood. Hard enough to regain control and stop my tears.

I met Riley's eyes, steeling myself against the pain I saw there and said, "You were working for Sinclair Security. Aiden asked them to put someone on me, and it was you."

My voice cracked, and I stared at the ceiling, fighting for control.

I would not let this break me.

He was a liar and a fraud, and I would not let him break me.

"Lise, it's not what you think. I swear I never meant for you—"

"Stop lying to me," I shrieked. "Just tell me the truth. Please."

My knees wobbled. I could feel myself losing it. I couldn't do this. I couldn't beg for the truth.

Not from Riley.

Not from Aiden.

Not from these men who'd sworn they loved me and lied to me instead.

A voice cut in, ice cold with fury. Jacob.

"Is this true, Aiden? Did you hire Riley to shadow Annalise when she started college?" Aiden was silent, and Jacob lost patience. His fist slammed into the top of the dining room table, sending silverware and china clattering. "Answer me. Did you? Did you do that to her?"

"He wasn't supposed to date her," Aiden said, his dark eyes hard when they landed on Riley. "He wasn't supposed to talk to her at all. He was just supposed to keep an eye on her. Make sure no one was bothering her."

Across the table, Charlie said, "Fucking hell, Aiden."

I had to leave. I had to get out of there. I wiped at my eyes again and unclenched my fists, dully seeing the blood that smeared my fingernails.

I wrenched the diamond ring off my left hand, scraping my knuckle. Each burst of pain barely penetrated the misery surrounding my heart. Riley reached for me, and I batted his hand away, hurling the ring at his face.

Out of reflex, he caught it before it hit him.

His eyes wide, he looked from the ring in his hand, smeared with blood, to my palms and fingernails. It had been years since I'd had to work that hard to keep from crying. My aunt and uncle's funeral when I was seventeen. It hadn't worked then either.

"For eleven years," I said, voice shaking, "my life has been on pause. I left you to keep you safe. Because I loved you. So much. I loved you so much. And I was so afraid I'd get you killed, so I ran."

"Lise, please," Riley said. He took a step closer, and I backed up. Jacob was on his feet a second later snarling, "Don't fucking touch her."

I ignored them both. "I thought I was protecting you. I thought the reason I couldn't move forward, the reason I was living half a life was because of him—the psycho who put you in the hospital, who won't stop sending me those fucking flowers. All these years, I thought it was him, that he was the one who took my life away. But then I came back, and you were here, and I realized—"

My voice cracked, and I swallowed hard. I had to finish it. I had to say this. "I realized that it wasn't him. It wasn't running that put my life on pause. It was being without you."

Riley made a choking sound, shifting as if to move, but Jacob blocked him. The words bled out of me in a hot rush.

"You were here, and I thought you hated me. And then you didn't, and I thought maybe we could do this. Maybe we could beat him and have everything we always talked about. A life. You and me."

I couldn't do it. I couldn't hold it together. Tears came so fast and hard I was blind with them. "And now I know it was all a lie. I don't even know who you are. You're a stranger. You're a stranger, and I'm a fool."

"Lise, no. I—"

That was all Riley got out before Jacob swung a fist into his jaw, sending him to the floor. I squeezed my eyes shut, vaguely hearing Charlie in the background yelling at Aiden and Jacob murmur something I couldn't make out. He slid his arm around my shoulder, pulling me close and pressing a gentle kiss to my temple as he said, "You're coming with me."

I nodded into his shoulder and let him lead me out of the house.

CHAPTER SEVENTEEN
ANNALISE

T buckled my seatbelt and leaned back into the plush leather seat of Jacob's luxury sedan. Shouts echoed behind me.

Riley and Jacob.

Jacob got in the car, slamming his door, and started the engine. We drove through the gates in silence, me wiping tears from my cheeks and Jacob sneaking glances at me.

Finally, he said, "What did you do to your hands?"

I uncurled my fingers and studied my palms, smeared with blood; neat red half-moons cut into my skin.

Jacob took a quick look and let out a breath. "I didn't think you still did that," he said.

"I haven't in years. Not like this." I curled my fingers back into fists. It wasn't as bad as it looked. My fingernails weren't long or sharp enough to do any real damage.

"You always hated crying in front of an audience," Jacob said quietly. "You and Charlie both. So strong when you shouldn't have had to be."

"I didn't do so hot with that today," I muttered. I'd

completely lost it in front of everyone, crying and scream-ing. I'd been out of control.

Jacob stopped at the end of the long drive and flicked on his blinker. His silver eyes, usually so cool, were warm with emotion as he looked at me. "You had a right to lose it." He opened his mouth to say something else, then closed it and shook his head.

"You didn't know?" I asked, tentatively. I wasn't sure I wanted the answer. Riley, Aiden, the Sinclairs—that was all the betrayal I could take.

"No," Jacob said in a flat, hard voice. "I had no idea."

He turned onto the main road and drove through Buck-head. The bright spring sunshine dappled the road, lighting the trees a brilliant green. We could've been in the middle of the country, but in a mile or two we'd turn out onto a busy city street.

Jacob's building, which he'd named Winters House as a poke at Aiden, was only a few miles away. A historic hotel, he'd converted it to a mixed-use development with retail on street level, a few floors of offices, and the rest very high-end condos.

Jacob lived in the penthouse, his real estate company was on the fifth floor, and Holden and Tate's gaming company, WGC, was on the fourth. Holden and Tate, my younger cousin and brother, shared the tenth floor, each of them in one of the building's expansive residences. Jacob's building was home away from home for the Winters family.

Jacob said again, "I had no idea. I didn't think he should let you live on campus, but with Vance and I both there it was hard to make a case for forcing you to stay home. You hadn't gotten any flowers or gifts in a while. Things were quiet. I was surprised Aiden gave in so easily, but it didn't occur to me to wonder why." The side of his mouth curved in a half smile and he admitted, "I was a junior in college, Lise. I had my head on school and girls."

"Not your younger cousin," I said.

"Exactly. Vance and I were both distracted. We should've paid more attention. I'm sorry—"

"Jacob, no. That was the whole reason I wanted to live on campus. I was tired of everyone worrying about me. Feeling like they had to. I wanted to live a normal life."

I slumped to the side of my seat, letting my head rest against the cool window of the car. Living a normal life hadn't worked out very well. A hot tear trickled down my cheek. I scrubbed it away in frustration. I hated crying.

No, it wasn't the crying I hated. Crying was fine. Sometimes it even felt good. A release. What I hated was the pain. The wrenching sense of loss. I was sick with it, my heart aching and my stomach rolling.

My phone rang in my pocket. I pulled it out and checked the screen. Riley. I pressed my thumb to the power button on the side and swiped the phone off. I had nothing to say. Not to any of them.

A thought occurred to me, and I sat up, looking over at Jacob. "Did we leave Abigail?"

Jacob's lips curved into the warm, sweet smile he reserved for his fiancée. "Kind of. She's getting our things together. Someone will give her a ride home when she's ready. I didn't want to wait."

Neither had I. "Thank you," I said.

"You can stay with us as long as you want," he said. "Security at my place is pretty good."

"I don't want to be in the way."

"Lise, you could never be in the way. Stay as long as you want. Do you want me to have Flynn barred from the building?"

"Yes," I said, without hesitation. The thought of facing Riley again left me queasy and fighting off the prickle of tears.

"Consider it done." Jacob pulled the sedan into the underground garage and parked in his reserved spot just in front of the elevators. He ushered me into the building, the elevator gliding up fast and smooth to the penthouse.

I'd always loved Jacob's penthouse. Where Winters House had a Mediterranean influence, Jacob's penthouse was old world Europe. Creamy walls, oil paintings, gleaming hardwoods, and antiques. He led me down the hall to their guest room, giving me a gentle shove in the direction of the bathroom.

"Get your hands cleaned up and wash your face. I'll make coffee and get some food together. You missed breakfast."

"I'm not hungry," I said.

"Eat anyway. You already feel like shit, being hungry will only make it worse."

I shook my head but did as he'd ordered, washing my hands and patting them dry. The tiny cuts in my palms had stopped bleeding during the short drive. My face, on the other hand, was a mess, my eyes swollen, cheeks blotchy and red.

I was drying my hands when I heard voices, Abigail's smooth, modulated tones and Charlie, agitated and talking fast. She fell silent when she saw me coming down the hall. They were all in the kitchen, Jacob pouring coffee, Abigail scrambling eggs at the big gas range. Charlie pulled a glass dish of cinnamon rolls from the microwave and slid it across the bar. Jacob placed a steaming mug of coffee beside the rolls and said, "Sit. Get some sugar and caffeine in your stomach."

I thought about protesting again that I wasn't hungry. I wasn't, but I knew they meant well. They couldn't fix this. No one could fix this. If feeding me would make them feel better, I wasn't going to argue.

The cinnamon rolls did smell good – yeasty and warm with spice. Whoever had made them hadn't been stingy with the cream cheese frosting. I wiggled a roll free from the pan and swiped my finger through the frosting.

"They're a day old, but they're still good," Abigail said, from the stove, sending me a gentle smile over her shoulder. Charlie came around and sat at the bar beside me.

"Are you going to yell more?" I asked.

"Do you want me to?" she asked, nudging my shoulder with hers.

I thought about it. I loved that she was mad on my behalf. I loved that she was here for me. It meant a lot, especially because I knew how close she was to Aiden. He'd practically raised her. She'd been ten when her parents died and only twelve when I'd dropped out of college and taken off.

I loved her, and I knew she loved me, but we weren't as close as we could've been. My fault. I wrote her, then emailed her over the years. I'd send her funny things I came across that reminded me of her, stuff like that. But it wasn't the same as being there the way Aiden had been.

Just thinking of Aiden sent a wave of nausea through me. I put the cinnamon roll down on the counter and shook my head.

In a small voice, I said, "I think I'm done with yelling."

Charlie wrapped her arm around my shoulder and squeezed me in a fierce hug. Before the affection could overwhelm my emotions, she let go, picked up her coffee and said, "Then just eat your breakfast."

Abigail slid a plate of scrambled eggs in front of me, and I ate. My stomach was in knots, but I must have been hungry. I finished the cinnamon roll, the eggs, and the coffee.

I put down my fork and stared at the empty plate, at a loss for what to do next. I'd had a plan. We'd had a plan, Riley and me. Without Riley, there was no fake engagement. Without Riley, everything fell apart.

I had to think. I had to figure out what to do. I didn't want to do anything except curl into a ball and cry.

I hadn't realized I'd been spinning fairytales of a life with Riley until they fell apart around me. Somewhere deep inside I'd been hoping there was a happy ending for us.

Knowing it wouldn't happen was tearing me to pieces.

I didn't have the energy to put myself back together.

"Come on," Charlie said. Her arm around my shoulders, she urged me off the stool and out of Jacob and Abigail's kitchen, tugging me down the hall to the guest room. At her urging, I climbed up on the big, black, canopy bed and lay back on the fluffy white duvet. Charlie kicked off her shoes and climbed up beside me. Picking up the remote off the bedside table, she clicked on the TV.

"Maggie swears by John McClain for a broken heart, but considering everything else that's going on, I think we'll skip the violence and explosions. We're going to watch a stupid, funny movie and not think about anything. If you feel the slightest urge for chocolate or ice cream, you let me know, and I'll get it."

I didn't want to watch a stupid, funny movie. Especially not the one she put on, which I knew would have as many fart jokes as sight gags. I let her do what she wanted. I didn't want to be alone, and I didn't want to talk. Might as well watch a stupid, funny movie with my cousin.

The alternative was to think about everything that had happened with Riley. I wasn't ready for that.

I tried not to laugh at the movie, but Charlie's giggles were infectious. She caught sight of my scowl and laughed saying, "I know, I know. It's ridiculous. Lucas made me watch it the other day. I told him I'd hate it because it's so dumb and then I laughed so hard I was crying."

"It really is dumb," I said, laughing again as the main character tripped over a mop handle and tumbled down a flight of stairs, rolling to a stop at the feet of the female lead. The lovable buffoon looked at her with an expression of such potent adoration that the laugh hitched in my chest, and before I knew what was coming, it turned into a sob.

Beside me, Charlie said under her breath, "Fuck." Her arm wrapped around me and she pulled me into her shoulder. Stroking my hair, she murmured, "It's going to be okay, Lise. I know it doesn't seem like it now, but I promise, it's going to be okay."

"All those years, Charlie. All those years I felt so guilty for leaving him. For that letter. And all that time he knew. He knew why I left. He had to know I lied and he never came after me. I felt so guilty. It ate at me. I loved him so much, and it was all a lie."

My breath strangled in my lungs, my throat tight with tears. I cried harder, sobs shaking my chest, making it impossible to talk. Charlie held me tighter saying only, "I know, Lise. I know."

I couldn't fight the despair pulling me under. Everything I thought I understood was backward. People I thought I could trust betrayed me.

I held onto Charlie and wept. It felt like hours until I wound down and when I finally stopped crying, I was exhausted. Charlie slipped from the bed and disappeared into the bathroom.

Belatedly I noticed the TV was off and the penthouse was quiet. She came back with a wet washcloth and wiped it across my cheek. My face was hot, my eyes swollen, and the cool, wet cloth felt like heaven.

Suddenly, I was embarrassed. "I'm sorry, Charlie, I don't want to get between you and Aiden and I didn't mean to—"

"Did you know Lucas and I broke up?"

At my look of shock, she shook her head. "No, a while ago. Before we moved in together. We were just supposed to be hooking up, and then I fell for him, and he walked away."

"What an asshole," I said with a watery laugh. Lucas couldn't have been more in love with Charlie. He adored her. I couldn't imagine him dumping her and moving on.

"Exactly," she said with a gentle smile. "He was a complete asshole, and he broke my heart. It's not the same; I'm not trying to say that. But don't apologize for crying all over me. I've been there. I know."

"Thanks, Charlie," I said taking the washcloth from her and holding it over my face. My eyes were so swollen it hurt to blink. I didn't think I had any tears left in me.

I let my lids slide shut, lulled by Charlie stroking my braid, and slipped into sleep.

I woke later to raised voices down the hall. Jacob and Aiden. Jacob saying, "She needs time, and you need to back off. She'll deal with you when she's ready. Not before. Just go home."

Only Jacob, and maybe Gage, would face Aiden down like that. I knew people said that Jacob was a shark, but to me, he was just Jacob, my older cousin and sometime partner in crime.

I didn't want to come between him and Aiden, but I

was grateful he was running interference. I was hollowed out, run dry, and I didn't have the reserves to deal with Aiden.

Aiden was the one who looked after us. Our defense against the world. I wasn't sure which betrayal was worse, Aiden's hiring Riley and not telling me, or Riley's for his lies.

I waited until I heard the door close, then got out of bed and used the bathroom. Washing my face and re-braiding my hair left me feeling marginally better. Less of a mess, at least.

I wanted to go out. I wanted to be alone. Walking down the hall, I tried to make a decision. Any decision. Jacob stood in the kitchen, his silver eyes going dark with concern as he saw me.

"I know I look like hell," I said. I'd washed my face and straightened my hair, but that didn't do a thing for my puffy eyes and splotchy face. Abigail, coming up the hall from behind me, said, "I have just the thing."

She passed me and went for the freezer, pulling out something that looked like Zorro's mask, except pale green. "Put this over your eyes for a while. It'll bring the swelling down."

I took the mask from her, holding it by the strap. Abigail gave me another of her gentle smiles. On the surface, she was a perfect match for Jacob—elegant and refined, a master at navigating Jacob's social circles. Underneath she had a core of steel and a warm heart.

"Do you want to be alone, or do you want company?" she asked.

"Alone. But—"

"But you're tired of being cooped up," she said. "Go up to the roof and get some sun. It'll make you feel better. I'm making chicken and dumplings for dinner. It'll keep until you're ready to eat."

I didn't protest as she herded me to the front hall and pointed me in the direction of the stairs to the private rooftop garden. Jacob watched her with an indulgent smile, saying only, "No one will bother you up there. It's a good place to think."

He was right. Potted plants surrounded the space, along with a dining table, grill, and a seating area complete with a fire pit. I sat in one of the teak recliners, laying back and turning my face up to the spring sunshine. The ice mask was covered in a velvety fabric that molded to my eyes, cooling my swollen skin.

I still wanted to curl up in a ball and cry, but I'd been there, done that. I had to decide what to do next. Normally, I'd be packing my bags. For the first time in years, running had no appeal, even with the mess my life at home had become.

I was done with running.

This fake engagement had turned into a disaster of the worst proportions, but I couldn't deny it had provoked my stalker just as we'd planned. If I ran, we'd lose all the ground we'd gained.

Letting out a sigh, I accepted that cancelling the fake engagement would be as useless as running. I could fire the Sinclairs and get rid of Riley. Spread the word that I was on the market again. That would solve the problem of Riley, but it would be giving the stalker exactly what he wanted.

If I ended the engagement, I'd have to wait before I tried it again—more time lost—and I'd have to find another fake fiancé.

I never wanted to see Riley again.

I wanted this to be over. All of it. Riley, the stalker, everything.

I sat there, letting the late afternoon sun bake into my skin, the mask over my eyes gradually warming, and turned the problem over in my mind. There was no ideal solution. No way to get everything I wanted.

I couldn't put the pieces of my heart back together. I couldn't roll back the clock. But maybe, if I was strong, if I had courage, I could finish this and set myself free.

A shoe scuffed the slate beside me. I reached up to tug the mask from my eyes and saw Jacob, holding two beers. Without a word, I reached out to take one, dropping the mask on the edge of the recliner. Jacob sat beside me and took a pull from his beer.

"Thanks," I said.

"Anytime. Your eyes look better. Abigail knows all the tricks."

"I like her with you."

"Me too," he said, his lips curving as he thought of his fiancée. "She's better than I deserve."

"Probably," I agreed, smiling a little myself and sipping the beer. It was crisply cold and bitter with hops, just the way I liked it.

I drank more and waited. Jacob took his time. We were halfway through our beers when he said, "Do you know what you're going to do?"

"I do," I said.

"Am I going to try to talk you out of it?"

"I don't think so. I think you'll approve."

"Tell me."

CHAPTER EIGHTEEN
RILEY

I turned into the drive to Winters House, reaching up to hit the remote for the gates. Slowing the car, I prepared to stop, not sure I'd be able to get in.

I'd left Winters House not long after the scene with Annalise. I wouldn't have put it past Aiden to change the codes and lock me out. I wouldn't even have blamed him.

He was no innocent in this mess, but neither was I. I'd had plenty of opportunities to come clean with Annalise and every time I'd put it off. Somehow I'd managed to convince myself that my lies weren't a big deal.

They weren't what was important.

I loved her. That was what mattered.

I winced as I remembered the agony in her eyes, the sheer undiluted pain as she'd realized the truth. I'd made a lot of miscalculations in my life, but none as bad as this.

Cooper heard it in my voice, probably already had a clue when he saw I was calling from the office on a Sunday. We'd worked together for over a decade. I couldn't hide anything from him. His response had cut to the bone.

"Get your ass back to Winters House and make it right,

you fucking idiot. You'd better fix this before she kicks all of our asses. I don't care how badly you fucked up your personal life; you have a job to do. You two were getting close to drawing this guy out in the open. You can't give up now. Suck it up and take what you have coming."

Lucky for me, Evers was out of town, sparing me his commentary. Knox, on the other hand, sent a text.

I knew you'd fuck it up. Fix it, or I'll shoot you.

I think he was kidding, but with Knox, it's hard to tell. I didn't care what any of them thought. The only person I cared about was Annalise. Her ring weighed heavy in the pocket of my jeans. I pulled it out and set it on the desk in front of me. The princess cut diamond sparkled under my office lights, the delicate, intertwined platinum bands so perfectly her.

I'd known it was hers as soon as I'd seen it, but that was nothing next to the way I'd felt every time I spotted it on her finger. It marked her as mine. My Lise. My love.

I'd spent most of my savings to buy this ring. All I wanted was to put it back on her finger. Not as a charade. Not as part of a job. I wanted her to wear my ring because she knew I loved her and she loved me back.

I'd been so close. I'd had her in my arms. I'd been inside her, been skin to skin, tasted her breath, felt her heart beat against mine.

For the first time in eleven years, I was whole.

I was home.

And I'd fucked it all up.

Now I had to fix it.

I made one more phone call and finished what I'd come to my office to do, setting in motion the first part of my plan to win back Annalise. I shoved the ring into the small watch pocket of my jeans. I wanted it close until I could put it back on her finger.

Before I went after Annalise, I had to settle things with her family. Assuming they let me back on the property. As the first set of black metal gates swung open, admitting me to the estate, the knot in my chest loosened.

I checked my rearview, making sure the gates closed securely behind me and made my way to the second set of gates protecting the inner courtyard of the house. I never had to reach for the remote. A friendly wave from the guard, one of ours, and I was on my way.

I left my car in the courtyard. I half expected Aiden to kick me out, telling me the job was over. I wouldn't go without a fight, and I wasn't giving up, but if Aiden wanted me out, I couldn't force him to let me stay.

I didn't bother to knock, letting myself in. I took a hard right down the hall and around the corner to Aiden's office. He sat behind his big polished desk, a crystal tumbler in front of him, half full of whiskey.

At the sound of my footsteps, he raised one dark eyebrow, his face blank, impossible to read.

I stopped in front of his desk, folded my arms across my chest, and said, "I'm not leaving. I'm not walking away from this job, and I'm not walking away from her. I know I fucked up. I know she's hurting and it's my fault, but I'm going to fix it."

I braced for an angry response, ready to shout the house down, to throw a punch, anything to prove to Aiden Winters, to the whole clan, that I wasn't going anywhere. The fight drained out of me when Aiden let out a breath and flung his hand toward the leather chair opposite his desk.

I sat as he stood. He crossed the room to pick up a crystal decanter and another tumbler.

"Whiskey?" he asked, not waiting for my answer. He poured three fingers into the glass and came back to the desk, bringing the decanter with him. Sitting, he slid the glass across the desk toward me and nodded at it. "I'd offer you the good stuff, but my family keeps stealing it."

I took a sip, the smoky, peaty flavor of the whiskey rolling over my tongue. I wasn't a whiskey connoisseur, but this was a hell of a lot better than what I usually drank.

"Where is she?" I asked.

"Still with Jacob. He said she was sleeping and Charlie was with her."

"I'm not walking away," I said, again.

"I'd think you were an idiot if you did," Aiden said, with a sigh. He took a sip of whiskey, seeming lost in thought before he said, "You know, I was only twenty when my parents died. When I came home and took over at the company. Took over the family. I'm barely three years older than Annalise."

"Seems like more."

Aiden let out a wry laugh. "Sometimes I feel a million years old. I did the best I could. I fucked up a lot. I managed things at the company pretty well, considering, but the rest of it—"

"You're not responsible for everything," I said. He made a dismissive sound and took another sip of the whiskey.

A few hours ago I was happy to blame Aiden for his share of this mess. Now, looking at him, seeing my own guilt reflected in his dark eyes, I couldn't bring myself to point the finger.

If he'd fucked up, so had I. His mistake was born out of

love. Mine came from fear. To my way of thinking, that let him off the hook. Mostly.

"I lied to you," he said. "I gave you her letter, and I lied to you."

"I know."

"I'm sorry," he said. "By the time I realized I'd made a mistake, it was too late to take back. You were too old for her, and you met her under false pretenses. You were only supposed to keep an eye on her. You were never supposed to talk to her."

"Why didn't you just fire me?"

"Would you have left her alone? If I'd gone to Maxwell Sinclair and had you fired, would you have disappeared?"

I took a long drink of the whiskey and set the tumbler on Aiden's desk. "No. I would have come clean with her. I would've told her the truth and waited until she forgave me for lying."

"Exactly why we didn't fire you. Lise has always known her own mind. As long as she wanted you, there wasn't much I could do about it. No sense in taking you off the job if you weren't going to leave."

"But then the stalker came after me, and you saw your chance to get me out of her life," I said.

Aiden didn't deny it. "You were too old for her."

"Bullshit," I said. "It wasn't my age. It was me. Who I am. Or who I'm not. I came from nowhere. I was a nobody. Not good enough for a Winters. Admit it. That's what it was about. I didn't have the right pedigree for Annalise, and the first chance you had, you got rid of me."

"You have got to be kidding me," a female voice said from behind me. I turned to see Charlie standing in the doorway of Aiden's office, her ocean blue eyes spitting fire. "Who do you think you are? Uncle William? I expect this kind of crap from him, but not from you, Aiden. You lied to Riley because you didn't think he was good enough for Annalise? How could you do that to her?"

Aiden gave his little sister a pained look and shook his head. She snagged his glass and sat in the leather chair beside mine.

"What were you thinking?" she asked, sounding bewildered as much as angry.

Aiden looked from Charlie to me and said, "I was thinking that I didn't know what to do. I was thinking that Lise couldn't shake the stalker, that this guy who was supposed to be protecting her had charmed his way into her bed. I was thinking that I was in charge of the whole fucking company, the whole family, and I had no idea what I was doing. And when she said she had to run to save Riley I thought it solved a lot of problems all at once."

"You could get her away from the stalker and me at the same time," I said. I didn't like it, but I could see his point.

Aiden leaned forward, bracing his elbows on his desk. "If I'd had any idea she wouldn't come home, that she'd keep running for over a decade, I swear I never would've done it. I figured she'd stay away for a few months, on the outside, and then she'd come home, and we'd regroup and figure out what to do."

He shot a guilty look at Charlie and went on, "You were too young to realize, and we didn't tell you, but two months after she left we started pushing her to come back. We had someone following her, someone from Sinclair. He got too close, and he spooked her. She dropped completely off the radar for over a year. She was a ghost, and we were terrified. After that, I was afraid to push too hard."

Charlie rolled the whiskey glass between her palms, staring into the caramel colored liquid before taking a long sip. "That's why you never said anything about Lucas, even when Uncle William did. That's why you stuck up for Jacob with Abigail. Because of what happened with Lise and Riley."

"Because of them," he agreed. "And because of Elizabeth. I learned firsthand that background and money don't make a marriage. Love is what counts." Aiden met my eyes. "I knew she loved you. I didn't believe you loved her."

"I did. More than anything," I said.

Charlie leaned forward in her chair and pinned me with a steely look. "Not enough. She gives you a letter, Aiden sends you packing, and you just walk away?"

"It was complicated," I said, knowing it was a weak excuse. Life was always complicated.

Aiden said I was too old for Annalise, but I'd been too young to understand what was really important. I'd been worried about the differences between us. Afraid I'd lose the job I loved—a job that would be very difficult to replace if I got fired for sleeping with the client. I'd let all of that pile up in my head, let it convince me Annalise had decided I wasn't good enough for her

What I should have done was burn the letter, tell Aiden to fuck off, and gone after Annalise.

"And what about now?" Charlie said, setting her jaw in a mulish scowl.

I wanted to be pissed at her, but I knew she'd spent the last few hours with Annalise. Charlie's outrage was on behalf of the cousin she loved, who'd been hurt enough.

I leaned forward, meeting Charlie's angry eyes, and said, "I love her. I have never stopped loving her. I'm going to do whatever I have to do to make her believe that."

Charlie settled back in her chair and finished off the rest

of her whiskey. "I hope you've got a good plan because right now she never wants to see you again."

I had the beginnings of a plan, but I was saved from explaining when Lucas Jackson leaned in through the office door. His unusual light green eyes landed on me for an almost imperceptible moment, his wink a flash, before he grinned at Charlie and said, "Princess, you done raking these two through the coals? We've got work to do. Let these dumbasses clean up their own mess."

She set Aiden's tumbler on his desk. "I'm going home with my husband. You two better figure out how to fix this. If you run Annalise off again, the rest of us will never forgive you."

Aiden watched her leave, shaking his head. When she was safely out of earshot, he said, "Thank fucking God for Lucas Jackson. Now it's his job to keep her out of trouble."

"I didn't believe it when Cooper said they were together. He was the president of a motorcycle club. And not one of the nice ones," I said.

"There are nice ones?" Aiden asked, raising one eyebrow. He shrugged a shoulder. "He was only with the Raptors to avenge his brother. He's actually pretty clean-cut if you look past all the tattoos."

I couldn't hold back a laugh. Lucas Jackson was clean-cut? Were we talking about the same guy? Lucas worked for Sinclair now, headed his own division, but he hadn't changed that much.

Aiden shrugged again. "Whatever. He'll kill anyone who looks at my baby sister the wrong way, and that's all I care about anymore. She's happy, and he'd do anything to keep her that way. You could say my criteria for acceptable mates has changed over the years."

"That's all I want," I said. "A chance to spend the rest of my life making Annalise happy."

"Good luck," he said, sardonically. "You have to get her to talk to you first."

He had a point. Fortunately for me, I had a plan.

CHAPTER NINETEEN
RILEY

"I was never here," Lucas said under his breath, sliding what looked like a cell phone into his jacket pocket. Breaking into Jacob's building wasn't a one-man job, even when I had access to the schematics for the security system. I could manage a little routine B & E on my own, but getting into the penthouse undetected required hacking skills beyond my reach.

"Appreciate the help," I said as Lucas turned to go.

"Charlie finds out, I'm blaming you."

He disappeared into the night, leaving me alone in Jacob's rooftop garden. Normal access to the penthouse was through the elevator, but overriding the main security system and the cameras would leave a trace, not to mention the elevator opened right into the foyer, providing no cover if Jacob or Abigail happened to be wandering through the penthouse for a late night snack.

The garden access let us skip the elevator, though it had required climbing up the fire escape. Good thing neither of us was afraid of heights. I had a five-minute window to pick the lock on the garden stairs and get into the penthouse before the door's sensor reset itself. That was the easy part.

I slipped into Jacob's penthouse, silently locking the door behind me, and made my way down the hall to the guest room. The penthouse was dark and silent. I'd studied the floor plans in my office a few hours before and knew exactly where I was going.

I found Annalise asleep in a big black canopy bed, half buried under a fluffy white duvet.

We needed to talk, but I didn't want to scare the hell out of her. I turned on the bedside lamp and waited. Her eyes flicked under her lids, her nose scrunching and then releasing as she gradually came awake.

"Lise, wake up. We need to talk."

I kept my voice low and soothing, trying not to alarm her, but she shot bolt upright, eyes flying wide. When she spotted me, they narrowed. but she didn't make a sound.

Not until she hissed, "Get out."

I held up my hands in front of me, palms out. "I will. I'll leave as soon as we talk. There are things you have to know. Things we have to work out. Then I'll go, I swear."

She was silent for a long moment before she sat up straighter, gathering the duvet around her like a shield. Inclining her head toward the armchair in the corner, as regal as a queen, she said, "Sit over there. I don't want you near me."

I'm not going to pretend her words didn't slice through me. I deserved her anger. The distance between us and her tear-swollen eyes were all the reminder I needed.

I'd hurt her. I'd made so many excuses for myself, had so many reasons, but at the end of the day it all boiled down to this—my bad decisions had broken her heart.

All I could do was hope there was a chance to fix it.

"I was never supposed to make contact," I said. I didn't know if I had the right words, but I'd start with the truth. "I was supposed to be on campus, keep an eye on you. I was not supposed to engage. You weren't supposed to know I was there at all. Your freshman year you never noticed me."

She stiffened, and a muscle on the side of her jaw flickered. She didn't like that, didn't like knowing I'd watched her for a year before I'd gotten careless and let her see me. She wasn't going to like the truth, but it was all I had to give.

"I didn't lie in my reports, and Cooper reamed me out when I admitted I took you out for coffee. Maxwell Sinclair threatened to fire me. You were my first assignment with Sinclair Security. I didn't want to lose the job—there aren't a lot of companies like Sinclair—but I couldn't be invisible anymore. Not to you. It got so you were all I saw. I'd close my eyes at night and dream of you. It started to eat at me that you didn't see me back. I'd see your smile, the way your eyes lit up when you'd talk to your friends, and I was jealous. I was greedy. I wanted that part of you for me."

"You didn't even know me," she said. "And it's more than a little creepy that you were watching me to protect me from a stalker and essentially ended up stalking me yourself."

When she put it like that, it *was* creepy. So much for the truth setting me free.

"I wasn't the one sending you flowers and scaring the shit out of you."

"No, you were the one following me and then lying to me about who you were." Her voice wobbled, sending a flash of pain through my heart.

"I lied," I admitted. "I lied to you over and over. I had a million ways to justify it—to myself, to the Sinclairs. I'm not going to excuse it. I was wrong. I finally talked to you, took you out on a date, and I lost my head. That's the only way I can explain it to you. I just fucking lost my head over you. I figured you'd be different in real life. We'd go out, you'd be boring, or annoying, and that would be it. You'd go back to being a client. A job. I led myself down a path, one lie at a time."

She wanted me in the armchair, but I couldn't sit still. I rose and paced at the end of the bed. She said nothing, just watched me, her eyes silently tracking me, back and forth.

"First I told myself I'd take you out for coffee, and that would be the end of it. Then I told myself I could keep you safer if I stayed close. That who I was didn't matter. That my intentions were good."

"You were still lying."

"I know. I'm not saying it was okay. I just need you to understand that I didn't have a plan to deceive you. It started small and grew, one lie at a time."

I shoved a hand through my hair, wondering if there was anything I could say that wouldn't make me sound like a creeper.

Probably not.

"Aiden was right. I was too old for you. Not just in years but the things I'd done, the things I was trained to do. You were too good for me. You were the oldest daughter of the Winters family. I was insane to think it could work. The Sinclairs wanted me off the job. Aiden wanted me off the job. I was completely fucking in love with you, and you didn't know who I was. The whole thing was a disaster."

"If you'd just told me the truth, we could've figured it out," she said, her voice low.

"You say that now, and looking back, yeah, maybe we could have. But at the time? At the time it seemed smarter to wait. Then it was too late, and you were gone."

So quietly I almost couldn't hear her, she said, "You didn't come after me. You knew why I ran. I thought I was keeping it a secret, protecting you, but you knew exactly what was going on. You had to know that letter was bullshit, and you never came after me."

"I didn't believe the letter at first," I told her.

I was torn. As angry as I'd been at Aiden Winters, I was oddly reluctant to throw him under the bus. Knowing Aiden had deliberately come between us would only hurt Annalise more, but I wouldn't lie to her again.

Carefully choosing my words, I said, "Aiden gave me the letter, and then he backed it up. I didn't want to believe any of it, but he told me that guy you left with was your high school boyfriend, that you needed a fresh start. I should have known he was covering for you. I should've known it was a lie. But half the time I could hardly believe you wanted me. Looking back, I think I spent most of our time together waiting for it to fall apart. It seemed inevitable."

"I told him to give you the letter," she said, dully. "I told him to make sure you didn't come after me. He could've told me who you were, what was going on."

"He fucked up. We all fucked up." I raised my hands in the air, helplessly. "He loves you, and he didn't know how to help you. I loved you, but I didn't believe in you."

Annalise rubbed the heel of her hand against her cheek, wiping away a tear. Fuck. The last thing I wanted was to make her cry again.

Her voice shaking, she said, "I appreciate you telling me the truth. Now I want you to leave."

"I'm not done."

"I think you are," she said, her voice stronger.

"No, I love you, Annalise."

"Don't—"

"What? Don't tell you I love you?"

"It's too late, Riley. We can't go back."

"I don't want to go back, Lise. We have a mess behind us. Lies and misunderstandings and so many years we wasted. I don't want to go back. I want to go forward. I love you. I want a life with you."

"Riley—" Her voice cut off, and she made a little choking sound. She drew in a long breath and said, "I don't believe you. This is still a job. I'm still a job. How do I know this isn't a charade to get me back home? How can I believe anything you say?"

I stopped my pacing and sank back into the armchair, bracing my elbows on my knees and staring her down.

"There's nothing I can say," I admitted. "I'm not going to ask you to trust me. Given the circumstances, that would sound ridiculous. I can promise you I won't lie to you, but you don't have a reason to believe that either. I can look you in the eye and tell you that I'm in love with you. I've been in love with you since before you knew I existed and I'll be in love with you until the day I die. But I can't make you believe me."

"Then I don't know what we're supposed to do," she said, studying the duvet in front of her, refusing to look at me.

"I do. Tomorrow, you're coming back to Winters House. Together, we're going to finish this job. We're going to pretend we're happily engaged until we drive your stalker crazy enough to come out in the open and then we're going to take that fucker down. We're going to set you free. And if you still don't believe that I love you, I'll figure out how to prove it to you. I know you love me and I understand that you can't trust me. Not yet. But you will."

"I already decided to come back," she said. "We've never been this close to catching him. I'm not backing down now. But things are going to change."

Cautiously, I asked, "What things?"

"For one, you're moving out of my rooms—"

"Lise, it's not safe—"

She made a cutting motion through the air with her hand. "It's safe enough. I don't want you in my rooms. That's my first condition. Non-negotiable."

I gritted my teeth and said, "Fine. I'll move into Jacob's suite. What else?"

"No more PDA. You can hold my hand, but no kissing, no snuggling, and I'm not sleeping with you again. Do you understand? I'm coming home so we can finish the job, and I'm using you to play my fiancé because starting over would be a huge waste of time. But I don't trust you. We're not together. If you can't work with that, I'll tell everyone we broke up, and I'll find another way."

I closed my eyes in resignation and leaned back into the armchair. I'd rather she'd jumped out of bed and thrown her arms around me when I told her I loved her, but I'd known it wouldn't be that easy.

She was coming home, and she was giving me a chance, even if she didn't want to.

Annalise loved me. To the marrow of my bones, I knew she loved me. Just as deep, she knew I loved her.

She was hurt, so fucking hurt, and it was my fault. She was afraid to trust me. I'd earned that. But as long as she was coming home, I had a chance.

This time, I wouldn't waste it.

CHAPTER TWENTY

ANNALISE

Riley was waiting for me at Winters House. I parked in the garage and went in through the kitchen, hoping to stay low key and out of sight. I'd made the decision to follow through with the fake engagement, but I wasn't happy about it.

Riley had carved my heart into pieces, and I was nowhere near ready to deal with him, much less pretend we were madly in love.

I stepped into the family room, hoping to sneak down the hall, and he was there, sitting in an armchair, a cup of coffee beside him, his laptop balanced on his knees. I gave him the coolest glance I could manage and breezed by saying, "I have to change."

I measured my pace as I walked down the hall. I would not rush. Riley would know I was running from him. All I had left was my pride, and that was hard enough to salvage after the way I'd lost it the day before.

No more crying. No more hysterics.

I had to focus on moving forward. We'd catch the stalker, and Riley would go away. Once he was out of my life, I could take a deep breath and set my mind and heart to getting over him.

He didn't follow me to my rooms. Inside, everything was neat and in its place, all signs of Riley wiped away. Relief lightened the weight on my shoulders. I'd told him to move out of my rooms, and he'd agreed, but I hadn't been absolutely sure he'd do it. If I was going to do this, I needed a sanctuary from him. I needed time to myself to shore up my defenses.

I showered and dressed, taking a little more time than usual with my makeup and hair. It wasn't about Riley. I wanted this charade of a relationship over as soon as possible, and the best way to do that was to get out there and let people see us together. We could start with going to Annabelle's and getting a mocha.

If that went well, we'd stop by Sloane's gallery and start that ball rolling. It was time to move on with my life, and that included exploring what, if anything, I could do with my photography. I knew how to wait tables, make a mean cappuccino, scrub a toilet, and take pretty pictures. I'd done all of the above to pay the rent, but I'd prefer to make a living off the pretty pictures if Sloane could sell them.

Ready to face the world, I went back to the family room to find Riley still bent over his laptop. He raised his head when I walked in, his hazel eyes probing and concerned. He was wearing his glasses again. I tried to ignore the tug at my heart.

It didn't matter how hot he looked in glasses.

He was a liar.

He'd lied about everything, from the beginning. I was holding out for a hot guy I could trust.

That wasn't Riley.

"I think we should go out," I said, crossing my arms over

my chest and staring him down. "I want to go to Annabelle's and get one of those mochas, and then I think we should stop by Sloane's gallery."

Riley nodded and gestured to the chair opposite him. I didn't sit until he said, "Good plan. And if we stop by Sloane's, she'll tell everyone and hopefully get this whole thing moving in the right direction. First, we need to talk."

I sat back in the armchair and crossed my legs, trying to look composed and unaffected. I don't think I pulled it off. It would've been better if I could bring myself to meet his eyes, but every time I did the emotions simmering there shook me off balance. I needed to hold it together. I needed to remember that I couldn't trust Riley.

I was a client. Our engagement was a job, and we had to finish it.

"I'm done talking about us," I said, looking at the wall behind him. "There's nothing to say."

"There's everything to say," he disagreed, "but you're not ready to hear it yet. I can wait. I don't want to talk about us. This is about your mother."

That took me by surprise. Why did Riley want to talk about my mother?

"At the engagement party," he said, "Melanie Monroe commented on how much you look like your mother. It started me thinking—what if this isn't just about you? What if the stalker has something to do with your mother?"

"My mother didn't have a stalker," I protested. "And I don't look that much like her."

"According to Melanie, you're practically a carbon copy."

"That's ridiculous," I said. "My hair is darker than hers, and I'm taller than she was. If you look at the pictures—"

"Pictures don't always tell the whole story, Lise. Melanie

admitted that your features weren't the same, but the way you hold yourself, your eyes, are exactly like your mother. I looked at pictures of you as a teenager, when this all started. Your hair was lighter then, and you hadn't hit your full height. At sixteen you looked exactly like your mother at twenty."

"My mother had been dead for seven years when I started getting the flowers and the notes. I don't see how they could be connected."

"No, you don't *want* to see how they could be connected. None of you do." Riley shut his laptop and set it on the coffee table. "Even the Sinclairs—you're all blind. You have too much history, and you're too close to see this all rationally."

"My mother—"

"Your mother had a lot of secrets. Maybe not from your father, but from everyone else. She had a child no one can find, and his father is a mystery. That's a big fucking hole in her life we know nothing about. The Sinclairs are running into roadblocks right and left trying to find this kid, and right now it's looking like Maxwell Sinclair is the one who put up those roadblocks."

"Maxwell's dead," I said.

I didn't want Riley to be right. I didn't want him to make sense. I didn't want this to be about my mother. In my memories she was perfect. Surrounded by flowers, her arms open for a hug, she was love and light and everything good from my childhood.

She had nothing to do with the crazy man fixated on me. Nothing.

Riley let out a huff of air in frustration. "Is he?"

"What do you mean, is he? Maxwell was in a car accident. He's dead. He's been dead for years," I protested, trying to ignore the niggle of doubt in my chest.

Riley worked for Sinclair Security. He'd been around when Maxwell was still running the company, and he'd been with them when Maxwell had died. I couldn't pretend I knew more about Maxwell's death than Riley did.

Proving me right, he said, "Maxwell Sinclair drove off a bridge. His body was never recovered. Maybe he's dead; maybe he's not. All I'm saying is that between your mother, your missing half-brother, Maxwell's supposed death, and your stalker, there are a lot of crossed lines and a lot of loose ends. All of you have been working on the assumption that your stalker is a stranger. Some random person fixated on you. It's possible. More likely than usual because you were in the public eye at a young age and any freak show could have seen you. But I don't buy it. This has been going on way too long, and this guy finds you too easily. My money says he knows you. Knows your family."

Every cell in my body rejected what Riley was saying. It couldn't be someone I knew. How could someone I knew torture me like this? Who could hate me this much? I didn't want to consider it was linked to my mother. The image I had in my head of her was a fairytale and one I held onto with both hands.

I knew she was human; I knew she had a past, she'd made mistakes. I just didn't want to face them. I wanted the fairytale. I wanted my perfect mother, who smelled of flowers, and hugged me tightly.

I drew in a deep breath and let it out slowly. Burying myself in memory was just another way of running. So was ignoring Riley. He had a point, and if I wanted this to be over, I had to be smart.

"We should go to their house," I said, slowly, hating the

idea. The house I'd grown up in, my parents' house, sat in the woods only a quarter of a mile away. I hadn't walked through the door in years, but if there was a clue about my mother's past, it was probably there.

Satisfied, Riley nodded and stood. "After Annabelle's and the gallery," he agreed. Reaching into his pocket, he pulled out the engagement ring I'd thrown in his face the day before. The big square stone caught the light, the platinum bands shining with a dull gleam, one of them sparkling with inset diamonds. It was a beautiful ring. The perfect ring. If you'd shown me a thousand rings, I would've picked that one.

I looked away, shoving my hands in my pockets. An impassable gulf stretched between my commitment to our fake engagement and the reality of putting that ring on my finger.

I had to wear the ring. Being seen in public with Riley and no ring would cause the wrong gossip. The point was to stir up the stalker by flaunting our engagement, not satisfy him with hints that there was trouble in paradise.

Bad enough if it somehow got out that Riley was no longer sleeping in my bed. Being seen around town without my impressive engagement ring defeated the purpose of having a fiancé in the first place.

I forced myself to hold out my left hand, squeezing my eyes shut as he took it in his and slid the ring on to my finger, carefully easing it over my scraped knuckle. I didn't look at it. I didn't look at him. Needing a second to get myself together, I said, "Let me get my purse. I'll meet you in the garage."

Riley seemed to understand that I needed space. He was quiet on the ride and said little once we were in Annabelle's. Annabelle herself was behind the counter, her long cinnamon hair pulled back in a messy bun. Her always-bright smile flared when she caught sight of me, and she dashed around the counter to pull me into a hug.

Rocking me back and forth she said, "I heard you were back! What took you so long to come in?"

Letting me go, she stepped back and gave Riley a long look, then smiled at me and said, "Oh, yeah. I heard all about this."

She lifted my left hand and studied the ring. To Riley, she said, "Nice work." To me, she said, "I'm short staffed today, or I'd sit with you guys. I know you're busy planning a wedding, and I'm practically chained to this place, but let's get together soon. I've missed you."

"Soon," I promised.

Soon this would all be over, and I could have a life. A life that included friends. Annabelle was just one of the people I'd missed over the years.

The line for coffee had grown behind us. We stepped out of the way, waiting only a minute before Annabelle gave us our drinks and sent us off with a wave.

The stop at Sloane's gallery wasn't as fun as seeing Annabelle. Sloane, in turn, kissed my ass, made snide comments about my looking old, gross comments about how hot my twin brother was, and sent Riley long, lascivious glances that left me itching to smack her.

I did not know how Maggie and Vance tolerated her. The weird thing was, Sloane's husband Rupert was a genuinely nice guy. He deserved so much better than this grasping, catty harpy.

We didn't linger at the gallery. I set an appointment with Sloane to bring in more of my work, accepted a sample copy of the contract to review, and took a spin around the space to admire the work she had displayed.

Half of it was Vance's, his metal sculptures dominating the airy gallery.

On the tall, white walls she'd hung various pieces ranging from paintings to collages, all of them well executed and interesting. All of them priced obscenely high. No photographs, but I could imagine how my work would fit into her collection. If her customers paid the prices she had marked, signing with Sloane could be a very good move for me.

Something to think about later.

Later when this was over. Later, when my life could start.

Sloane would be merciless when Riley and I called off the wedding. I pushed that thought aside. What did I care what Sloane had to say? Nothing. I didn't care. I'd be happy when both the stalker and Riley were out of my life. I had to be.

CHAPTER TWENTY-ONE
ANNALISE

T sipped my mocha on the ride home, savoring the rich, sweet chocolate underlain by the bitter bite of coffee. Annabelle had a gift. I knew my way around a portafilter. I'd worked as a barista enough to know the difference between competence and talent.

I was good, but Annabelle could craft coffee drinks that made my taste buds roll over and beg for mercy, especially when she brought out the chocolate. I could live on her mochas. The drink was a nice distraction from our destination.

Riley pulled around the side of Winters House and reached for the remote to open the garage door. "Keep going," I said, gesturing to the narrow extension of the driveway that led past the garage, past the main house, to the two cottages on the east side of the property where Mrs. W and Mr. Henried—the gardener—lived.

Slowing, Riley followed the drive past the pool and pool house to the cottages. While the pool house matched the main house in style, with its warm cream walls and red tile roof, the cottages, set into the woods out of sight of Winters House, had a different look altogether. Instead of Mediterranean, like Winters House, they were built in a craftsman style. Wide front porches, stained shingles, stone work on the steps and around the foundation. Homey and welcoming.

My father had chosen the same style for his house, albeit on a much grander scale. We followed the road past the cottages, circling behind the pool and gardens of Winters House. The woods closed around us, blocking out the midday spring sunshine. Growing up, I'd loved these woods, playing beneath the trees, climbing them with my brothers and building forts with fallen branches.

I'd felt safe here, unaware of the danger that could lurk in the shadows. After my parents died, I'd wanted the graceful discipline of the main house. The manicured gardens over the wild of the woods. I hadn't ventured this close to my parent's house in years. Not from the driveway, and not down the path through the woods.

Riley drove around the last curve of the drive, and the house appeared, nestled in the trees, looking as if we'd walked out the door only hours before. He pulled to a stop in front of the porch and studied the house.

"Not what I was expecting," he said. "No one lives here?"

"No. None of us—" I broke off, swallowed hard. Trying again, I said, "Mrs. W and Mr. Henried take care of it, but no one lives here."

I could understand his confusion. The garden beds in front of the porch were neatly weeded, the bushes trimmed and the peonies in bloom. The house itself was in perfect condition. I'd forgotten how beautiful it was, the way it nestled into the trees, the stone pillars and cedar shingles glowing with warmth.

Like the cottages, it was a craftsman style, but my father had been a Winters, and our house had been no cottage. Built on a grand scale, it had a deep wraparound porch, arched windows with hand carved shutters, and a slate roof accented by the flash of copper gutters and downspouts. Inside, the great room soared two stories, with a massive stone fireplace on one end and a view of the woods on the other.

Pulling the house keys from my purse, I opened the door of the SUV and jumped out. As far as I knew, nothing had been touched in the house in over a decade. Maybe not since we'd moved out. I'd come back a few times as a teenager, missing my parents, but the house was too empty without them.

The air inside smelled stale and flat. The interior was in perfect condition, the furniture uncovered, magazines still arranged on the coffee table, but the house still felt abandoned.

The front door opened into a foyer, the staircase to the second floor on one side and the hall to the kitchen and family room on the other. I ignored both and walked straight ahead into the great room. I didn't know what I was looking for. Anything personal would be in the master bedroom, or my father's office. I wasn't ready to face those rooms yet.

I stood in the center of the great room, Riley beside me, and turned in a slow circle, absorbing my childhood home. It had been years, but something was off. Deliberately, I turned in a second circle, studying the room—the pictures on the mantle, the leather couch and matching armchairs, and rustic style coffee table. The reading nook with book-shelves and chaise lounge, the door to my father's office, the half wall dividing the great room from the kitchen.

Everything looked the same, but something was missing.

I crossed the room to the fireplace and studied the mantle. My mother had filled it with family photographs. Everyone was there—her parents, my father's parents, their wedding pictures. My brothers and I, Uncle Hugh, Aunt Olivia, my cousins. There had barely been any space left when I was a little girl, and still, she found spots to add more.

Some of the photographs were missing. The picture of my mother taken the day she graduated from medical school. The one of her holding me in the hospital, my dad in the background holding Vance, my mother looking weary, her blue eyes shining with joy.

"What is it?" Riley asked, examining the photographs along with me.

"Some of the pictures are missing," I said. I stepped up onto the stone hearth to get closer to the mantle and pointed to the empty spaces. "Here and here."

"Pictures of your mother? And you?"

"Yes," I confirmed. I discovered another spot missing a picture, one of me on my first day of kindergarten. I could see it in the back of my mind—my hair the same platinum as my mother's and pulled back into two tight braids. I'd been wearing a red pinafore with a butterfly stitched on the front, my grin half excited and half terrified.

"Would your aunt have taken some of the pictures to the house?" Riley asked, gently.

I shook my head. "Aunt Olivia loved pictures as much as my mom did," I said. "She had a ton of her own. She left these here, she told me, for us. For when we were ready to come home. To go through all of it."

"And you never were?" Riley asked, surprise in his voice.

I reached out a finger and stroked it down the side of a gilded frame holding a picture of my parents on their wedding day. "No. Gage and I were gone. Until the last few years, Vance was more interested in drinking. Tate was so young when they died, he doesn't really remember living here. If Olivia and Hugh were still alive, it would've been different. I think we could have faced it. Maybe one of us would've come home already, would've been living in this house. Instead, we all fell apart."

"Someone was here. Someone took those photographs. The question is," Riley said, taking a slow survey of the house, curiosity in his eyes, "what else did they take?"

We searched the whole house, but other than the missing photographs, it was impossible to pin down what might be gone. After so many years I had no idea what had been in my father's desk drawers or my mother's dresser.

Riley shook his head at the carelessness of leaving her jewelry in its cabinet in her walk-in closet, unlocked in an empty house. He was right. To anyone else, the diamonds and gold would've been too valuable to leave unguarded. Gage had her wedding ring, had given it to Sophie, but the rest of it—they were just rocks and metal.

The people inside were the real treasures of a home. There was no one here but ghosts.

I left Riley in my father's closet and went to check my old bedroom. I was half afraid I'd find something weird, like flowers or a note, some message from whoever had been in the house, but everything was untouched, perfect.

It looked as if eight-year-old me had skipped out just that morning and could walk in any second. My hair ribbons were tied neatly beside the mirror of the little girl's white vanity table, snapshots from summer camp still tucked into the side of the mirror.

I sank onto the edge of the bed, blinking hard, fighting back tears. I loved this house. We'd been so happy here. We shouldn't have left it like this, abandoned. My parents wouldn't have wanted that. They'd designed every inch of our home, created it out of love as a haven for their family. It would've broken their hearts to know that we'd turned our backs on it.

But they hadn't known they'd die here, murdered on a cool spring night by a killer who would never be caught. They hadn't known they'd leave us, or that Uncle Hugh and Aunt Olivia would follow them less than nine years later.

"You okay?"

Riley stood in the doorway. I shrugged a shoulder and shook my head, unable to answer and unwilling to meet his eyes.

"I like your room," he said. "It looks like you. Were you taking pictures even back then?"

I watched him at my dresser, studying the ancient and very basic SLR camera sitting on top. It had been my first, a gift from my grandfather. I'd had to save up my allowance to get the film developed and I'd carefully framed each shot, afraid to waste them. That simple camera and the cost of developing the pictures had taught me so much about photography.

I'd stopped taking pictures for a few years after my parents had died, unable to open myself up enough to get interested in hobbies. When Aunt Olivia bought me a camera years later, she'd gotten something newer. Something with no memories attached.

"I think I was always taking pictures," I said. "I started

with my mom's 35mm, bugging her to let me hold it every time she took it out. Everything always made more sense through the viewfinder."

Riley stroked a finger across the top of the camera. When he sat on the end of the bed beside me and wrapped his arm around my shoulders, my heart squeezed hard, but I leaned into him. Just for a minute, I needed his strength.

I didn't want to be here anymore. I didn't want to miss them like this. The house was too much the same. It looked as if any minute they'd come in, telling us to hurry up for school or set the table for dinner. I half expected to hear my mom's voice, calling up the stairs for us to get a move on before breakfast got cold.

A tear slid down my cheek. Riley said only, "Lise," and held me tight to his side. I let my head rest on his shoulder, giving myself just a minute. A minute to breathe in his woodsy, spicy scent. A minute to let him hold me.

I wished that they were still here.

I wished things hadn't gone so wrong with Riley.

I wished I'd never left home.

A thousand wishes for things to be different and not one of them would come true.

The minute was up far too soon. I forced myself to stand, to step away. He reached for me, and I dodged him, twisting from his hand.

"I can't," I said, keeping distance between us when he would've moved closer. "I can pretend with you in public, but not when we're alone."

"I'm not pretending, Lise. I—"

I squeezed my eyes closed shutting him out. I couldn't do this, couldn't hear his excuses right now. Not in this house, surrounded by all I'd lost.

Riley cut off and fell silent. Moving to the door, he said, "Let's go. There's nothing to see here."

I followed him out, more than ready to leave. At that moment I would have happily agreed never to enter the house again. If I'd known how soon I'd be back, I would have started running and never stopped.

CHAPTER
TWENTY-TWO

They were all there when I walked in, arrayed around the dining room table at the end closest to the fireplace. Aiden, of course, had taken the head of the table. The seat to his left was empty, presumably saved for me. The seat beside that was occupied by Gage.

Sometimes the men in my family could be overbearing, but on days like this, I appreciated the way they looked out for me.

I sat between my brother and my cousin and busied myself pouring a cup of coffee from the tray in the middle of the table. Cooper sat directly opposite me, on Aiden's right, and Knox beside him. Riley was on the end, a notebook and open pen in front of him.

He pulled his glasses out of his shirt pocket and put them on as he glanced down to the notes on the page, picked up his pen and made a slight correction. I tried to ignore the flip in my belly.

What was it about those glasses? And the scruff on his cheeks, not quite thick enough to be a beard. His untucked white button-down, sleeves rolled up, made him look almost

227

professional until I got to the worn jeans and motorcycle boots.

I wanted to hate him.

He'd played me. Lied to me.

But he was still Riley. My Riley.

He glanced at me, his hazel eyes narrowing on my bare left hand. The engagement ring was on my dresser. We weren't planning to go out until later, and I didn't see the point in wearing the ring at home.

We weren't engaged. The ring was a prop. It meant nothing, but seeing it on my finger depressed me. I could put on a front for everyone else, but I knew the truth. I wanted that ring to be real. I wanted all of it to be real.

Was it better or worse that I'd had one night with him? One night where I really believed in love. In forever.

I couldn't decide.

My aching heart said it was worse to have tasted heaven only for it to turn sour. My brain repeated the old platitude about better having loved and lost, blah blah.

I'd loved and lost him once. I could have skipped doing it a second time.

I curled my hand into a fist and hid it under the table, pretending to ignore Riley's scowl.

"Where are we?" Cooper asked, getting everyone's attention. Aiming the tip of his pen at me and then Riley he said, "You two went out yesterday, pumped the gossip machine through Sloane. Any action since then that we haven't heard about?"

Riley tapped his pencil on the pad of paper. "Nothing since the yellow hyacinths and begonia on the seventeenth. Abigail is working on a benefit next week, co-sponsored by the Winters foundation. It would be a good opportunity to be seen."

"I thought all the tickets were spoken for," I said, remembering Abigail mentioning it at dinner the night I'd stayed with them. I wasn't a big fan of formal affairs. I wouldn't have anything to wear. But Riley was right; it would be an excellent place to be seen. All the best gossips would be there.

"I asked her to hold back a few tickets, just in case we needed them," Aiden said.

"Sophie and I will go," Gage offered.

"So that's settled," Cooper said, making a note. "Between now and then?"

"I have some ideas for lunch, dinner out," Riley said. "What do we have from the flowers?"

"No trace evidence worth a damn," Cooper said. "We still don't know where they came from, and the account that paid for the delivery goes back to a prepaid credit card and a dummy email."

I looked from Cooper to Knox. "I don't understand how after all this time we have no clue who it is. How many times has he sent me flowers? He's here somewhere. He's watching me. You guys are supposed to be the best. How does he keep getting away from you?"

"Lise," Cooper said, looking pained, his voice placating. "I know this is frustrating. We're going to get this guy. He's been different than other stalkers we've dealt with. More careful. He resists escalating, getting sloppy. These last few weeks are the closest we've come to pushing him into making a mistake."

"He hasn't made one yet," I muttered, under my breath.

"No, but he sent three arrangements in less than two weeks. I'd call that an escalation," Knox said.

I looked across the table at Riley, meeting his gaze for less than a second before my eyes skipped away. "I just want this to be over. Tell me what to do. I'll do anything. I don't care if it's dangerous. Just tell me what to do."

Riley leaned forward and pointed one finger at me. "No. No way, Lise. The idea is to push him into escalating. To push him into getting sloppy. All you do is pretend to be happily engaged to me. Safely engaged to me. You're not going to *do* anything."

"Do you have any idea how hard it is to be passive? To do nothing? I admit running away from home and staying away was not a great plan. But at least it was doing something. This is just—waiting. Waiting and hoping. It's driving me nuts."

"Lise, I know you're frustrated," Cooper said again, "but—"

"She's not wrong," Riley said, interrupting Cooper. Cooper shot him an annoyed look, one Riley ignored. "We've been doing the same thing for over ten years. Protecting Annalise, trying to figure out who's sending the flowers and the gifts. None of it's working. We're looking in the wrong direction."

"What do you mean, Riley?" Aiden said.

"I mean, I don't think Lise's stalker is a stranger. I think it's someone she knows. I think it's someone all of you know. And I think it has to do with Anna Winters."

Riley sat back, apparently waiting for a response. He got nothing but blank stares.

"Riley, that's a stretch, don't you think?" Cooper asked, his voice strained as if he were trying to be patient. "Annalise had a lot of media on her when she was younger. She was an uncommonly pretty little girl in the middle of a scandal, and it shouldn't have surprised anyone that she drew the wrong attention. I don't know why you think this has to do with Anna."

"And I don't know why you're so resistant to the idea that it might," Riley shot back. "This isn't the first time I've brought it up and every time you shoot me down. Annalise looks like her mother. And there's a lot we don't know about Anna Winters."

"Are you suggesting we investigate my mother?" Gage asked, his voice tight.

The vein in his neck throbbed. Gage was pissed. I didn't like the idea either. My mother was dead. Her secrets were hers, and they'd died with her. The idea of digging in to her past felt wrong. Disloyal.

But... Before I could tease out the logic, Riley put it into words for me.

"Your mother and father were murdered," he stated baldly. "Unless you believe the murder/suicide story?" he asked, one eyebrow raised, knowing none of us thought for a second my father had killed my mother and then himself. It was the police department's favorite theory, but there was no way it was true.

"No, but—," Aiden said.

Riley cut him off. "There were no signs of forced entry. Whoever killed them, your parents let the murderer in the house. It could've been a stranger, but what stranger would've come all the way to their door? I know no one used the gates back then, but their house isn't exactly in plain sight."

"My father looked into it," Knox said. "There was nothing to find."

"That's bullshit," Riley said. "I liked your father, but he was twisty as hell, and you know it. Just because he didn't tell you what he knew about the murders, doesn't mean he didn't know anything."

"Watch it, Flynn," Cooper said, his ice blue eyes narrowed dangerously.

"No, I won't, goddammit. This plan puts Annalise's life on the line. We're using her to push this guy, and if there is even the slightest chance he had anything to do with the murders, we have to be smart. We have to be fucking careful. We cannot afford to be blind."

"Yeah, well, it sounds like you're accusing our father—," Cooper started to say.

"I'm not accusing Maxwell of anything except having information he didn't share," Riley said. "You know, you said yourself that his fingerprints are all over Anna's missing son. My guess is she asked him to hide the kid, and he did. But the truth is we don't know. There are a lot of people who were involved with Anna and James, Olivia and Hugh."

"Who do you think we should be looking at?" Aiden asked, quietly.

"I don't know," Riley said. "But all of you assumed it was a man leaving those pictures of the murders, and it turned out to be Marissa Archer. A socialite from the country club wasn't on my list of suspects either, but there you go. Perfect example. Here's another one, did you know your uncle William used to date Anna when she was still Anna Marlow?"

"No way," I said, in disbelief. Uncle William and my mother? "When? She and my dad started dating in college."

"Before that," Riley said.

"How did you find that out?" Knox asked.

"It was in your father's files on the murders," Riley said.

"And what the fuck were you doing going through our father's files?" Knox demanded, his voice rising.

"What you should have done years ago. Looking for any

information that would help me figure out what the fuck is going on."

"You had no right—"

"I had every right," Riley shouted, surging to his feet. "Are you serious? Do you think there's anything I wouldn't do to keep Lise safe?"

Riley and Knox glared at each other, Cooper looking between them, his eyebrows knit together. I couldn't tell if he was going to break up the fight or jump in. My head was reeling.

Uncle William and my mother? Maxwell Sinclair hid my missing half-brother? So many secrets. So much I didn't know about my parents.

"Settle down, both of you," Cooper said. "Riley's got a point."

"It's not William," Knox said, dismissively. "I'll grant you, it does look like our dad had something to do with hiding the kid, and we don't know why. We're working on it. But just because he's mixed up with that doesn't mean he has anything to do with Lise's stalker. Anna Winters died a long time ago. Years before the stalking started."

"Eight years," Riley clarified. "And at sixteen Lise was a dead ringer for her mother. The hair, the eyes—I've seen pictures."

"That doesn't prove anything. It's a guess. You're trying to pull together random information—"

"That doesn't mean I'm wrong," Riley said.

"Doesn't mean you're right either. But if you want to play that game, maybe it's you," Knox said, evenly.

"What the fuck does that mean?" Riley asked.

"It means there were three different times over the last eleven years when you were in close proximity to Annalise just before she received a delivery of flowers."

Riley shook his head in disbelief. "No shit, Knox. She was one of my cases. I was keeping an eye on her. I was in close proximity to Lise more than three times over the last eleven years."

"True," Knox said. "But the three times I'm thinking of weren't part of her casework."

"You're wasting time," Riley said. "You know it's not me. This started way before I knew her, before I knew any of you."

"I know you've been in love with her for twelve years. I know it was enough to get you to risk your job, more than once. Looking back, maybe you signed on with us, maneuvered your way onto her case because you were already obsessed with her. Maybe you've been in love with her a lot longer than twelve years."

"Stop," I said, the word erupting from my mouth while my brain was still reeling from the accusations flying back and forth across the table. "Riley is not obsessed with me. He's not in love with me. Stop being an ass, Knox. None of us wants to think this is someone we know. But he's right. It could be anyone. Have you looked in on Marissa Archer lately?"

Marissa Archer had been caught leaving pictures of my parent's murders for us to find. She'd started with Jacob, then moved on to Vance, and had finally been caught trying to break into Charlie's house. We still weren't exactly sure why. When she'd been arrested, she told Charlie the real murderer was still out there, but as soon as her son and her lawyer got to her, she'd stopped talking. The last I'd heard she was safely contained in a private facility for the mentally ill.

Aiden's voice was hard when he said, "No change. She's not talking. Literally. The last report was that she'd suffered a psychotic break and wasn't expected to recover. She's a dead end."

"So there's no way she's orchestrating flower deliveries from her padded cell?" I asked, only half kidding.

"No," Cooper said, shortly.

"Maybe it's Sloane," I offered, trying to lighten the mood.

"Wishful thinking," Gage muttered under his breath.

"I know, right?" I whispered back.

Riley shook his head at me, the side of his mouth quirked up in a half smile. "You don't want it to be Sloane," he said. "She's planning to make you a ton of money."

"There is that," I agreed. "Anyway, if she was the stalker, she'd be after my twin, not me."

"Maybe if she was, Maggie would take her down, once and for all," Gage said.

Maggie did not appreciate the way Sloane tried to hit on her husband. Vance loved his wife and actively disliked Sloane, but it still bugged Maggie. It bugged me too, and Vance was my brother, not my husband.

"So what do we do now?" I asked. Joking aside, if we were going to look at people we knew, the suspect list swung from zero to more than I could count.

"I want to go back to the house," Riley said. "Lise and I were there yesterday, and there were pictures missing from the mantle. We didn't stay long." He shot a careful glance at me. "But I need to go back and look again. There may be more missing than just a few pictures."

"I'll go with you," Knox said.

"So will I," Gage said. "I was almost eleven when they died. I may remember better than Annalise what belonged where."

"Gage," I said, quietly, reaching out and taking his hand

in mine. I squeezed his fingers, not knowing how to put into words what I'd felt being in that house again. The longing. The memories. The sense of a life interrupted, lost to tragedy and time.

I couldn't decide if I'd wanted to curl up on the couch in front of the fireplace or never set foot in the house again. All these years we'd told ourselves Winters House was home. And in a way, it was. Our fathers had been brothers and best friends. My brothers and I had been running tame in Uncle Hugh's house since we could walk. Aiden and his siblings had been the same in our house.

But Winters House wasn't really my home. That house in the woods with its shingles and stone—that was home, and it hurt to be there.

Low enough so only I could hear him, Gage said, "I haven't been in the house since I came back. I want to go. I want to see if I can help."

"You don't have to stay if it's too hard," I said, squeezing his hand again.

"I won't. I promise," he said. Gage was trying to make me feel better, but I knew he would stay no matter how painful it was. Leaning over, he kissed me on the temple and said, "I have to stay to keep Knox from riling up your boy."

"He's not my boy," I muttered.

Gage just laughed and got up looking at Riley and Knox in turn. "I have to get into the office later today. Let's go do this."

"Don't leave the house until I get back," Riley said to me.

I rolled my eyes in response. I wasn't going anywhere unprotected. Knowing the stalker had been in my parent's home, had taken pictures off the mantle and who knew what else, had left me more freaked than usual.

Cooper, Aiden, and I watched the other three leave. As soon as they were gone Aiden said to Cooper, "You planning to take another pass through your father's files?"

Cooper gave him a long, steady look. The two of them had been friends almost as long as they'd been alive. They were tight, but Cooper had been thrown by his father's presumed death and further messed up by learning that Maxwell had something to do with hiding my missing half-brother. I could understand. None of us were eager to start digging into our parent's pasts.

They were dead, and we didn't want to risk our happy memories. The truth was a pretty ideal. In reality, it could be ugly. And pointless. How much did I really want to know what had happened to them?

"I think I have to," Cooper said. "I missed William and Anna dating in college. It must've been a side note or something because I can promise you it's not front and center in any of the files or I would've known."

"We're all a little fucked up over our parents," Aiden said.

"Truer words," Cooper agreed. "But, Flynn is right. We have tunnel vision. All of us. The harder we look for the baby Anna gave up, the more the search turns in on itself. It's not an accident, and it's got my father's fingerprints all over it. God knows I loved him, but Flynn's right about that too. My dad was a twisty bastard. Good father. Sometimes even a decent husband. But he had very specific ideas about loyalty and honesty. We did not always have the same view of right and wrong."

"Do you think he's dead?" I asked Cooper. "Your dad?"

Cooper sighed. "I don't know. I want him to be alive, but if he is, and I get my hands on him, he'd better have a good fucking explanation."

I stood and pushed my chair back. "I'm going to my room to mess with my camera, start sorting through all those pictures. If Sloane's serious about showing my work, I need to have some work put together for her to show."

"Lise?" I met Cooper's eyes. "Put the ring back on. Even in the house."

I nodded and left the dining room. I felt like I was on a treadmill and an invisible hand had just cranked up the speed. I was sprinting to keep up with no idea where I was going or what would happen when I got there.

CHAPTER TWENTY-THREE

ANNALISE

The second house search was a bust. Gage said it looked as if someone had been through my father's desk, but it was impossible to tell when, or what they were looking for.

It would have been perfectly natural after he died for my uncle or aunt to have gone through his things looking for paperwork to settle the estate. That applied to pretty much everything in the house. If we'd been hoping they'd discover something concrete, we were all disappointed.

We were back playing the waiting game, and my nerves were stretched tight. I was used to feeling free. As free as anyone could be, that is. I'd always had a job, and rent to pay, but when I wasn't working, I hadn't had any obligations.

Living on the run had been lonely, but it also meant that the only one in charge of me was me. Now that I was home, I had a whole crew of people who loved me and were more than happy to tell me what I could and couldn't do. I loved them right back, but they were making me crazy.

My camera cradled in my hands, I snuck down the hall

toward the french doors, hoping to sneak out across the terrace and into the gardens. I wasn't going far. Not even out of sight of the house. I just needed some air.

The peonies were almost gone, and I wanted to photograph them while I still could. I'd always loved their rich, sweet scent, the delicate pink of the blooms and the wild abundance of petals. They came and went so fast if you didn't catch them you'd have to wait a whole year until they bloomed again.

"Where are you going?" Riley asked from behind me.

I couldn't help my startled jerk, almost dropping my camera at the sound of his voice. "Just outside to take some pictures."

"I'll come with you," he said.

"No, I just want some air and some quiet," I said.

Riley looked around the silent house and raised an eyebrow. Okay, it wasn't quiet I needed so much as to be away from him.

"You're not wearing your ring," he said in a low voice, his eyes on my left hand, on my bare ring finger.

"I forgot," I said.

We both knew I hadn't forgotten. I was doing my best to keep my emotions under control. To keep my head in the game and off Riley. Seeing that ring on my finger didn't help.

Riley's eyebrows pulled together, then relaxed as he said, "Take your pictures. In a few hours, we'll leave to go shopping for the benefit. I made reservations for dinner. You'll want to dress up a little."

"Fine," I said. I could have asked where we were going, but I didn't care. The point was to get out and be seen together. Whatever restaurant Riley had chosen, it was guaranteed to be filled with people who would spread the word of our romantic dinner. My stomach turned at the thought.

"Lise—" Riley started before the ring of his phone interrupted him.

I knew that ring tone. The gate house. My stomach cranked tight. Here we go, I thought, bracing.

"What is it?" Riley asked, brusquely. "What are you doing at the gatehouse?" He was quiet for a beat then said, "Bring it up."

He shoved his phone in his back pocket and gave me a considering look.

"Another delivery?" I asked.

"Yes. But different. A small box. And it wasn't dropped off. The guard found it."

"Found it? Where was it?"

Different was good if it meant the stalker might make a mistake, but this was weird.

"Knox was in the guard house. He's bringing it up."

"Why was Knox at the guard house?" I asked.

Riley shook his head and turned for the front door. I followed him. Together, we watched Knox's black SUV come up the drive, through the courtyard gates, and pull to a stop in front of the door. His expression was unreadable as he got out of the car, carrying a clear plastic bag containing a small black box.

I stared at that box in expectant revulsion as if it was an explosive timed to go off any second.

I didn't want to see. Didn't want to know what was inside.

I had to. It would be all too easy to hand everything over to the men, to let them shut me out. This was my life, messed up as it was, and I had to know.

We stepped back to let Knox in, following him to the

dining room. He took a seat, setting the plastic bag, and the black box inside, on the dining room table. Putting on a pair of protective gloves, he said, "Don't touch it. I need to get back to the office and have it checked for prints and trace."

Gripping the box at the corners, leaving as much surface area as possible untouched, Knox drew the box from the plastic bag and set it on top.

"Have you opened it?" I asked.

Knox shook his head. "Not yet. We scanned it. My guess is earrings or a necklace."

He opened the lid of the black velvet jeweler's box, and my knees turned to water. I sank into the chair beside Knox and let out a long breath.

The diamonds in the box shone like fire against the black velvet, small, perfectly shaped stones, set in platinum, arranged in the shape of lilies. Two of them. Knox had been right; it was a pair of earrings. The last Mother's Day present we'd given her before she died, chosen by Gage, Vance, Tate, and I, and paid for by my father.

My breath hitched in my chest, and I drove my fingernails into my palms. Old habits die hard, but the pinch of pain in my hands did the trick, driving back the tears that threatened to well in my eyes. Tears wouldn't do me any good.

"How did he get these?" I asked, my voice shaking only a little.

"You recognize them?" Riley asked, gently. His hand rubbed soothingly across my shoulders, settling on the back of my neck. I didn't answer aloud, only nodded.

My hand floated forward, fingertip almost touching one of the sparkling diamond petals before Riley took my wrist and drew it back.

"Don't touch them. We'll get them tested and give them

back to you as soon as we can, but until then, don't touch them."

I nodded again. Stupid. I knew better, and Knox had reminded us not to touch them. I just... They were my mother's. We'd seen them in the jewelry store and all four of us, for once, had immediately agreed she had to have them. Even Tate, only five years old, had pointed at the diamond lilies and said, "Those. Those are mama's flowers."

She'd worn them almost every day after we gave them to her. Now they were here, delivered by an unseen hand, stolen somehow. When? It looked like Riley had been right about our leaving the jewelry unsecured. What else was missing? Aunt Olivia might have known, but with her gone, there was no telling.

"The guard never saw who delivered them?" Riley asked.

"No. We've been having some trouble with the exterior cameras, the signals flickering, so I came by to take a look. A gift bag was sitting on a stone just off the drive, about twenty feet from the guard house."

"And the cameras didn't catch it?" I asked. Riley's hand squeezed the back of my neck in reassurance.

"No. The signal goes fuzzy, blinks, and when it comes back the bag is on the rock."

"How is that possible?" I asked, turning to look at Riley, and then at Knox.

"It's not," Knox said.

"Did you call Jackson?" Riley asked. To me, he said, "It's possible but unlikely. There are devices that can scramble the signal, but they're hard to get a hold of. If our stalker is using one, he or she has access to tech above and beyond what the average citizen can get his hands on. Even the average wealthy citizen. Lucas would know where we should look."

"I'll talk to him when I get back," Knox said, closing the black jeweler's box and sliding it back in the plastic bag. "He needs to take a look and tell us if someone is scrambling the signal, or if it's something else."

"What kind of something else?" I asked.

Knox leveled his dark gaze on Riley. "It's starting to look like an inside job," he said in an even, emotionless tone.

Riley went stiff. "Don't dance around it, Knox. Say what you're thinking."

"I think that you were in that house twice this week. You had plenty of opportunity to lift these earrings. You absolutely had the opportunity to plant them on the rock."

"And the cameras? I'm not a systems guy," Riley said. His hand dropped from the back of my neck and he stepped away from the table, crossing his arms over his chest.

"Who knows?" Knox said, shrugging one shoulder. "We've got the equipment. Maybe we should do an inventory and see what's missing. Even if you didn't take it from the supply room, you know where to get it."

Riley looked from Knox to me. His eyes searched mine, waiting for something. I sat there, frozen, Knox's accusation barely registering. It wasn't possible that Riley was the stalker. Memories flashed through my mind; Riley in the hospital all those years ago, Riley holding me after a delivery of flowers.

I couldn't believe Knox was right. But Riley had lied to me about who he was, lied about so many things. Was I just a fool who wanted to believe so much that she ignored the obvious?

Riley was done waiting for me to speak. Raising one

eyebrow, he said, "What do you think? I don't hear you jumping to defend my honor, Lise."

I stared up at him, the accusation in his hazel eyes striking a blow to my heart. My gut shouted, *No.*

No way Riley had anything to do with this. He'd never hurt me intentionally. I wanted to tell Knox to go to hell. To stop wasting our time looking at Riley, when all Riley had ever done was defend me and try to keep me safe.

I opened my mouth to speak, and nothing came out. I wanted to believe Riley.

I *had* believed Riley. I'd fallen for everything he'd ever said to me right up until he'd admitted it had all been a lie. He'd been lying to me from the day we'd met.

When it came to Riley, my instincts were all wrong.

At my silence, pain flashed through Riley's eyes. With a hard nod of his head, he said, "Fine. I don't know why I'd be surprised. When have you ever believed in me? The first time we hit a rough spot, you sent your brother to dump me and took off. That's your M.O., isn't it? Things get hard, and you run. You shut down, lock me out."

"That's not fair," I protested.

"Who said any of this was fair? I lied to you at the beginning. I'm sorry for that. But we have a second chance. How many people ever get a second chance? And you're throwing it away because of a mistake I made over a decade ago. You don't have the guts to take a risk."

"That's not fair," I repeated, this time in a whisper. "You're twisting things. You didn't just lie once, a decade ago. You kept lying until I caught you a few days ago. Big difference. And I didn't run away because I was afraid of the risk, I ran to keep you safe, you asshole. Maybe it was wrong, but I did it because I loved you."

"If that's the story you want to tell yourself," Riley said.

"From where I'm standing, this is the same thing all over again. You want to believe Knox? You want to think I'm the one doing this? Have at it. I'm not going to beg you to believe in me. I shouldn't have to. And when we catch this guy, and you have proof it's not me, don't come asking me to give you another chance."

He turned and left the dining room. His boots echoed through the entry hall, followed by the slam of the front door.

Knox picked up the plastic bag holding the black jeweler's box. "Stay inside. Set the alarm behind me. I don't like that this guy was so close to the house. Until Riley gets back, keep the alarm on, and don't go anywhere."

"Got it," I said.

So much for photographing the peonies. I wanted to ask him if he really believed his accusations against Riley. Before the question could fully form in my mind, I knew there was no point in asking.

What Knox thought didn't matter.

I was afraid to trust Riley. Afraid to trust myself. But I knew, down to my bones, that Riley would never hurt me. Not like this. He'd lied. A lot. But sending those flowers, my mother's earrings, fabricating his own accident and near overdose. There was no way.

I followed Knox to the door and watched him drive away, Riley in the passenger seat of the big black SUV. When Riley came back, I'd talk to him. We couldn't go on as we were, and he was right. If I wanted any kind of life, with or without him, I had to stop running. I had to stop being afraid to risk my heart.

Easier said than done. I locked the door and set the alarm, the quiet suddenly oppressive. Abel was at the market. Mrs. W was running errands. Sophie and Aunt

Amelia were out with Charlie, but they'd said they'd be back for lunch in an hour or so. The house was big, but rarely empty, especially since Sophie and Aunt Amelia had moved in, even less so since Gage had come home.

Any other day I would have savored the quiet, but the specter of the stalker coming so close to the gatehouse to leave his gift of my mother's earrings made me uneasy. The alarm system, with its cameras and motion sensors, was a safety blanket. What if he'd gotten to more than the cameras? What if he had a way around the door or window sensors? What if he was inside the house?

Panic had my heart racing. I took a deep breath, then another, and walked down the hall to my rooms in a measured, controlled pace. Knox would not have left if he thought the alarm was compromised. Sophie, Mrs. W, Abel, Amelia, and Charlie would all be home soon.

In the meantime, I had work to do. I sat at my desk and flipped open my laptop. Time slipped away as I flipped through the photographs I had stored there, evaluating each one, trying to decide what was worth a second look.

The stiffness in my neck felt as if I'd been sitting there for hours, but it couldn't have been that long. When I heard the beep of the alarm being deactivated, I stood and stretched. I'd go help Mrs. W unload her purchases, maybe help Abel make lunch if he'd let me.

I'd barely cleared my bedroom door when an arm came up, closing around my neck, cranking tight against my windpipe and cutting off my air. My mouth gaping like a fish, I reached up to claw at my captor. A sharp sting flared behind my ear, growing, heating, spreading through my veins like fire, leaving me weak and dizzy.

My vision blurred and swooped as I was turned upside down, hanging over a shoulder, my hair swinging, almost dragging across the hardwood floor. Where were we going? Down the hall? Did I hear the door close?

My head spun. I thought I smelled freshly cut grass, flowers. The damp, loamy scent of the woods. Where was the sun? I couldn't get my bearings, couldn't force my mind to function.

I blinked, trying to clear my eyes, seeing only the blur of dark shoes below lighter pants, hearing only the shuffle of feet and the heavy sound of breathing. My vision faded to grey and my brain shut down before I could save myself.

Was I dying? I could be dying. I wasn't ready. I wanted my second chance.

A second chance to save myself.

A second chance at everything.

Chapter Twenty-Four

Riley

This wasn't the first time Knox had gotten on my nerves, but it was the first time I'd considered swinging my fist into his face. He was driving, so I held back. I didn't for a second believe that he thought I was the stalker, so what the fuck?

"What was that about?" I demanded. "Why the fuck would you make Annalise think I took the earrings or fucked with the cameras?"

Knox slid his eyes in my direction for a long moment. "I didn't say it was you. I just pointed out that you had the opportunity."

"Yeah, but why? You don't think it's me," I said, watching his face. I maybe, possibly, saw the corner of his mouth twitch. Knox had a first-rate poker face.

"Maybe I do," he said.

"Fuck you," I said, without heat. "I don't need you confusing her. She's confused enough as it is."

"That's on you," he said. "You had the perfect chance to tell her the truth when you talked her into this fake engagement. You're the one who confused her. I told you to fix it. You're not fixing it."

"And you are? By telling her I'm the stalker? How the fuck is that helping?"

Knox laughed. "Did I say I was helping? What makes you think I'm on your side?"

I let out a grunt of irritation and stared through the front windshield, again fighting back the urge to plant my fist in his face.

"Annalise is like a sister," he said, the taunt gone from his voice. "We grew up together, and however fucked up my family is, the Winters family is on a whole other level. The money, the murderers, the paparazzi. It's fucking chaos, has been ever since Anna and James died. I was just a kid, but I remember like it was yesterday. One minute we're all the fucking Waltons—"

"I don't think the Waltons lived in mansions in Buckhead," I interrupted.

"Whatever. You know what I mean. Bedtime stories and picnics. Happy family shit. The next Anna and James are dead, the police are saying he killed her, and Hugh has to keep the gates shut because everybody wants pictures of the grieving kids. Just when things started to calm down, some psycho starts sending notes and presents to Annalise. She's had a shit time of it."

"I know. I know all of this," I said, annoyed. Knox scowled at me.

"No, you don't. Not really. And maybe you think that once you find this asshole sending her flowers you'll get rid of him, convince her to forgive you, and you two will have smooth sailing. Walk off into the sunset and get your happily ever after."

I didn't take the bait. I wasn't going to admit that's exactly what I was thinking.

"If it were that simple,' Knox said, "I'd have kept my mouth shut. But whoever ends up with Annalise—that guy is going to have to be willing to fight for her. She's going to have to be willing to fight for him. Because her life is always going to be complicated. She'll always be a Winters. No matter what their last name is, her kids will be Winters. If either of you is going to run scared, might as well find out now."

"You're an asshole," I said, knowing he was right about all of it. "When did you get so talkative? I don't think I've ever heard you string this many words together."

"Fuck you."

That was more like it. "That doesn't explain why you were trying to pin the stalking on me. That's fucked up, Knox."

"You're both idiots," he said, shaking his head. "I was hoping she would defend you. The fact that she didn't tells me how much you fucked with her head by lying. I figured the two of you would gang up on me, but instead, you turned on each other. You've got a lot of work to do. And you might want to figure out exactly what you want from her. If you're not going to step up, then back off and let her go."

"I'm in love with her," I said.

"No shit. But love isn't enough."

"What more is there?" I asked.

Love was fucking huge, so big my chest burned, my lungs got tight when I let it loose, let myself really feel everything inside me for Annalise. How could that not be enough?

Knox gave me another of those sidelong looks. "When you figure it out, maybe you'll be able to get your girl back."

I didn't have an answer for that, so I kept my mouth shut and stared out the window. We were almost to the Sinclair Security building. I needed the distraction of work. I needed answers about those earrings. We neared the mirrored building that housed the Sinclair Security offices.

The company took up most of the four-story structure. When I'd first signed on with Sinclair, they'd owned the building but leased most of it to other tenants. As Maxwell had become increasingly distracted by other things and his sons had taken over, Sinclair Security had expanded. Now only the first floor had outside tenants. The rest was all theirs.

Knox pulled into the underground garage. I followed him to the elevator, then down the hall to Cooper's office, a floor above my own. Cooper was on the phone when Knox opened his door. Cooper took one look at us and ended his call.

"What happened?" he asked. Knox answered by dropping the plastic bag containing the black jeweler's box onto his desk. Cooper pulled gloves from his desk drawer and eased the box open, leaving it in the bag. His ice blue eyes warmed, then went dark as he recognized the earrings.

"How did you get these?" he asked, examining the earrings with narrowed eyes.

Knox explained about the gift bag left on the rock. When he got to the cameras, Cooper held up a finger to stop him and picked up the phone. "Jackson. In my office. We have a problem with the security at Winters House." A pause. "Cameras. Get in here."

He hung up the phone and gestured for Knox to finish.

When Knox was done, he pointed to the earrings and said, "Do you remember these?"

Knox shrugged. "Not really. Lise did."

"She would. She and her brothers picked them out," Cooper said, sadness lurking in his eyes as he slowly closed the velvet box, hiding the diamond lilies.

"How do you remember that?" Knox asked.

"Anna lost them," Cooper said. "Or she thought she did. I overheard her telling Mom about it. She didn't want James or the kids to know they were missing and she couldn't figure out where they could be. I didn't remember them. What eleven-year-old notices his friend's Mom's jewelry? But Mom commented that Anna wore them every day. She went over to the house to help her look."

"Are we sure they didn't find them?" Knox asked. "Maybe they did, and these disappeared later."

"Maybe," Cooper said. He picked up the phone and dialed. After five rings, a female voice answered.

"Mom, Cooper. I have you on speaker."

"Cooper," the woman crooned, "You never call me anymore."

"I know, I'm sorry, mom. Work has been really busy."

"You're just like your father," she said, a wobble to her voice. "Always working. Never any time for me."

At her plaintive tone, Cooper's jaw tightened. Knox turned to look out the window. I didn't know Lacey Sinclair well. We'd only met a few times before her husband's car drove off that bridge, presumably with him inside. She'd moved to Florida shortly after, where she seemed to be spending her days playing cards and drinking gin.

"I'll try to get down there soon," Cooper said. "Or maybe you should go to Vegas for a vacation. Axel would love for you to come visit."

Knox let out a choked laugh and shook his head at Cooper, who sent him a devilish grin. The fourth Sinclair brother, Axel, ran the western division of the company out of Las Vegas and he most definitely would not appreciate his brothers siccing their mother on him and his wife, Emma.

"Ooh, that would be fun, I'll call him this afternoon," Lacey said.

"Mom, I need to talk to you about Anna Winters," Cooper said.

"Oh, Cooper. Do we need to rehash all of that? You know I don't like talking about Anna." Her voice wobbled again, this time I thought as much from emotion as alcohol.

"Mom, it's important. Do you remember a pair of earrings that went missing? The flowers the kids gave her?"

"The diamond lilies." Lacey exhaled a watery sigh. "She was heartbroken when she lost them. She couldn't imagine what could have happened to them. You know Anna didn't grow up like us. She never got used to having diamonds, and she was so careful with her jewelry. We looked everywhere."

"So you never found them?" Cooper pressed. "I remember her telling you they were lost, and you saying you'd help her look. But you never found them."

"No, we didn't. And we looked. Everywhere. Olivia helped. Oh, it was so silly, trying to keep it from James and the children..." She trailed off and then, her voice almost crisp, she asked, "Why are you asking about Anna's earrings? What's going on up there?"

Cooper hesitated, sharing a look with Knox. Silent communication passed between them, and Knox gave a shrug of one shoulder. Cooper looked back down at the phone on his desk and said, "Annalise is still having problems—"

"Annalise is home? You boys never tell me anything. Is she staying, or—"

"She's staying, mom but she's still having trouble. Remember the flowers? And the gifts?"

"Oh, that was so silly. So much fuss over a few flowers."

My hand fisted at my side and I had to remind myself that Lacey Sinclair was half drunk and didn't mean most of what she was saying. Knox paced to the window and looked out, making a sound in his throat that was almost a growl.

His voice coated in ice, Cooper said, "It's not silly, and it's more than a few flowers. Whoever it is has been following her back and forth across the country. People have been hurt, mom."

"What do you mean *people have been hurt?*" She asked, sharply. "It was only ever flowers, a few presents. Every girl should have a secret admirer."

This time Knox did growl. I paced across the room, trying to put as much distance as possible between me and the flighty, tipsy voice coming through the phone speakers.

His voice so tight his words were choppy with tension, Cooper said, "He sent Lise those earrings, and we're trying to figure out how he got them."

"Oh, well, I can't imagine. Anna lost them so many years ago."

"Okay, thanks, Mom. I'll call you tomorrow." Cooper stabbed a finger at the phone and hung up on his mother. Knox opened his mouth, but before he could get a word out, Cooper lifted his hand and said, "Just let it go Knox. This isn't about mom."

I tried to clear my head of anger at Lacey Sinclair and her thoughtlessness. "What are the chances Anna lost those earrings, and they just happened to turn up over twenty years later?"

Knox said, "Zero. I don't believe in coincidence."

"Neither do I," Cooper said. "My bet is Anna never lost the earrings. They were stolen, probably right from her jewelry box. If she was careful with her jewelry, like mom said, she wouldn't have left them sitting around."

"Someone with access to the house. A close friend," I said. "That narrows it down."

"Not necessarily. James and Anna didn't entertain as much as Olivia and Hugh, mostly because the big house was better suited for it, but they had a Christmas party that year. Lots of people in and out of the house. I remember because all of us kids were invited, but we got in huge trouble for playing in the snow in our dress-up clothes." He looked at Knox. "Remember? It snowed that year right before Christmas."

"You nailed Vance in the face with a snowball," Knox said with a grin. "He had a black eye for a week. The moms were so pissed."

"Dad thought it was funny," Cooper said, shaking his head.

"So did James and Hugh," Knox said. "That was the last —" Knox fell abruptly silent. Cooper cleared his throat.

Getting us back on track, I asked, "When did Anna lose the earrings?"

"Shit. I didn't think to ask that. I'll have to call her back," Cooper said with an aggrieved sigh. He picked up the phone, then set it back down when Lucas Jackson stepped into the room.

"I talked to the gatehouse about the cameras," he said, "and checked the feeds. That's what took me so long."

"And?" Cooper asked, eyeing the phone, impatient.

"It's electronic interference, not someone hacking the feeds. Whatever they're using, it's high-end. Not easy to get your hands on."

"Is it something we have?" Knox asked. When he caught my glare, he said, "Relax, I'm just asking."

Lucas looked from me to Knox, then shook his head. "It is, but all our equipment is accounted for. Whoever this is, they're either very well-connected—NSA, covert ops, shit like that—or they're involved with some really sketchy people."

"So, who do we know who would've had access to Anna Winter's jewelry box in nineteen ninety-five and is connected with the kind of people who could provide this level of tech?" Cooper asked.

The four of us stared at each other. The first criteria wasn't that hard. A lot of people would've had access, especially considering the Christmas party that year. But the second?

"Fuck," Cooper said, putting all of our thoughts into one word.

Lucas's phone beeped in a distinctive trill that sounded like bells. "Charlie," he said, under his breath. He pulled the phone from his back pocket and answered. "What's up, Princess?" He fell silent, dark brows drawing together, green eyes suddenly intent, focused as a laser beam. After what felt like an hour he said, "We're on our way. You, Sophie, Amelia, and Mrs. W go straight to the gatehouse and stay there. Understand me, Princess? Do not go wandering around. Do not stay in the house, even if the alarm is on. Go to the gatehouse and stay with the guards. Text me when you're there. Promise me."

Whatever Charlie said must have satisfied Lucas because he hung up the phone and shoved it back into his pocket. "Annalise is missing. Charlie, Sophie, and Amelia planned to eat lunch with her at the house. When they got there, Annalise wasn't there. Purse and camera are in her room, car keys on the board in the garage. Mrs. W thought she was with Riley."

I was already headed to the door, Cooper, Knox, and Lucas right behind me. Cooper clamped one hand on my shoulder and said, "I'm driving. Lucas, you see if you can access the camera feeds from the car, see if we can catch anything. She can't have gone far. We'll find her."

We would. I wouldn't stop until we found Annalise, no matter what it took. I just had to hope I wouldn't be too late.

CHAPTER
TWENTY-FIVE
ANNALISE

The room smelled like funeral flowers, waxy and sickly sweet. Light flickered, golden and soft.

Wrong.

Something was wrong.

My eyelids weighed a thousand pounds. I fought against their easing shut, fought against the lethargy in my muscles, the fog in my brain.

Feet shuffled on the carpet. A flick and hiss. Sulfur. I stared through the tangle of my eyelashes, fighting to open my eyes, struggling to put the pieces together. The smell. The light. Candles. Someone was lighting candles.

I blinked and tried to focus. White cotton with pink and green embroidery filled my vision. Climbing roses embroidered on my bedspread.

My stomach rolled as I realized where I was. My parent's house. My bedroom. And I wasn't alone.

I flexed my fingers. Wiggled my toes. I didn't think I'd been out that long, but I didn't really know. I wasn't wearing a watch, and the windup clock on my bedside table hadn't been set in years. Candlelight flickered in the room, but a beam of sunshine fell from the window across the bed.

If the sun was still up, I didn't think too much time had passed. A few hours, but no more. Maybe a lot less.

Staying still, I listened to the sounds of feet shuffling on the carpet. Another flick and hiss. Why all the candles? The smell was nauseating, the floral fragrance heavy and cloying. Maybe it wasn't the candles. Maybe it was fear. Or the drugs. I remembered the hallway—the arm around my neck, the stinging pain of the needle and everything going fuzzy.

I was in serious trouble. I shifted on the bed enough to reassure myself that I wasn't restrained. I was trying to decide if I should pretend I was still unconscious, or try to move, when a familiar voice said, "I know you're awake, Annalise."

I knew that voice, but I couldn't make myself believe. The puzzle pieces wouldn't fit. Gathering my strength, I rolled to my back, bracing my palms at my sides, sitting up in halting jerks. I dipped to the side and had to catch myself before I fell over, my body still weak, sluggish from the drugs.

"Careful, sweet girl. You don't want to fall off the bed and hurt yourself."

I couldn't look at him. It was horrible enough to know he'd brought me here. I couldn't look yet. My eyes on my knees, I braced my palms and pushed myself backward until I could lean against the headboard. When I was pretty sure I wasn't going to fall over again, I looked up.

Uncle William stood at the end of my bed, a box of matches in one hand, the charred stump of a used match in the other. His eyes should have been filled with the kindly affection I'd known my entire life, and they were, but behind that familiar expression burned something else.

Something mad.

Something dark. Hungry.

I flinched from him, though he hadn't made a move. As if everything were normal, he said, "Just give yourself a few minutes. The drugs will wear off. They weren't very strong, only enough to calm you down. I didn't want a fuss while we were still in the main house."

"Why are we here?" I asked, my voice shaking.

William set the box of matches on my vanity, laying the burnt stub beside a pile of others neatly arranged, side-by-side. White pillar candles glowed from every flat surface in the room—my vanity, my dresser, my bedside tables, even my camp trunk beside the closet. Beneath some, brass candlesticks gleamed in the flickering light. Some he'd placed without a holder, letting the wax drip to pool on the wood. The room was stuffy with them, the heat and scent dizzying.

He'd placed bundles of flowers between the candles. The purple-pink blooms of heliotrope. Eternal love. Blood red roses. The classic flower of true love. Roses should have been romantic, not terrifying.

William pulled out the white chair at my vanity and turned it to face the bed. He sat, his posture upright, one leg crossed over the other, as composed and proper as if he'd been in the formal living room of Winters House.

"I thought it was time we talked," he said.

"Talked about what?" I asked. My eyes slid to the door of my bedroom, half open, the hallway outside teasing me. So close, but William had positioned the chair so that he was almost exactly between me and the door.

"Don't play stupid, Annalise. I have you here in your bedroom, carried you through the woods while you were unconscious. I think you know where we stand."

"I don't think I do," I said, slowly.

I wasn't playing stupid.

Was he fucking kidding me? Okay, yes, the fact that he'd drugged me and carried me to my childhood home, laid me on my bed, brought me flowers, and lit a bunch of candles, pointed strongly to him being my psycho stalker.

I got that part.

I wasn't even close to being able to understand where we stood with each other.

The only thing I knew was that William stood between me and the door. Anything else he was going to have to explain, slowly and clearly, because I had no fucking clue what was going on.

"Annalise, you've been playing games with me," he said, patiently. "I understand women like to play games. I do. But I'm tired of it. It's been too many years. I'm getting old. You're getting older. I'm done dancing around each other. I'm ready for the next step."

"And what's the next step?" I asked, absolutely certain I did not want to know the answer.

William shook his head gently, as if in amusement, and said, "For us to be together, of course."

"What the hell does that mean?" I asked. The moment the angry words left my mouth, I knew they were a mistake. The darkness in William's eyes flared to life, freezing my heart in my chest.

Be smart, I told myself. *You're alone in a room with a seriously crazy man. Think. This is not the time to lose your temper. Stall him.*

Softly, I said, "I'm sorry, I just don't understand. You want us to be together?"

"I thought it was supposed to be your mother, you know. All those years ago. So much pain. I was so in love with her."

"With my mother?" I asked, prompting him for more. I'd seen enough movies. I knew I was supposed to keep him talking. Let him get out all the crazy and buy myself some time. Time for Charlie and Sophie to come home and realize I wasn't there. Time for Riley to find me.

"You never knew," he said. "I couldn't let her go. I couldn't let her out of my life, so I had to pretend. Pretend to be her friend, their friend. Pretend I didn't remember how it was. But I remembered everything. She was my light. She was my love. Everything was perfect and then she left me. For him." Rage simmered in his voice, darkened his eyes.

"When?" I asked, desperate to know despite my fear.

"Freshman year of college," he said, with a sigh. "I saw her on the first day, standing in line to register for classes. I bumped into her, and she turned around and looked at me with those blue eyes—" he let out a long breath, his gaze hazy with memory. "I asked her out right there, and for the first semester, we were inseparable. Then she went home over Christmas break, and when she came back, she broke it off."

"I'm sorry," I said, helplessly. I wanted to ask what had happened, if that was when she started dating my father, but I didn't want to push him the wrong way. I didn't know what would set him off.

"So was I. She came back only until spring break, and then she went home. She told everyone her mother was ill. I believed her, the bitch. But the whole time she was writing letters to James. Writing letters to my best friend and having my fucking baby."

I heard a shocked sound of surprise and realized it came from me. I slapped my hand over my mouth. I'd known my mother had had a child before she married my father, known she'd given him up. Charlie had found the adoption papers in the attic. But we'd never known how it happened or who the father had been.

"I'm sorry," I said again. I didn't want to say I was sorry; I wanted to ask him how he'd known, and what he'd done about it, and why he hadn't tried to take the child.

"She should have told me," he said, sending me a look so full of yearning and pain, sadness flashed through me before fear drove it out. "We would've gotten married. We would've had the perfect life. But she said we'd never be happy together, and the baby would be better off with a mother and a father who were ready for children. She said there were so many people who desperately wanted a child, and she wasn't ready to get married or be a mother. She wanted to be a doctor, and she didn't want me." His face collapsed on itself, twisting into a scowl. He barked out, "She had no right."

"How could you stay friends with her after that?" I couldn't help asking.

William looked at me, and his eyes softened. "If you can ask me that, you don't really understand love, Annalise. I hated her for leaving me. I hated her for taking my child. For destroying my dream of a happy family. And I hated James for stealing her heart from me. But it was easier to live with the hate than to live without my Anna."

"You killed them, didn't you?" I asked, my throat tightening on the words. It seemed so obvious now. Love twisted into hate, turned to rage and death.

But William's eyes widened in shock. "No. No, Annalise, no. Never. I was so angry. So angry with both of them. But I never would've hurt Anna. I thought about James. Considered it. A car accident, or a fire. Thought about how I could do it without getting caught. But I couldn't quite bring myself to cross that line."

"Then who?" It seemed impossible to believe that with all this crazy obsession they'd been murdered by a random intruder.

William's shoulders slumped, and he looked down at his hands. "I didn't kill them, my sweet girl. But it was my fault they died. I've lived with the guilt for so long. So long."

"How was it your fault? Who killed them?" I tried to restrain my shout, but the words spilled from my lips.

"That stupid bitch. Always in the way." William's head bobbed from side to side in a loose nod.

"Who?" I said again, control over my temper slipping. I needed to know who it was, what had happened, and I was forced to sit and wait while this crazy man tripped his way down memory lane.

"Marissa," he said on a long exhalation.

"Marissa Archer?" The socialite acquaintance of my parents who'd been caught leaving us pictures of the murder scene?

"Marissa," he confirmed. "That crazy bitch, she's lucky the police got to her before I could."

"Why would Marissa kill my parents?" I asked, lost in confusion. None of this made sense.

"We dated in high school. Knew each other our whole lives. I broke it off right before college. She was going to Vanderbilt, and I wanted to stretch my wings, live a little before we settled down. We expected we'd end up together, get married, but we didn't make any promises." He raised one shoulder in a half shrug and glared at me. "I didn't make her any promises."

"But she assumed?" I couldn't help pushing. Now that I had a hint of the truth, I needed more. I needed it all.

"That crazy, obsessive bitch," he said with a dismissive sneer. "She couldn't let go, even when I told her I was in love with Anna. Then when Anna started dating James, Marissa thought she could have me back. But after Anna, no woman was good enough. I fucked Marissa when I got lonely. She used to look a little like your mother—blond, blue eyes—but it wasn't the same."

"She killed my parents because she was jealous?" I asked, hating the uselessness of it all. So much anger and heartbreak. So much selfishness.

"In a way," he said, appearing lost in thought.

I glanced out the window, trying to gauge the time by the light. Not close to dusk, but that didn't tell me much. It could be just after lunch or hours later. I was betting on it being earlier. Charlie was expecting me. I'd be missed. I just had to hang on until someone looked here. Just hang on.

Keeping William talking was creepy, but not a hardship. I'd waited half my life for answers. I was going to wring every sick, twisted detail from William before this was over.

I had no doubt I'd get away from him. No matter what he had planned, I wasn't going to die. I refused.

"What does that mean, 'In a way'?" I asked, drawing him from his reverie. He looked at me in mild surprise.

"Anna, you know what it means."

CHAPTER TWENTY-SIX

ANNALISE

S hit.

I did not like him calling me Anna.

Whatever that meant, it couldn't be good. Escalation. It sounded so scientific, so analytical. Now that I was face to face with it, it was chilling. Whatever loose grip William had on reality, it was sliding away from him.

"I want to hear it from you," I said.

His eyes warmed, his lips curling in a gentle smile. "She never understood, Anna. She thought if she could get you to tell her where the child was, she could retrieve him and the three of us would make a family together. As if I could ever accept her as my wife. As if I'd want that bastard child."

Confusion swept through me. Didn't he want the baby?

"I thought the baby was yours," I said.

"I would have taken him then, Anna. I told you that. We could have married, told everyone he was early. But once you married James, had children with him, there was no way to bring the bastard you birthed back into our lives. Better to leave him wherever Maxwell put him."

"You don't know where he is?" I asked.

"The only one who did was Maxwell. But Marissa didn't believe you. She was furious about it. She said you slapped her and she lost her temper. Shot you, then James when he came for her. Killed you both by mistake like the stupid bitch she is."

Marissa. I couldn't picture it, couldn't imagine the woman I barely remembered having so much anger in her for my mother that it erupted into murder.

"And Uncle Hugh? Aunt Olivia? Was that Marissa, too?" The murders had been so much alike we'd always assumed the killer had been the same person.

William's eyes wouldn't meet mine. They fixed on the candles on my bedside table, the white wax dripping down the brass holder, streaming to the carpet below.

Slowly, he said, "That was a mistake."

The grief in his voice, real and raw, tore the breath from my lungs. "Why?" I cried. "Why kill them?"

"Because they knew," he roared. "They knew all of it, Marissa let something slip—probably on purpose, the cunt—and they knew. They were going to make it public, tell the investigators, sully your memory by telling everyone you'd had a bastard child. Tell everyone you'd rather give your baby up than marry me."

A fresh wave of horror washed over me. "You killed Uncle Hugh and Aunt Olivia to protect your reputation? To avoid gossip?"

He slammed his fist down on his knee and shouted, "To protect you. To protect your memory."

Forgetting his delusion that I was my mother, I said, "She was dead. She was dead, and you killed two people just to stop a little gossip."

"You don't know what you're talking about. I loved you, and you ruined everything. You and that fucking brat you gave up. All those years, even at the end with Maxwell, working so closely together, he refused to tell me where he hid the baby."

"You were working with Maxwell? At Sinclair Security?" I couldn't keep track, wasn't sure what was fact and what was William's version of the truth.

He let out a condescending laugh. "Of course not. We had other business. Things had slowed down at the firm. They were edging out some of the older partners in favor of young blood, but I will not be dismissed." He slammed his fist into his knee again in emphasis. "Maxwell had some... opportunities. Unsavory, I'll admit, but profitable. We were spending a lot of time together at the end, but still, he wouldn't tell me."

"Did you kill Maxwell?" I couldn't help asking.

"Of course not," he said, as if the question were ridiculous, obviously forgetting that he'd just confessed to murdering my aunt and uncle and covering up the murder of my parents.

"The business with Maxwell," I said, slowly, putting pieces together as I spoke, "the unsavory people...is that where you got whatever you used on the cameras?"

William gave me a sly smile but didn't answer.

"But you've been looking for the baby all this time," I said. "Even though you don't want him?"

"He's a loose end." William leaned forward, bracing his elbows on his knees, a sweet, gentle smile spreading across his face. "I didn't understand until your sixteenth birthday. She called you Annalise, but she might as well have given you her name. You are her. Just like your mother. Made for me. And I realized, Anna was lost to me, but I could have you."

Bile rose in my throat. I pressed my back into the headboard of my bed, revulsion driving me as far from William as I could get.

I inhaled slowly, fighting for calm.

I needed to keep him talking, needed to buy myself time.

Time for Riley to find me.

I realized, in the midst of this madness, that I had no doubt he would. By now Riley must know I was missing, and he would never give up, never stop. He was coming for me; I just had to hold on.

He'd been right. I hadn't trusted him. I hadn't seen that he'd lied for the same reason I'd run all those years ago. Because he was afraid to trust me. Afraid I'd turn him away, exactly the way I had. We'd both been wrong. Both been too afraid to be honest. Too afraid to believe.

I needed another chance. I had things to say to Riley, and I was not going to let William Davis steal Riley's love from me the way he'd already stolen so much. William didn't want me dead. If I could keep him talking, keep him distracted, I might be able to find a way out of this.

"That's why you started sending me things? Because you wanted us to be together?"

"I knew you'd understand my flowers," he said. "I chose them so carefully, collecting them from here and there. Anna was the one who taught me what they meant. I knew she would've taught you. All I had to do was claim you like I should've claimed her. I waited. I was patient. I gave you time. Even let you travel, see the country, sending you flowers along the way to remind you who you truly belonged to. I'm not angry about this game with Riley. I knew what you were telling me."

"What was I telling you?"

"That you were ready. You weren't going to marry him.

He's so far beneath you he isn't even worth considering. But you've never grown out of that teenage rebellion. Teasing me. Taunting me. I understand you better than you understand yourself, Anna."

William rose to his feet and walked to the end of the bed, looming over me even from several feet away. I was defenseless, and there was nowhere to run. The candlelight flickered in his eyes, illuminating the twist of emotions. Love and anger and lust.

I swallowed hard, tasting vomit in the back of my throat. A bulge distorted the front of his gray flannel pants, and I went dizzy, lightheaded with panic.

I would die before I let him touch me. I didn't want to die. I wanted to live, but I wasn't sure I could live through that. My eyes raced around the room, searching for a weapon, but there was nothing. It was a child's room. Stuffed animals and hair bows wouldn't protect me from William.

Desperate to keep him talking, to keep him away from me, I asked, "And your son? What are you going to do when you find him?"

William leaned forward, bracing a knee on the end of the bed. "He shouldn't exist. I'll get rid of him," he said, calmly. "And you and I can start anew. We'll have our own baby after we're married, just the way we were meant to all along."

"You're fucking insane," I whispered. William only laughed, a low, satisfied sound. He thought he'd already won. In his head, we were as good as married, my belly already round with his child.

I twisted to the side, gathering myself to lunge off the bed when he moved to block me, laying one hand on the comforter, then the other, crawling up the bed toward me. I kicked out with my bare foot, my heel glancing off his shoulder as he dodged me.

A grin stretched across his face, manic, exhilarated by the chase.

His hand closed around my ankle and yanked, dragging me down the bed and spreading my legs. I kicked with the other foot, catching him hard in the ribs. He let go of my ankle and let out a low, "Oof," before lunging to close his hands over my hips and pull me down the bed.

I rolled, twisting, flailing my arms, reaching for something, anything. My fingers closed around a pillow, and I swung, the pillow bouncing uselessly off William, careening into the air, knocking candles across my dresser to the floor.

He pinned me to the comforter, his breath hot on my cheek as he whispered, "I've always loved your spirit. This time, I'm going to break you, Anna. And when I'm done, you'll belong to me. Finally."

Light flashed in the corner of my eye. I looked to see flames climb the curtains on either side of the dresser, spreading in seconds to devour the ceiling, jumping to the swag on the other window, flowing across the carpet from the candles on the floor.

For a frozen moment, I watched in horror before I registered William's erection pressing into my leg, growing harder as I twisted against him, fighting to push him off.

His hands were on my jeans, yanking at the button, his weight holding my torso immobile. My legs kicked uselessly, my heels bouncing off the bed, toes jamming into his shins. He couldn't get leverage to pull my jeans off and still hold me down. He tugged at the denim, first over one hip, then the other, baring my skin inch by inch.

The smoke detector screamed a high pitched wail, first in my room, then in every room, the sound filling the house like the heavy smoke from the fire. I'd seen a grease fire once in a restaurant where I'd waited tables, knew how fast the flames could move. The future had narrowed to minutes if we didn't get out of this room. Out of this house.

My heart thudded, my body wild with panic, arms swinging, legs kicking. I caught him with a punch to the cheekbone, and he reared back, freeing me just enough to scramble to the side of the bed. With a roar he lunged over me, dragging at my jeans, pulling them almost off one hip.

My arm flailed, fingers reaching, desperate for one last chance, for something, anything. I couldn't see. The air burned my lungs. The tip of my finger grazed cold metal, and my heart surged.

Forgetting my jeans, I dug in my feet and pushed another inch toward the side of the bed, my fingers closing around the candlestick. I let myself fall limp, let William turn his attention back to dragging off my clothes and then I swung.

The candlestick struck him in the temple, and he toppled onto his side, his hand reaching for me as he fell. I rolled in the other direction, tossing the candlestick toward the open door, stumbling to my feet, coughing in the thick smoke as I yanked my jeans back up with both hands.

Running for the safety of the hall, I scooped up the candlestick and took off, William's footsteps pounding behind me.

Chapter Twenty-Seven

Riley

The SUV pulled up to the gatehouse, coming to a rolling stop just long enough for Lucas to leap out. He'd stay with the guard and the women until we gave him the signal that the property was secure. My heart pounded, my nerves drawn tight with fear for Annalise. I wanted to jump out of the SUV, go tearing through the house calling her name, but that wouldn't do any good.

Charlie, Sophie, and Amelia had already searched Winters House, along with Mrs. W. Annalise wasn't there. If she'd left the estate, it hadn't been in a vehicle or the guard would have seen it. She was here somewhere, but not in the house.

I walked through the front door, across the entry hall, to the terrace doors and stepped outside. The gardens were serenely beautiful in the afternoon spring light, the flowers swaying in the breeze, the lawn perfectly cut, the beds edged with precision.

Not a blade of grass was out of place. There was no sign of Annalise.

I stood still for a moment, my hands braced on my hips,

the weight of my gun at the small of my back reassuring. I wanted a target, a focus for my fear, for my fury. Someone had dared to take her, had forced her from her home. As soon as I found her, I'd make them pay.

"To the cottages or into the woods?" Cooper asked.

Going with my gut, I said, "Woods."

If I had been right, and this was about Anna, the house in the woods was as good a place to start as any. We took off at a jog, me in the lead, Knox and Cooper just behind. We'd just passed under tree cover, slowing to accommodate the lack of light and uneven ground, when Cooper's phone rang.

He listened for a few seconds and then said, "Call the fire department. When they get there, show them the way back. We'll clear the house if we can."

Fuck the bad light and uneven path. I put on a burst of speed, calling over my shoulder, "Fire department?"

If the house was on fire, and Annalise was inside, I didn't have a second to waste.

"Alarm went off at the house. Just a minute ago."

Fear was an icy ball in my chest as we cleared the woods. Smoke poured from the roof at the back of the house. We couldn't see flames yet, which might be a good sign. I wouldn't know until I found Annalise.

The front door was bolted, the handle refusing to turn. Stepping back, I drove my heel into the door beside the lock. It lurched under my blow, the bolt tearing halfway through the wood. I tried again, throwing all of my weight into my heel. Wood cracked as the door gave, swinging open to reveal a smoke-filled entry hall.

A shout echoed from the second level. I raced for the stairs, hearing Cooper tell Knox to check the first floor. Feet sounded above, running. A heavier tread followed, further away.

The thud of my feet on the stairs drowned out the noise from above. I pulled my shirt up over my mouth, trying to filter the thick, acrid smoke. My eyes teared, blurring my vision. Looking up through the rail of the banister, I caught sight of Annalise sprinting down the hall, a brass candlestick in her hand, William Davis a pace behind her.

With one long arm, he reached out and caught her hair, wrapping it around his fist and yanking her back. Her feet went out from under her, her back hit the floor, and her head bounced on the hardwood with a hollow thud.

Davis was on her a second later, dragging at her jeans. Primal, white-hot fury raged through me.

He didn't get to touch her.

He didn't get to hurt her, to scare her.

Not for one more second.

Bracing my hand on the post of the banister at the landing, I vaulted around the turn, clearing half of the upper stairs just in time to see Annalise bring up the candlestick and slam it into the side of William Davis's head.

My gun was in my hand before I made the conscious decision to shoot. Annalise drew back and struck him again, driving him off of her. She scrambled back, deeper into the smoke, out of view. Davis lunged to his feet a second after I cleared the top of the steps.

He didn't see me. He was blind to everything but Annalise, pursuing her down the hall with single-minded devotion.

He never saw my gun come around, never saw my finger tighten on the trigger. When the bullet caught him in the shoulder, the expression on his face was pure, undiluted surprise. He went down in a crash of long limbs and lay unmoving.

"Cover me," I shouted to Cooper and went for Annalise. Stowing my gun, I caught sight of her in the thick smoke of the hallway and scooped her up, carrying her away from the fire and away from William Davis.

I held my breath as I jogged down the stairs and out of the house, only taking a breath when we hit clear air. Lise's coughing almost drowned out the wail of the fire engine.

I carried her to the edge of the circular drive, leaving plenty of room for the engines to get to the house. In the distance, I heard Cooper directing the firefighters to a dry hydrant at the back of the house.

Knox strode our way.

"We need a bus," I said, over the sound of Annalise's deep, wracking coughs.

"Incoming," he said. "Just went through the gates." He studied Annalise and then asked, "She hurt besides the smoke inhalation?"

I thought of her unbuttoned jeans, Davis's hands clawing at her. Pressing my lips to her ear, I said under my breath, "Did he hurt you? Anywhere? Don't try to talk, just nod or shake your head."

Vehemently, she shook her head, her hair spilling over my arm, dull with soot and smelling of smoke. I tightened my arms around her and said, "Okay. Paramedics are on the way. We're going to get you checked out at the hospital. You're okay. It's going to be okay."

Lise turned wide panicked eyes to the house, to the smoke billowing from the roof and licks of flame on the shingles.

Knox reassured her, "Cooper studied the schematics when we upgraded the security at the main house. There's a dry hydrant connected to a cistern behind the house. If they can get enough water out of it, they should get this under control. We've had a lot of rain this spring. That'll help." To me, he said, "What happened up there?"

I looked at Annalise, her bloodshot eyes and tear streaked face.

I said only, "Davis."

"William Davis?" Knox asked, incredulous. Seeing the way Annalise's eyes squeezed shut, the hitch in her chest interrupting her wracking coughs, he said, "Fuck."

The ambulance came down the drive, sirens screaming, saving me from having to tell Knox to shut the fuck up. Lise needed medical attention. She needed to feel safe. She needed to be far away from here before anybody pressed her for details on what had happened in that house.

No one was going to make her talk until she was ready. If they tried, they'd have to go through me.

I put her in the ambulance myself, climbing in with the paramedics over their objections. I stayed out of the way as they put an oxygen mask over her face, moving to take her hand after they were done. She opened her mouth as if to speak, but I shook my head. Brushing her hair off her forehead, I said, "Later. We'll have time later. I'm not going anywhere."

A tear dripped down her cheek, cutting a line through the soot on her face. I wiped it away with the side of my thumb. "Everything's okay now."

They took her away from me when we reached the hospital, wheeling her out of the ambulance and rolling her down the hall into the ER. They had to check her out, and I would only be in the way, but letting her out of my sight tore me up. I'd left her alone for an hour, and Davis had gotten to her. I never wanted to leave her side again.

I paced the waiting room, ignoring Knox, trying to beat back my irrational desire to storm down the hall and demand to see Annalise.

I never thought I'd be so relieved to see Aiden Winters. The second my eyes fell on his drawn face I said, "She's okay. They're checking her out, but she's okay. No burns, no injuries other than the smoke."

"You're sure," he said.

A wry chuckle rumbled in my throat, surprising me, and I said, "I'm guessing you can get more information than I can, considering one of these wings is named after your family, but the paramedics felt good about her condition. Why don't you make yourself useful and go badger an update out of them."

Without responding, Aiden strode past me to the front desk. He never raised his voice, but the nurse picked up the phone and made a call immediately. A few minutes later Aiden was back.

"Follow me."

Knox fell in beside us as Aiden led us deeper into the hospital, up a floor, and down another hall to a private waiting room. When the door was closed, Aiden said, "The nurse couldn't get an update, but someone will be here as soon as we can see her."

"What did Cooper tell you?" Knox asked, carefully.

"That Flynn saved Annalise's life. That the cistern behind the house was full and the damage to the house won't be bad, all things considered." As if it was an afterthought, he added, "William Davis is dead."

"I thought I hit him in the shoulder," I said.

"You did. But in the confusion no one mentioned to the firefighters there was someone in the house and by the time they got up there, Davis was dead."

"The smoke," Knox murmured.

Aiden nodded. Looking at me he said, "What else do you know?"

Again, I thought of Annalise's unbuttoned jeans. I kept my mouth shut. This was her story to tell, not mine, and I'd let her tell it the way she wanted to when she was ready. Davis was dead, and she was free.

We had all the time in the world.

CHAPTER TWENTY-EIGHT

RILEY

Annalise's fingers tightened around mine, my first hint she was awake. After what had felt like a lifetime, but had been more like forty-five minutes, a nurse had come to tell us that she was resting comfortably in a private room and we could see her, but to be aware that her throat was very sore and she shouldn't talk.

I'd seen fires before. I knew how quickly they could overtake a structure, how deadly the smoke could be. A few more minutes up there and Annalise could have been on a slab next to William Davis.

She might have had burns in her lungs. Her throat might have swollen shut, forcing them to intubate her to get oxygen into her body. For such a necessary organ, the lungs were terrifyingly fragile. I'd seen enough to know how lucky she was.

If she hadn't been a Winters, they would've discharged her already. We all knew they'd chosen to keep her overnight because no one wanted to make a mistake with a high-profile patient. Not one of us complained, except for

Annalise, who'd argued with wide, frustrated eyes but had followed the doctor's directive not to talk.

She'd been put to bed with oxygen tubes in her nose and had fallen asleep not long after. Her family had crowded into the room to reassure themselves that she was okay, then allowed Aiden to shepherd them out. He'd said to me, "You're staying?"

"I'll bring her home tomorrow," I promised.

He'd given me a sober nod and said, "I owe you everything." Then he was gone, taking with him the rest of the Winters clan with their loud voices and endless questions.

Aiden owed me nothing. I would've done anything for Annalise. My conscience was perfectly fine with shooting William Davis and not the least bit concerned that he'd died in that house. All I had to do was remember his fingers tearing at Annalise's jeans, and I wished I'd shot him more than once. I wished I'd shot him in the balls, the fucking psycho.

Lise's fingers squeezed mine again. Her eyes fluttered open, bloodshot and swollen. She opened her mouth to speak, but all that came out was a hoarse croak.

I pressed a fingertip to her lips, holding them closed, and said, "Don't try to talk. Your throat is a mess from the smoke, and it will heal faster if you don't talk. Hold on one second."

I got up and grabbed a whiteboard and dry erase marker I'd gotten from the nurses while Annalise had slept. Too much had happened to condemn her to silence, but she'd heal faster if she let her throat rest.

"Do you want to sit up a little?" I asked. She nodded, and I adjusted the bed, raising her to a half-reclining position and handing her the dry erase board and marker. She grabbed it and started to write.

· · ·

MARISSA ARCHER KILLED MY PARENTS.
  In love with William. Jealous. Crazy.
  Hugh and Olivia found out.
  William killed them.
  In love with my mother. Wanted me to take her place.

SO FEW WORDS TO SUM UP SO MUCH PAIN. A FAMILY shattered over jealousy and obsessive love. Annalise used the edge of the sheet to wipe the board clean and wrote, *William?*

"Dead," I reassured her. "The smoke. We were focused on getting you out of the house, the ambulance, and Cooper was helping the firefighters get hooked up. None of us thought about Davis still in the house."

Beneath his name she wrote, *Did you shoot him?*

I nodded. "In the shoulder. It wouldn't have killed him. You both breathed in a lot of smoke before you got to the hall. I could barely see you when I pulled you out. A few minutes after that, visibility was probably zero. Even if we'd told them he was there, they might not have found him in time."

Annalise stared at the whiteboard, the black marker hovering over the surface. She let out a shaky breath and wrote, *I don't care. I'm glad he's dead.*

"So am I," I agreed.

Maybe, if we were better people, we'd feel compassion for a clearly disturbed man who had fallen over the edge. William Davis had been the cause of so much death, pain, and heartbreak. I couldn't bring myself to feel anything but relief that he was gone.

If the Winters family wanted to have a party to celebrate his funeral, I'd be right there with them, popping the champagne cork and setting off the fireworks.

Lise wiped the board blank again and wrote,

I'm sorry.

"Nothing to be sorry for, Lise." I reached up to tuck a strand of hair behind her ear.

She shook her head and scribbled,

Let you think I didn't trust you.

I was scared.

I cupped her chin in my hand, urging her head up so I could meet her eyes. "Me too," I said. "I was scared too."

She wrote again, her hand moving over the whiteboard in fast, loose strokes.

Love you. Always. Always loved you.

"Me too," I said. "I never should have let you leave. I should have known that letter was a lie. I should've told Aiden to go to hell. I should've believed in you because I loved you. Because I knew who you were."

She shook her head, tears spilling from her eyes, leaving tracks through the smudges of soot the nurses had missed when they'd cleaned her up. She picked up the pen to write, but I closed my fingers over hers and said, "Just listen, for a minute. Please."

Her fingers went lax on the pen, and she looked at me, her eyes searching. Waiting.

"I fell for you so hard back then," I said. "You scared the hell out of me. I didn't know which way was up. I wasn't supposed to talk to you, and I couldn't stay away. I risked my job, and I didn't even care, but the whole time I was so sure it was going to end. I convinced myself you were too good for me, and when I got your letter, when Aiden gave me that lame-ass story about you running off with an old boyfriend, I let myself believe him because it was what I'd expected to hear in the first place."

Lise turned her hand and grabbed mine, pulling at my arm, reaching for the pen.

"Let me finish, Lise." Her blue eyes pained, she fell still. "I blew it back then. And I blew it a second time when you came home and I lied to you again about who I was and how we met. I don't have an excuse. It was fear and bullshit just like the first time. I told myself I was over you. Then I told myself it didn't matter. I was lying to you, and I was lying to myself. What we have between us, that's the only thing that matters. I love you. I've loved you since the day you almost spilled your coffee on me. I will never stop loving you."

She tugged her hand from mine and went for the pen again. I held it out of reach, over her head and said, "One more thing, and then it's your turn."

She dropped her hand and glared at me.

"I will never lie to you again. Not because it's easy. Not because I'm afraid. Not because I forgot to take the trash out. Not for any reason. I swear. If you can't do anything else for the rest of your life, you can trust me. I know why—"

Lise lunged up and snatched the pen from my hand, yanking her oxygen tubes out of place. She sat back and shoved the plastic prongs back in her nose. Scratching furiously on the whiteboard she wrote,

My fault too. I shouldn't have run.

Never trusted you, and I should have.

Not going to run again.

I trust you.

I know who you are. I know your heart.

Love you.

I pulled the whiteboard and pen from her hands and set them on the table beside the bed. Digging into the small watch pocket of my jeans, I pulled out the ring I'd put on her finger barely two weeks before. The ring she'd thrown in my face.

Holding it up in the light, I said, "I bought this for you. Not for the job. For you. The job is over. William is dead, and you're safe. For the first time since you were sixteen, you have choices. I'm asking you to choose me. Choose me and let me spend the rest of my life making you happy."

She held up her left hand and mouthed, *yes*.

I slid the ring onto her finger, where it belonged, and stood. I nudged her hip, and she slid over in the narrow bed. Climbing in beside her, careful not to tug on the oxygen tubes, I settled my head on the pillow next to hers, not caring that she smelled of smoke.

She was safe. She was alive. And she was mine. Forever.

Her lips parted, and I pressed a kiss to them, stopping her words.

"Let your throat rest. You have plenty of time to talk later."

A disgruntled noise rumbled in her throat. I tried to hide my smile, but she saw it in my eyes and hers narrowed in annoyance.

I kissed the line of her jaw and murmured, my lips brushing her skin, "Is it wrong that I'm enjoying getting the last word? Getting all the words?"

She made that irritated sound again, and this time I laughed. "Don't worry, as soon as your throat is healed you can talk my ear off. I'll listen to you all day if that's what you want."

Mimicking my earlier action, she pressed her fingertips to my lips, holding them closed, and mouthed, *I love you*.

I caught her fingers in mine and held them, resting our

hands on her stomach, my legs tangled with hers, our heads touching on the pillow.

"Go to sleep, Lise. When you wake up in the morning, I'll take you home."

With a contented sigh, she rubbed her forehead against mine and let her eyelids slide shut. I watched her sleep, my own eyes heavy, the sparkle of the ring on her finger like stars in the night sky, their light imprinted on my memory, following me into sleep.

EPILOGUE
ANNALISE

A few days after I was released from the hospital, I wandered into Aiden's office after dinner. He sat behind his desk, the newspaper spread before him, an empty glass of whiskey in his right hand. His eyes rose to meet mine, and there was a pained expression on his face.

We hadn't had a real conversation since the day after Gage and Sophie's wedding when I'd discovered Riley's lies, and Aiden's betrayal, and had left the house with Jacob.

He'd been avoiding me. And maybe I'd been avoiding him, too. I'd forgiven Riley, but I hadn't let Aiden off the hook. Not yet. It was time. That didn't mean I was going to make it easy for him.

My throat was still sore from the smoke. I'd been cleared to talk, but only if I kept it short. I dropped into one of the big leather chairs in front of Aiden's desk, raised one eyebrow, and said, "Well?"

Fortunately for my sore throat, Aiden didn't need any more prompting than a single word. Unfortunately, he was terrible at apologies.

"You know that I'm sorry," he began.

I shook my head and stared at him. He stared back.

Finally, I said, "It wouldn't hurt to say it."

At the gravelly sound of my voice, Aiden winced. "Hell, don't talk. You sound terrible." I narrowed my eyes and crossed my arms over my chest. "Okay, Annalise, I'm sorry. I'm sorry I hired Sinclair Security to spy on you. I'm sorry I was paranoid and overprotective. I'm sorry I lied to you and didn't tell you that your boyfriend was working for me." His voice softened, and his eyes were sad as he finished, "I'm sorry I played a part in keeping you from Riley. If I could do everything over again, there are so many things I would change, but trying to push you two apart is the biggest. I—"

I waved my hand in the air to cut him off. I'd wanted an apology. I didn't need him to put on a hair shirt and grovel.

"I'm good, Aid. I love you, too."

My older brother's voice sounded from behind me. "That's it? You're not going to make him beg?" Gage dropped into the chair beside me and propped his ankle on his knee. To Aiden, he said, "After what you put me through when I came home, that's all you're going to give Annalise?"

Aiden shifted in his seat uncomfortably. He still felt guilty over the way he'd treated Gage, and Gage had no problem poking at him over it.

"Leave him alone," I said to my brother. "You know he's got that overdeveloped sense of responsibility. He probably lays in bed at night and tortures himself over all the things he thinks he's done wrong."

Aiden rose and carried his tumbler to the decanter of whiskey in the corner of the room. From the stiff set of his shoulders, I knew I'd struck home.

"Anyway," I went on, "I thought of the perfect way he can pay me back."

"Really?" Gage said, a mischievous light in his eyes. "What are you going to ask him for? A boat? A car? Make it a Bentley. I can see you driving a Bentley."

The laugh burst from my raw throat, and I slapped my hand over my mouth to hold it in. Shaking my head, I said, "I can buy my own Bentley, thank you very much. I haven't spent a penny of my own money in eleven years. Aiden's been busy making my trust fund grow while I was working under the table, scrubbing toilets and slinging coffee."

"Good point," Gage said. He tilted his head to the side and studied Aiden. "Then what are you going to ask him for?"

"I want him to let me fix him up," I said with a smile.

Both Aiden and Gage's eyes widened in horror. Aiden was the first to speak.

"No fucking way, Lise. I get that you're in love, everyone's in love, and you think every single person should be paired up. I get it. I'm happy for you. Thrilled. I'll throw you the biggest wedding Atlanta's ever seen if that's what you want, but stay the hell out of my personal life."

"I want you to be happy, Aiden," I said. "And you have terrible taste in women."

"She's got you there," Gage said. "You always go for the icicles. So proper, and so chilly."

"Butt out," Aiden muttered.

"He's been having a lot of late meetings lately," Gage commented to me. "I think there's something going on at the office."

Aiden gritted his teeth, his words tight when he said, "I told you to stay out of it, Gage."

Ignoring Aiden, Gage said, "It involves a blond with purple eyes, but that's all I can get out of him."

"Periwinkle," Aiden murmured. "Not purple, periwinkle." Then, realizing what he'd given away, he scowled. "And there's nothing going on with her. Just business."

I leaned forward, intrigued. "Really? What business?"

"None of yours," Aiden said, in that tone he used when he wanted people to do his bidding.

Gage gave Aiden a long, measuring look before turning to me and saying, "I'll keep you posted. But, I didn't stop in to needle Aiden. I wanted to talk to you about something. Both of you."

"Is everything okay?" I asked.

"Everything's great," Gage said. "I wanted to talk to you about the house. We can't leave it the way it is. The damage from the fire wasn't as bad as it could have been, but with the roof half burned away, we had to get repairs started as soon as possible, or a good rain would do worse than the fire. Charlie sent over a crew to put temporary patches on the roof, and we've got clean up scheduled to deal with the mess from the water and the smoke."

"I didn't think about that," I admitted. "But it's not that bad? My room must have been destroyed."

"Pretty much," Gage agreed. "The rest is mostly smoke and water damage. We're still waiting on the insurance adjuster's report."

He and Aiden exchanged a long, heavy look. They were keeping the official business from me. I knew the police had judged William's death an accident, as well as the fire, but that was it. There had been a few reporters at the gates when Riley brought me home, but nothing like what I'd expected. From what I'd been able to glean from eavesdropping, the police weren't interested in anything a dead man had said about crimes long buried in the past.

I was the only witness to William's confession, Marissa Archer was locked in a sanitarium, and William was dead. As far as the powers that be were concerned, case closed.

I would have thought that would bother me, but strangely, it didn't. Demanding that William be blamed for Uncle Hugh and Aunt Olivia's murders, trying to pin my parent's deaths on Marissa, would have created a media frenzy none of us wanted to deal with. We knew what had happened. Those responsible were paying for their crimes, William with his life. That was enough.

Gage went on, "Regardless of what the insurance company says, we need to decide what we're going to do with the house."

"You and Sophie?" I asked.

Gage shared a look with Aiden and then shook his head. "We prefer to stay here. Sophie doesn't want to leave Amelia, and there's plenty of room. Vance and Maggie aren't going anywhere. Maggie wouldn't leave her grand-mother's house voluntarily, and Vance would never ask her to."

"Tate?" I asked, my heart suddenly racing.

"He—we—think you and Riley should take it. If you want it. After everything that happened, we'd understand if you didn't."

I could see his point. Our parents had died in that house. But then, Uncle Hugh and Aunt Olivia had died in Winters House, and none of us had abandoned it.

Everything that had happened with William in my bedroom had been a nightmare, but my bedroom was destroyed. I'd never have to see it again as it had been. When the clean-up was done, it would be like a brand new room, all the ugly memories purified by the fire.

Riley and I could bring the house back to life. As I thought about it, my heart swelled. It was time to move forward. Time to live again. And part of that was bringing my parent's memory into the present.

"I'll have to talk to Riley," I said. "He's got a place, and we haven't really talked about where we're going to live."

Gage stood and clapped a hand on my shoulder, squeezing once. "No rush. Charlie's ready to jump in and rebuild what was damaged, whenever we figure out what to do with it. But while you're talking to Riley about the future, don't mention Aiden's offer for the biggest wedding in Atlanta. Jacob and Abigail's will be enough of a circus. Don't even think about eloping, but I can say from experience, a small wedding is perfect."

Riley and I hadn't done much talking since I'd been released from the hospital. Every time I tried to string more than a few words together, he scowled and handed me another mug of herbal tea with honey.

That was okay. My throat did hurt, and I wasn't going to turn down a little pampering. That, and I didn't have much to say. William Davis was dead. We were all reeling at the knowledge that a man we'd considered as good as a second father had torn our family apart.

It was so bizarre, so hard to absorb, that we'd all been a little quiet. The grief at learning of William's betrayal mixed with the relief of finally knowing what had really happened to our family had left us quietly reeling.

None of us had ever believed the story of two identical murder/suicides, but without the truth, the specter of that story hung over us. Haunted us. Now we were free to move forward. To be happy.

I was more than happy; I was over the moon. I was with Riley, we'd untangled the lies and fears between us, and now we could just be. I was perfectly content to sit beside him, propped up against the headboard in bed, or on the couch in the family room, and watch TV, or work on my laptop while he was on his, all the time sneaking sidelong glances and drooling over how hot he was in his reading glasses.

I didn't need long, heartfelt conversations. I just wanted to be with him and do normal, everyday stuff. That was my idea of heaven, and I'd landed smack in the middle of it.

I gave myself a day or two to mull over the issue of the house, before I brought it up to Riley.

First, because I wanted to make sure I really was okay with living there. That scene with William was over, but it had been horrifying while it lasted. And while I'd had a very happy childhood in that house, my parents had died right there in my father's office.

Could I walk into that room every day and remember the good times rather than the bad? I didn't want to make a commitment, get Charlie started on remodeling or encourage Riley to sell his place unless I was sure.

And second, I didn't want to try to have such an important conversation with Riley scowling at me for straining my throat. So I behaved myself, sucked on lozenges and drank buckets of honeyed tea while I thought about the house and enjoyed being around my family, knowing I wouldn't be chased off by an unexpected delivery.

The simple freedom in knowing that I could stay, or go, but I could make my own choices out of desire rather than fear—that was bliss. I was in no rush to worry about the rest of my life when the present was better than my wildest dreams.

When I finally did bring up the house to Riley he only smiled and said, "It's a great house. If you're okay with it, I think it would be the perfect place to raise a family."

"What about your place?" I'd asked, not wanting him to feel obligated.

I'd only been to Riley's condo once, but it was centrally located in midtown, not far from the Sinclair Security build- ing. Modern and open, with plenty of space, it was the opposite of my parent's homey craftsman style house in the woods. It also had the benefit of privacy.

The house in the woods was secluded, but it was a quar- ter-mile from Winters House. Living in the Winters estate would put me close to my family, but Riley might want a little more space from the rest of the clan.

When I brought up my concerns, Riley just shook his head. "I can handle your family," he said. "And you've been away from them for long enough. Anyway, my condo was an investment. I'm not attached. Charlie's got her broker's license. She can sell it, and we'll stay at Winters House until our house is ready to move into."

"Really?" I'd asked, looking up at him, drinking in the love in his eyes and the affectionate smile turning up the corners of his lips. He hadn't shaved in a while, and his scruff had turned into a beard. I'd never been into facial hair on guys, but Riley's was soft to the touch and gave him a roguish air that made my knees weak. I loved the way it felt under my fingertips and against my skin when we kissed.

"Really," he said, bending down to press his lips to mine.

Our house. That's what we started calling it, and just referring to it as ours, rather than my parent's, birthed a sense of ownership, of new beginnings. We decided against any major remodeling, other than updating the appliances, and Charlie set her crew to repairing the fire and water damage.

We never really had a formal conversation about the wedding. Despite Aiden's offer, I had no interest in a big wedding. I'd loved Gage and Sophie's wedding. Just friends and family at home.

Riley had added only one stipulation. He wanted to be married in the great room of our house in the woods after the renovations were complete. That had sounded like a dream to me. All we needed was for Charlie to tell us the date the house would be done and we'd be good to go.

Well, that and a dress. I'd dragged the girls, alternately Charlie, Sophie, Maggie, Abigail, and even Josephine and Emily to almost every shop in town, but nothing was quite right. Charlie finally gave us a date only a few weeks away, and if I didn't find something, I'd be getting married in jeans and flip-flops.

I was starting to worry I'd never find a dress when Mrs. W stopped me after our fifth unsuccessful dress excursion and said, "If you have a few minutes, I'd like to show you something upstairs."

"Sure," I said, following her all the way up to the attic.

I hadn't been in the attics in years. They sprawled above the second floor, almost a full level except for the slanted ceilings. Room after room of storage.

Mrs. W kept them ruthlessly organized, or so it appeared, but as she led me past stacks of plastic storage containers she explained, "I didn't want to say anything until I found it. I knew it was here, but everything got rearranged a few years ago, and somehow, I misplaced it. I didn't want to get your hopes up unless I was sure."

She led me around the corner and headed for a storage container that had been set to the side, the lid partially open. Leaning over, she reached inside and gathered something in her arms. I heard the rustle of fabric, and she stood, holding before her a wedding dress.

I recognized it instantly. I'd seen it in pictures, remembered sitting in my mother's lap, her arms around me as we looked at a photograph of her and my father on their wedding day. This was her dress, and it appeared to be in perfect condition.

I raised my hand to my mouth and took it in, the full skirt, strapless bodice made demure by a boatneck overlay of Brussels lace that extended to long sleeves. I had almost the same figure as my mother, and I knew just by looking that the dress would suit me as perfectly as it had suited her. But—

Reading my mind, Mrs. W said, "I already checked the hem, and there's more than enough to let it down. Try it on," she urged, holding it higher. I peeled off my T-shirt and jeans in a flash, not shy around Mrs. W. She'd been taking care of us since we were children and I had nothing she hadn't seen before.

She'd already opened the buttons going up the back, and dropped the dress over my head, settling the layers of white silk around my legs.

"I'm only going to button every few buttons," she said. "If I do all of them we'll be here for the rest of the day."

When she had me fastened into the dress, she stepped back and turned me around. Her eyes got wet as she looked at me in my mother's wedding gown, and she shook her head in awe.

"You look so beautiful. So much like her, but exactly like yourself." Glancing around the attic room her face fell in dismay, "There's no mirror up here. I didn't think. When is Riley due home?"

It was the middle of the day on a Wednesday, so not for a few hours. Everyone was out except for Sophie and Amelia. "Stay right there," Mrs. W ordered before she disappeared down the stairs at the other end of the attic. A moment later she was back, gathering up my discarded clothes and pulling a wisp of white lace from the storage container.

"Come down to Sophie and Gage's room."

I didn't have to lift the skirts much to walk. They would definitely need to be let down a few inches for the dress to truly fit, but I felt like a princess with yards of silk rustling around my legs and my arms covered in white lace almost to my fingertips.

Sophie and Aunt Amelia were waiting for us in the dressing room of Sophie and Gage's suite. Sophie's eyes lit when she saw me, and she exclaimed, "Oh, you look just like Grace Kelly."

I barely heard her. I caught sight of myself in the full-length mirror and was transfixed. The dress was perfect, and Mrs. W had been exactly right. Wearing it, I looked like my mother, but also like myself. And with her dress, I could have her by my side on my wedding day.

Aunt Amelia, her voice shaking a little, said brusquely, "No, Grace's dress went all the way to her neck. James loved Anna's shoulders and collarbone, and he asked that whatever dress she wore, she leave them uncovered. She had the designer do the boat neck instead, just for him." Amelia let out a sigh and said, "You look so beautiful, Annalise. It's just perfect."

As Mrs. W arranged the lace veil over my hair, Amelia cleared her throat and said. "We've been driving all over town trying on dresses. Why didn't you tell us you had this upstairs?"

With the same starchy tone she always used with Aunt Amelia, Mrs. W said, "I wanted to make sure I could find it, and that it was in good condition. You've seen the attics.

Everything had been moved around, and it took me a while to locate it."

Before they could start arguing, I stepped in. "It doesn't matter. I'm glad I tried on all those other dresses because none of them were right and this one is."

Looking at Mrs. W, I saw tears in her eyes. "Thank you," I said, and she let out a sniffle. Mrs. W would be horrified to cry in front of the family. Breaking the mood, I said the first thing that popped into my mind.

"Who knows? Maybe you can wear it next."

Her eyes flew wide, and I winked at her. Riley had told me about catching her and Abel in the kitchen after, he was sure, they'd been kissing. Mrs. W's cheeks flushed hot pink, and her eyes dried.

"Don't be silly, Annalise. I'm far too old for romance."

"That's not what I heard," I teased.

Surprising me, Aunt Amelia cut in to say, "You're never too old for romance, Helen. You should tell that man 'Yes' and put him out of his misery."

Sophie and I stared at them in shock. Amelia clearly knew things that we didn't.

Mrs. W's pink cheeks went brick red, and she shook her head, spreading the skirts of the wedding dress, shaking out the wrinkles, and refusing to meet our eyes.

"I'm thinking about it," she said under her breath.

"Hhmph, thinking about it too slowly is what I say," Amelia said.

Mrs. W pinned her with a steely glare and said primly, "Then it's a good thing I didn't ask your opinion, Amelia. I'll go get a dress bag, and we can pack this up to take to the seamstress. It won't take her long to make the adjustments. I don't think it needs fitting anywhere but the hem."

And that was that.

I had a dress, and we had a wedding date.

The few weeks between finding the dress and marrying Riley passed in a blur. I had Dave Price review Sloane's contract. He made a few changes, she agreed, and I signed on the dotted line. Then I panicked and spent the next few days glued to my computer, sorting through pictures, editing the few I decided on, and generally freaking out. Everyone thought it was hysterical that I was more nervous about selling my photographs than I was about getting married.

I couldn't explain it. I'd wanted to be a professional photographer for most of my life. While I hadn't had a real show in a gallery, put out a coffee table book, or even worked taking portraits at the mall, I'd sold some pictures here and there as I'd bounced around the country. But I was nervous about my photographs. Would anyone like them? Would everyone say Sloane only took me on because I was a Winters? Was I really any good? Just the thought of my work hanging in Sloane's gallery for anyone to see had me shaking with nerves.

But not marrying Riley. Every time I thought of our wedding, all I felt was eager anticipation.

Ever since I'd left Riley in that hospital bed, I'd abandoned the dream of a life with him. I'd been absolutely certain that dream had no hope of ever coming true. Now he was mine, and I was his. I had Riley back. We were getting married. We'd even had a few conversations about kids. We both wanted them, and neither of us was getting any younger. I'd already made an appointment to have my IUD taken out. We'd wasted enough time. We didn't want to wait another moment to start our lives together.

I found I had not the slightest trace of nerves when it came to marrying Riley. Not when we set the date. Not when I tried on my dress at the final fitting. Not on the morning of our wedding.

In my whole life, I'd never been more certain of anything than I was about marrying Riley Flynn.

Aiden gave me away. As he walked me through the foyer of our house, into the great room and up to the fire-place where Riley stood waiting, I felt only a bone-deep certainty that I would love Riley every day for the rest of my life, and he would love me in return.

I grinned like a fool through the ceremony, and Riley grinned right back. When the minister pronounced us husband and wife, he dipped me over his arm and kissed me for so long the minister murmured, "I said *kiss the bride* not consummate the marriage."

Everyone burst out laughing, the minister included. Riley took my hand and pulled me through the great room, calling over his shoulder, "See you in a few."

The reception and dinner were back at Winters House since our dining room didn't have enough space to seat everyone and our kitchen wasn't quite big enough to feed the entire Winters family.

I followed Riley, my fingers twined with his as he guided me up the stairs to our bedroom. The second floor still smelled faintly of fresh paint. At the end of the hall, Riley swung open the door to the master bedroom and led me inside.

Sometime that day, while I'd been busy getting my hair and nails done for the wedding, someone—maybe Riley— had moved my big brass bed back where it belonged. Every-thing else in the room was new. We'd wanted a fresh start.

The past had dictated enough of our lives. All of us were ready for the future.

Riley pulled me into his arms, tipping my face up to his. "I wanted you to myself for a few minutes, Mrs. Flynn."

The name shivered through me, filling my heart with joy. Mrs. Flynn. I might have doodled that name in my psychology notebook all those years ago.

I twined my arms around his neck, falling into the love in his familiar hazel eyes.

"You set me free," I said.

Riley shook his head. "We set each other free."

He backed me toward the bed, his lips tracing mine, his hands working the buttons on the back of the dress. Laughing, I dipped my head back to free my mouth.

"Riley! We can't. It'll take too long to get my dress back on."

He was undeterred. "They can wait. I'm sure Mrs. W and Abel have plenty of hors-d'oeuvres to keep them busy. I'll be fast."

My breath hitched as the dress sagged from my shoulders. Riley had quick fingers. "What if I don't want you to be fast?" I breathed as he tugged the dress off and lowered me to the bed.

"Then we'll be late. I don't care. I just want to make love to my wife."

I had no argument with that. I wound my arms around his neck and pulled him close, murmuring in his ear, "Take your time, Mr. Flynn. I'm all yours."

And I was. That night, and forever.

Turn the page for a sneak peek of Aiden's story, Compromising the Billionaire

SNEAK PEEK
COMPROMISING THE BILLIONAIRE

CHAPTER ONE
Aiden

"You wanted to see me, sir?"

She hovered in the doorway, balanced on her toes as if preparing to flee. In her crisp navy suit and tightly pinned chignon, Violet Hartwell was the picture of a corporate professional. Only her dangerously spiked heels gave her away. Navy to match the suit, they were the only sign that Violet liked to live on the edge.

I gestured to the chair on the other side of my desk and said, "Yes, Ms. Hartwell, please sit down."

My eyes were glued to the length of her legs as she crossed the room, her stride as smooth as if she were barefoot.

I waited until she took the seat in front of me, smoothing her skirt demurely and crossing her feet at the ankle. She met my eyes with one bold look before dropping them to the surface of my desk.

Interesting.

She was daring enough to apply for a job at Winters Inc. using a fake name. Daring enough to sneak around after hours poking in my files. But not daring enough to look me in the eyes.

That was for the best. I had a plan, and her eyes were a distraction. I wasn't going to get sidetracked trying to decide exactly what shade they were. Weeks of watching her and I hadn't quite figured it out. Depending on her mood, the light, what she was wearing, they fell somewhere between the deep blue of a summer sky and the lavender of dusk.

But Violet wasn't here so I could obsess over her eyes.

Violet was here to walk into my carefully laid trap.

Once she did, I'd have all the time I wanted to obsess.

"Ms. Hartwell, you've been with us for what — two months now?" I asked, shuffling through the papers on my desk as if reviewing her resumé. I wasn't. The papers had nothing to do with Violet, but she didn't know that.

"Yes, sir," she said, politely. Carefully.

"And you're enjoying your work with Winters Inc. so far?"

"Yes, sir," she said again, meeting my eyes with a quick, wary glance.

She was nervous.

She should be.

"Your supervisor says you're sharp, detail oriented, and able to juggle multiple projects easily."

That hadn't been all he'd said. According to Carlisle, Violet Hartwell was ice cold, with laser focus. A perfect machine, contained and efficient. Polite, but not friendly. Distant. Reserved. He hadn't been happy to hear I planned to steal her from his division.

"That's very flattering, sir," she said, her eyes scanning the surface of my desk. What was she looking for? She was hyperalert, those dusky lavender eyes taking in every detail from the way I'd arranged my pencils to the labels on the manila folders beside my monitor.

Ever since a second review of her paperwork had pinged Security's attention, I'd had my eye on her. I was almost positive she wasn't working for a rival company. If one of my rivals sent someone in, they'd make damn sure their spy's ID would hold up.

Security had been watching, monitoring her trips to the file room, taking note of her attempts to hack into my email. She was better than I would've expected from an amateur, but my security team was the best.

I could've fired her. That was the easiest solution to the problem of Violet Hartwell, or whatever her name was.

I should have fired her.

I had too much to do, way too much going on, to deal with her myself.

I'd planned to have Security deliver the news and escort her from the building. Then, either by happy accident or some plan on her part, we'd shared an elevator for six floors.

I can't remember the last time I was so acutely aware of a woman.

She'd stood a mere three feet away, wedging herself into the corner of the elevator, her back to the wall. Curious, I'd studied her out of the corner of my eye. A strand of her pale blonde hair had escaped its twist to curl around her ear. As far as I could tell, she wore little makeup. The unadorned pink curve of her lower lip captivated me.

Even white teeth bit into that plump lip as she'd snuck sideways glances at me from those captivating eyes and pretended to review one of the files she carried.

Violet put so much energy into ignoring me, the force of it drew my eyes like a magnet.

I couldn't tear my eyes from the curve of her hips in that trim little suit, the length of her legs ending in another pair of those ice pick heels. The suit was well cut, more professional than feminine, but it couldn't hide the generous breasts beneath her primly buttoned blouse.

She'd smelled of flowers. Sweet peas, like the kind that grew on the arbor in the back gardens of Winters House. Sweet peas that brought back cool spring mornings, the simple joy of playing in the woods with my brothers and cousins as a child.

The nostalgic scent wrapped around a woman I suddenly needed to see naked knocked me off balance. I wanted to take a step closer and inhale her. I wanted to hit STOP on the elevator and peel that sedate suit from her body.

In an instant, she'd shifted from nuisance to puzzle, and I needed the answer. Who was this woman with the bombshell body beneath the professional facade? Why was she at Winters Inc? And why was she so interested in me?

I'd scrapped my plans to hand her off to Security. Violet Hartwell had moved to the top of my to-do list.

I watched her sitting on the other side of my desk and waited to see if she would fill the silence between us. Most people did, unable to help themselves, babbling on and on just to fill the empty space with words. I can't tell you how much I've learned just by keeping my mouth shut at the right time.

Violet was immune to my ploy. Her hands rested in her lap, fingers laced together, a neutral expression on her face. She would've been all cool composure if not for the avid curiosity in her eyes as she studied the surface of my desk.

For some unknown reason she was looking into me. I

had no problem using that to maneuver her into giving me exactly what I wanted.

"Violet, have you heard I've been looking for a new administrative assistant?"

"No, sir, I hadn't heard. Don't you already have a staff of four?" The first thread of trepidation wound through her voice.

"I do," I agreed. "But I find that even four of them can't keep up, and I've been interested in adding a fifth. I asked my department heads to keep an eye out for a suitable candidate, and Carlisle recommended you."

I hid my surge of triumph as her eyes went wide with shock. She hadn't seen that coming. But you know what they say — keep your friends close, and your enemies closer.

Violet Hartwell wanted access to me. I was going to give it to her, and then I was going to watch every single thing she did until I figured out her game.

She thought she could get the best of me.

She'd learn how wrong she was.

"I appreciate being considered," she said, smoothly, "but I don't think I'm qualified. I'm a project manager and —"

"Carlisle seemed confident that your skills would transition perfectly to fit my needs. Are you saying you're not interested? It's quite a promotion."

Not so much a promotion as a trap.

To a legitimate employee, working in my inner circle would be a dream come true. I'm Aiden Winters, CEO of Winters Inc. Most top-tier business school graduates would commit murder for the chance to take one of those desks outside my office.

For just a second, before her cool façade slipped back into place, Violet looked like she was ready to bolt. I couldn't help but enjoy the irony. She couldn't say no because turning down the opportunity of a lifetime would draw far too much attention, and attention was the last thing she wanted.

From what my investigations had uncovered, Violet wanted to be left alone to quietly do her job and snoop around on me in her spare time. A promotion to my personal team would make anonymity impossible.

Her eyes flared wider, their gorgeous purple shade vibrant against her creamy skin. When they narrowed, I knew that she knew. Carlisle had only good things to say about Violet, but she'd done nothing that would justify such a major promotion.

There was only one reason I'd offer her a newly created role on my team. I imagined I could see the gears turning in her mind as she studied me. Was she weighing her options? Trying to find a way to turn down the promotion that wouldn't expose her own ulterior motives?

I was about to find out if Violet truly lived on the edge. Now she knew I suspected her. Would she take the job and keep spying on me, or would she run?

Her eyes met mine, and behind that neutral expression, I saw the burn of defiance. I was about to get my answer, and I had a feeling it would be the one I was waiting for.

"I... I'd be honored, sir," she said, with just the slightest hitch before her words fell into place. It shouldn't make my cock twitch every time she called me 'sir,' but it did. So cool. So contained.

There was a world of meaning in the way she said 'sir'. I wanted to hear it again, over and over. And now I would.

I was the spider to her fly. I'd have plenty of time to learn everything I wanted to know about Violet Hartwell.

I stood and held out my hand, forcing Violet to stand as well. Her slim fingers slid across my palm, her grip surprisingly firm, her skin soft and warm. As she leaned forward, a wave of sweet pea scented air drifted to me, and I caught a glimpse of the shadow of her cleavage before she straightened.

Yes.

I was going to learn everything I wanted to know about Violet Hartwell.

Everything.

"You have a three o'clock meeting with HR to discuss your new position, salary, increased benefits and the rest. I'll expect you to start here tomorrow morning."

"But my projects —"

I cut her off with a wave of my hand. "Carlisle has everything under control. Tomorrow, Ms. Hartwell."

She gave a brisk nod and turned for the door, her chin jutting up just a little, that hint of defiance leaking out.

With her back to me, I didn't try to hide my in-depth study of the way her ass swayed when she walked. If she looked this good in that modest suit, I couldn't wait to see what she looked like stripped to her skin. If things went the way I planned, sooner or later I would.

I was so distracted by Violet's ass I didn't notice my cousin Gage until he stepped into the room and pinned me with a hard look. Shutting the door behind him, he crossed the room and dropped into the chair Violet had so recently vacated.

"What the fuck, Aid? You were staring at her ass like you were going to leap over your desk and jump her. Isn't she an employee? She's in Carlisle's division, right? Did she come on when we acquired the company we folded in or is she new?"

I sat and leaned back in my chair, crossing my arms over my chest, not trying to hide my grin of satisfaction.

"She's new. She came on about five weeks after we acquired CD4 Analytics. She had experience in data mining and project management, and Carlisle said she's been an ideal employee."

"But?" Gage probed.

"But her paperwork doesn't wash. We didn't pick it up when we hired her or she never would've gotten the job, but the security review caught something off with her last name. We've been watching her. She's been looking at files that have nothing to do with her division. Trying to hack email."

"Do you know who sent her in?" Gage asked.

"I think she's working for herself."

"What does she want?"

"That's the interesting thing," I said. "So far she seems to want me. She's poking into my emails. My files. I decided the best way to deal with her was to give her exactly what she wants."

Gage leaned forward. "I don't like this, Aiden. If she lied on her application, fire her. If she's digging around where she shouldn't be, fire her. Don't bring her into your inner circle."

"I have a plan," I said, trying to deflect.

Gage ignored me. "I saw the way you were looking at her. I've never known you to get involved with an employee. It's asking for trouble, and you know it. We have a zero-tolerance policy for harassment here. You know that; you set the fucking policy."

"I set the fucking policy because we are not that kind of company. But Violet Hartwell is not a regular employee. She's a spy, here under false pretenses, and whatever she wants, it has to do with me. You should've seen her face when I offered her the job. There was a moment of sheer panic when I knew she wanted to run.

She was happy buried in Carlisle's division digging away for whatever it is she's looking for. Now she has to deal with me."

"I don't like this," Gage said again. "Why don't you just put the Sinclairs on her, find out what she's up to, and then fire her. I can't emphasize enough the part about firing her."

"Oh, I put the Sinclairs on her. Cooper's been digging away. He hasn't uncovered her real name yet, but the condo she's living in is owned by a shell company. They still haven't uncovered the real owner."

"You're not firing her because you want to investigate her or because you want to fuck her?" Gage asked, studying me with curiosity.

I couldn't blame him. I was all business. Outside of my family, this company was my life. I would destroy anyone who threatened it. But Gage knew me better than anyone, and he'd already figured me out.

"Both," I admitted. "And like I said, she's not off the table because she's not a real employee. At best she's a spy. At worst she's a criminal. Either way, she's fair game."

"You have women lined up to date you. Why don't you go fuck one of them?"

"I have," I said. "I'm bored."

Gage gave me the smug smile of a man who went home every night to the warm bed of the woman he loved. Gage and Sophie were newly married, and so far it looked like the honeymoon would never end. They lived with me in Winters House, our family home. The place was huge, and still, I managed to walk in on them at least once a day. They couldn't keep their hands off each other.

On top of that, I'd been watching my cousin Annalise falling head over heels for her first love, had watched every other member of my sprawling family pair up, and if I was being totally honest, all that love and devotion had left me feeling restless.

I was happy for them. No, I wasn't happy. I was fucking ecstatic. Our family had been through more than its share of rough times. All the money and power in the world can't fight death. It can't undo murder. We'd lost Gage's parents when we were children, and then my own when we were teenagers.

The Winters family had been plagued by scandal and loss and grief for too many years. The only thing that made it better was seeing the people I loved find their own happiness, one by one.

Gage was right; I never had any trouble finding a date. I was adept at fending off the fortune hunters, and when I wanted a woman, I had one. Lately, the idea of taking out one of my regular companions had lost its luster.

Maybe it was all that true love in the air, but I wanted something different. Not what my family had. Not what Gage had.

Winters Inc. was wife, mistress, and child all in one. After my family, the company had been my sole focus since my father had died. I had no plans to change that.

"What do you mean, you're bored?" Gage asked. I should have known he wasn't going to let me off the hook.

"I mean, I'm bored." I shrugged a shoulder and tried not to think of that peek of Violet's cleavage. Getting her into bed would be tricky. She was smart, and she was on her guard. She hadn't given me a single sign that she was attracted to me, but that shell of hers was so well practiced, I already knew I'd have to work for it. Good. I liked a challenge.

Knowing Gage wouldn't give up, I went on, "I'm intrigued, okay? She's not a corporate spy, but she's up to something. She's looking for information on me, but when I offered her the chance to work by my side she balked. I want to know why. If I can talk her into bed while I'm figuring it out, all the better."

Gage let out a sigh of defeat. "She's your type, that's for sure."

"I don't have a type," I said.

"Really? So she's not a carbon copy of Elizabeth?"

No one in my family had liked my first wife. If I tried to look at Violet objectively, I could see why Gage would say that. She had the same cool composure, the same icy blonde hair, even the same elegant sense of style.

But Elizabeth had been cold to her core, something I wish I'd found out before I married her. Violet was an entirely different creature. I'd seen that hint of defiance, the way she'd raised her chin when she strode out of my office. She was scared and against the ropes, but she wouldn't give in.

Elizabeth was a stone sculpture, hard and frigid all the way through. Not Violet. I'd glimpsed the woman hiding behind the mask. The need, the defiance. I was betting there was passion beneath that perfect exterior.

I was going to expose it.

And I wasn't going to justify myself to anyone.

"She's not Elizabeth, Gage," I said with finality. "I've got this under control."

"That's what you say now." He stood. "I'm keeping an eye out for complaints to HR. If this ends up in a lawsuit, I'm letting you swing."

"It won't," I promised. "I'm giving her exactly what she wants. Me."

ALSO BY IVY LAYNE

Don't Miss Out on New Releases, Exclusive Giveaways, and More!!

Join Ivy's Readers Group @ ivylayne.com/readers

THE HEARTS OF SAWYERS BEND

Stolen Heart

Sweet Heart

Scheming Heart

Rebel Heart

Wicked Heart

THE UNTANGLED SERIES

Unraveled

Undone

Uncovered

THE WINTERS SAGA

The Billionaire's Secret Heart (Novella)

The Billionaire's Secret Love (Novella)

The Billionaire's Pet

The Billionaire's Promise

The Rebel Billionaire

The Billionaire's Secret Kiss (Novella)

The Billionaire's Angel

Engaging the Billionaire

Compromising the Billionaire

The Counterfeit Billionaire

THE BILLIONAIRE CLUB

The Wedding Rescue

The Courtship Maneuver

The Temptation Trap

ABOUT IVY LAYNE

Ivy Layne has had her nose stuck in a book since she first learned to decipher the English language. Sometime in her early teens, she stumbled across her first Romance, and the die was cast. Though she pretended to pay attention to her creative writing professors, she dreamed of writing steamy romance instead of literary fiction. These days, she's neck deep in alpha heroes and the smart, sexy women who love them.

Married to her very own alpha hero (who rubs her back after a long day of typing, but also leaves his socks on the floor). Ivy lives in the mountains of North Carolina where she and her other half are having a blast raising two energetic little boys. Aside from her family, Ivy's greatest loves are coffee and chocolate, preferably together.

VISIT IVY
Facebook.com/AuthorIvyLayne
Instagram.com/authorivylayne/
www.ivylayne.com
books@ivylayne.com

Made in United States
Cleveland, OH
08 February 2025

14128701R10181